Sasquatch
Profiler

By

Daniel L. Simmons

Sasquatch Profiler

Conspiracy Theory Publishing

LCCN: 2018903860

ISBN-13: 978-0692118122

Introduction

One day in mid-August, on a family outing atop Skyline drive, which overlooks the Palouse in northern Idaho and eastern Washington. During this back-wood drive, I alerted everyone to a chimerical sighting of the North American Sasquatch. After the hysteria subsided, my Uncle suggested I write a short story involving my abduction by Bigfoot. Pondering this suggestion for a few months, I sat down at my computer and tapped out a short story which kept growing. By the time I had finished, the story had expanded into a novel. Besides, how could I write anything short when it comes to Sasquatch.

This voice vibrated at the base of his skull, within the reptilian portion of his brain. "Know this; a warrior creates his enemies to conquer and, without this dynamic, the warrior would not exist. Strive for a world without warriors. When confronted, stand as strong as a granite wall, be impenetrable. Do not allow the warrior within your mind to defeat you. This way the warrior cannot turn you into his enemy."

Chapter 1

Dark Woods

In total darkness, one's perception changes. Hearing becomes the essential sense. Touch second and then the sense of smell. A night in the deep forest with no sounds alters this order. The darkness surrounds you, pressing its darkness into your skin, penetrating the skin, becoming part of the body. It was as dark as it was before God created light. The silence was a vacuum; one's ears created a humming-type of ringing in the void. But the odor in the air was overwhelming, damp with the musty smell of the dense forest. Anxiety crept into the reaches of one's mind, searching, seeking something tangible, desiring to hear or to see something. The smell of the thick forest and biting cold were the only realities here. In the distance, one could detect a dim light and a faint chiming sound.

At the far end of the watershed road, was a light blue Jeep Cherokee. Slightly off the road, driver side tires in a small ditch, listing the vehicle to that side. The driver's door was open and pushed up against a tree. The fading dome light and chiming from the open door were all that disrupted the dark, silent forest. Headlights came from down the road toward the direction of the Jeep. Bouncing and tossing, and tossing and bouncing, pitching in the ruts and potholes in the narrow tire tracks of the Forest Service road ZT 145, up the Cedar Creek Watershed. Not a road but a worn trail from a few, seldom taken excursions to this part of the forest. The lights from the oncoming truck shined from the wet path, making them appear as elongated angels of salvation. The glow around the headlights looked like halos. The lights came to an abrupt stop just behind the Jeep.

Then came the sound of the truck door opening and slamming, and the click of a flashlight as it came on and cast a white laser beam through the darkness. Chief Ranger Notworst was following up on a sighting by two hikers earlier in the evening. The hikers stated they had looked over the Jeep but quickly left when they heard a loud screeching sound along with a horrid stench. Making haste, they headed to the nearest ranger station to get help. Lucky for Dave Notworst, they found him at Ranger Station 5 just sitting down for supper. The hikers urged Chief Ranger Dave Notworst that someone immediately needed to look into the situation.

"Light blue Jeep Cherokee," Dave said to himself and out loud, "Looks like that crazy fool Dan Simmons has got himself in deep this time!" Muttering to himself, Dave said, "Nothing I can do tonight in this darkness; I'll send Search and Rescue in the morning; I hope the stupid idiot survives the night." Chief Ranger Dave Notworst jumped back in the driver's seat, shoved the gear shift firmly to the right and up, forcibly putting it in reverse and bouncing the truck backward down the Cedar Creek Watershed road ZT 145. Finding the nearest turnaround, he about-faced the vehicle, driving nose first back down the road to station 5 to eat his cold dinner. Thinking to himself as he drove, "What has Simmons done now?" Under his breath and through his teeth, Dave mumbled, "That guy just spends too much time out in the forest taking pictures, and of what? He never tells anyone what he is up to; a kook, that's what everyone was saying."

Chief Ranger Notworst reached into his pocket and retrieved his cell phone; pushing the start button, he saw the screen come alive, "No Service" glowed in the upper corner.

Shoving the phone back into his pocket, he reached for the 2-way radio. "Calling Search and Rescue, come in, Oscar." Dave paused and waited, then again said, "Search and Rescue, this is Ranger Dave Notworst, come in, Oscar." Waiting again and then becoming impatient, Dave spit loudly at the mic in his hand, "DAMN IT, COME IN SEARCH AND RESCUE!"

There was a crackling sound, then shortly a "Yeah, Yeah, this is Search and Rescue" came back Oscar Madison from the tiny speaker in the dashboard. Then again, a crackle; "Whaddaya want, Dave?"

Dave calmed down and said less forcefully, "We need your assistance; we have a lost visitor in the park. I need you to assemble a search party so we can get started first light."

Another crackle came out of the speaker, "Whaddaya got, Dave?"

Dave calmly stated, "Well, looks like we've got a sightseer up Cedar Creek road; he left his car and must have gotten lost; could be trouble; he may have left in a hurry." He continued, "Have your crew assembled and meet me at the station at 4 am sharp; I want to be up the creek at first light."

Crackle, pop, Oscar came back with, "Sounds like your sightseer already is."

"Funny, Oscar, let's keep the wisecracks to a minimum if you can."

Oscar came back, "Right! Whaddaya know about the missing visitor?"

Not to sound unprofessional, Dave said, "It appears to be Dan Simmons' Jeep up there."

Oscar came back, "Maybe we should just leave him up there this time?"

Dave snapped back, "Let's keep the opinions to ourselves; we are on an open frequency here. We got someone lost out there, and we need to do our job. Over and out!"

Buzz, buzz, buzz. Buzz, buzz, buzz. Buzz, buzz, buzz. Chief Ranger Dave Notworst reached over to the center of the nightstand and tapped the top of the clock. Sitting up in bed, yawning wide and detecting how bad his breath was, he quickly closed his mouth. Taking his two index fingers, he wiped the crusted and dried gook from the inside corners of his eyes. He looked at his fingers, and then he wiped them on his stained T-shirt. Stepping out of bed, he was shocked awake by the cold floor. Standing and stretching, he quickly headed to the bathroom to relieve himself. As he passed by, he looked into the mirror and realized why he was still single. Thinking out loud, he said, "I wouldn't want to wake up to that every morning either." When he finished his morning routine, he moved to the kitchen to put on a pot of coffee. Filling the coffee pot with water and Folgers, he lit the stove and slid the pot onto the burner. Dave then headed back to the bedroom to change into his uniform. Thinking to himself, "Better wear the .45 on my hip today".

Chief Ranger Dave Notworst was sitting on the toilet when Oscar Madison pounded on the front door. "Hey, Dave, you up yet? Let's hit the road."

Dave shouted back, "Give me a minute; I'm on the hopper."

Then Oscar yelled back, "Well, get the paperwork done so we can get on the road. The sun is going to be coming up, and the tracks are getting cold."

Dave Notworst threw the Field and Stream magazine on the counter and yelled back, "Okay, keep your shirt on."

Chief Ranger Dave Notworst was a tall man, almost brushing his ranger hat on the top door casing as he stepped out the door. The brim of his flat military style hat pointed down as he looked Oscar in the eyes. "How many guys did you get?" he asked Oscar.

Oscar looking back up at Dave said, "I got only three this morning, and two more coming this afternoon. Did you call the Sheriff's office and make a report?"

Stepping off the porch, Dave spoke as he walked, "No, I

can't make a report for 24 hours; it's up to us to find Dan Simmons; we need to find him before another nightfall." Dave added, "Who did you get?"

Oscar, much shorter than Dave, tried to keep up with his long stride as he talked, "I got Pete Davis, Tommy Wells, Joe Ferguson. Sue Farnsworth and Bill Sale will be up about noon."

Dave frowned and said, "Great, Pete Davis is such a nimrod; well, let's get moving, time's a-wastin'."

Chief Ranger Dave Notworst addressed the group, "This is what I have to go on; I had two shook-up hikers stop by my office last evening around 7, telling me about this Jeep that was left on the side of the Cedar Creek road ZT145. Keys still in it and the door flung open against a tree. They seemed pretty shook-up and were glad to be back at camp. I suspect it's Dan Simmons' Jeep; well, I am sure it is. I was up and looked at it in the dark last night and didn't see any signs of a struggle but what I did see were footprints in the mud like he was headed up the hillside on a dead run. Any questions?"

Pete Davis had a cock-eyed smile on his face which looked like a Jack-O-Lantern because of his missing front tooth.

Pete spoke up, "I gots uh questions."

Dave frowned and said, "What?"

Pete squinted a little and rolled his top lip up a bit exposing that hole that once held a tooth. One lost in a fistfight. Most likely due to one of his smartass questions. The teeth that were left were stained from tobacco, but that didn't keep him from smiling in his cock-eyed way.

Pete said in a slow drawl, "Hey, Notworst, are you the big hot dog on this outing, or is Oscar?"

Gritting his teeth Notworst barked back, "Pete, do you hear that sound? It's the sound of someone losing a greasy tooth. Now get in your truck and let's go!"

Walking towards the truck with his back turned, Pete said, "Well, I guess it's Oscar leading the pack today."

Then Pete started singing, "My baloney has a first name; it's O-S-C-A-R ..."

Dave and Oscar headed for Dave's government green truck; there was a succession of truck doors slamming and engines starting. Soon it was headlights through clouds of dust and the roar of engines. All headed for ZT 145. Two right turns, one left and then a final right turn onto ZT 145; it was still dark out, but the sky was starting to lighten. By the time they reached Dan Simmons' Jeep, they could see without the headlights of the truck; they had arrived at just the right time in the morning.

Once all of the caravan had arrived, Dave motioned for everyone to gather around. He addressed the group again, "Okay, fellas, Oscar is going to direct you because you are all trained in Search and Rescue; I am here to assist the best I can. So, Oscar, what is the plan of attack?"

Oscar cleared his throat, "Ahem, well, guys, I had a quick look around the Jeep and looked at the tracks before they got messed up. I can see that Dan Simmons was headed up the side of this gully just to the east of the Jeep; looks to me like he was moving up the hill as fast as he could, so there was some urgency in his actions. So, Pete, I'd like you to unload your four-wheeler and follow this trail on up ZT 145 where it turns into an old pack trail, but I think you can circle back and make it to the top of the ridge just above us. When you get to the top, wait for the rest of us to make the hike up the hillside."

Oscar, staring right at Pete, said somewhat sarcastically, "Got that, Pete?"

Pete came back with a salute and a, "Yes! Sir!"

Pete went to unload his four-wheeler, and Oscar continued, "Okay, the rest of us will spread out 15 feet apart and climb the hill. Keep sight of each other; we don't need to look for more than one person today." Oscar nodded his head towards the group, "Got it? Any questions?" Everyone shook their heads in agreement. Oscar said, "Oh, everyone double check your water and food supply. Joe, do you have the first aid kit in your pack?"

Joe Ferguson was the town pharmacist from North Bend. Joe was quiet but tall and strong. Joe stated, "I'm fully packed."

Oscar said, "Okay, Men, let's get going. I don't want to be climbing that hill when the sun hits us." Finishing out his instructions, Oscar told them, "I will be in the center where Dan's tracks are visible, and two of you on my left side and Dave you on my right." They all started up the hill, Oscar scrutinizing the tracks before each step he took, making sure his were beside them and not smack-dab on the top of them.

Just 20 minutes into the hike up the hill, two shots rang out and a group of roused, startled birds flew out of the trees directly above them.

Dave blurted, "Pete! Oscar, did you tell Pete he couldn't shoot any deer when we are on a search mission?"

Oscar looked up the hill at Dave and said, "Yes, but you know Pete."

Oscar shook his head and started back up the hill. The sun was beginning to peek through the trees the cold air was starting to warm, making the hike uphill very exhausting. Everyone stopped, and some of the guys sat on the hillside and took a quick break. Except for Oscar; he was surveying the valley below and the opposite side of the draw for any signs of activity. Above them was the low engine rumble of Pete's four-wheeler; they were close to the top.

Dave's voice was strained from the hike, and he was out of breath, but he forced out an "Okay Men, let's get going and finish this climb."

Oscar reached the top first, and there was Pete sitting sideways on the four-wheeler. Then came Joe Ferguson, followed by Tommy Wells, a young man still in his twenties; then followed Chief Ranger Dave Notworst, all out of breath but still charged with energy because it was still early in the day.

When he had caught his breath, Dave looked at Pete and asked, "What was all the shooting about, Pete?"

Pete returned his stupid cock-eyed smile and said, "There was a huge bull moose in the trail and wouldn't move. I yelled, and the dumb thing just stared at me, but he shore made tracks when I fired a couple of rounds; he even left a steaming calling card on the trail." Pete added, "I guess he didn't want to come to dinner."

Then Oscar shouted, "Dave, come over here and take a look at this!"

Feeling the effects of the hike up the hill Dave was walking like John Wayne in an old Duke movie, his .45 swinging back and forth as he walked.

Reaching Oscar, Dave questioned, "What do ya see, Oscar?" Oscar looked up at Dave and then back at the ground, catching Dave's eyes, making him look down too.

Oscar pointed out, "Look! Dan's tracks stop right here; they don't go any farther."

The soil was soft from rains the day before, and tracks were easy to spot and so was the absence of them.

Dave said, "What? That's impossible; where did he go? There's no tree to climb; it's like he spread wings and flew off."

Oscar, looking back at Dave, stated, "How can we track someone without a trail?" He added, "I've done some damn good scouting in my day, but I'm stumped here."

Dave looked ahead, about 15 feet away, to where a torn piece of red flannel shirt lay. He went over and picked it up, and said, "It looks like there's dried blood on it."

Oscar spoke in a quiet voice, "I am worried he may be hurt." He walked over to where Dave was standing. Oscar then added, "This is not a good sign; no tracks and a wounded man lost. Let's hope he has some survival skills and some basic gear."

Dave looked Oscar in the eyes and said, "I know Dan well enough to know he knows his way around. I think he was chasing something or something was chasing him."

Oscar came back with, "And it looks like they met up right here."

Dave felt confused, "Let's take a few minutes here and retrace our steps, just to see if we missed anything."

"Agreed," replied Oscar.

As Dave and Oscar are mentally retracing everything they have seen, Tommy Wells approached them. Tommy wrinkled his nose, "You guys smell that; it smells like there is some dead animal rotting around here someplace."

Oscar spoke up, "Yah, but it doesn't smell like a dead animal to me; it's sweeter and more pungent, like a gorilla cage at the zoo."

Dave added," Yup, definitely scat, but some nasty smelling scat." The smell seemed to be getting stronger in the direction they had walked.

The sky was partly cloudy, and the clouds were moving quickly above, momentarily blocking the sun. Dave's sweaty body felt a chill and goosebumps formed on his bare arms. Oscar shrugged his shoulders to the cold and Tommy shook as a chill ran up his spine. There was a crack of a breaking limb in the near distance. Dave looked at Oscar, finding Oscar staring back at him, eyes wide open, small blue irises in a field of white. Then came a scraping sound on a tree below them on the opposite side of the hill they had just clambered up. It was scraping like an elk or moose would do with its horns.

Oscar said, "Must be that moose Pete scared off."

Then, twenty yards in front of them came another scraping sound and then another just over the hill where they had just ascended. The scraping sounds were all around them, and then the many scraping sounds started scraping in unison. Pete stood up and stepped off his four-wheeler, with his rifle butt resting on his hip and the barrel pointed to the sky. The five men stood motionless, all of them looking off in different directions as the rhythmic scraping sounds now surrounded them.

A low short growl like a grunt came from one direction below the brush-line in front of Dave. Then a growl-grunt came from the other side of the circle of men. Now the growl-grunting was coming from all directions. Along with the rhythmic scraping, the growl-grunting surrounded them, like some guttural chanting. Dave was starting to feel nauseous and dizzy from the scraping and growl-grunting trance-inducing sounds. Pete hoisted the .30-30 to his shoulder, pulled back the bolt action ejecting a spent cartridge, whirling it to the ground sticking butt end out of the mud. In a second swift motion, Pete shoved the bolt forward injecting a new round into the chamber. Pete eyed down the sites sweeping the rifle barrel across the brush-line in front of him looking for movement. But there was no movement, nothing, and the sounds had stopped, the forest was once again silent.

The five men stood there, backs toward each other, and facing out from the circle. The silence was deafening; no one spoke a word---in a state of shock from what they had just witnessed. A lone red-tailed hawk far above screeched and soared across the sky, breaking the silence.

"What the hell was that?" Dave blurted, as he looked at Oscar. "What the hell was that scraping and grunting?" Dave added.

Pete spits on the ground, wiped the remainder from his two-day-old beard with his sleeve and said," All my years in these woods, I ain't never heard anything like that."

Oscar spoke up, "I'm with Pete. I have never heard anything like that either."

Joe Ferguson cleared his throat, "I heard some old timers talk about something similar, like the old Swede. He told stories about some big hairy creatures walking the woods. You know over at Murphy's Pub; the old Swede would bend everyone's ear with stories about the creatures he'd seen."

"Okay, okay, let's stop the fairy tales; we have a mission, and we need to keep on track," Dave said, bringing everyone back to reality and the Search and Rescue mission at hand. But Dave too was weary of the sounds, unsure of what it was.

Dave looked down at where the casing from Pete's rifle had landed in the mud. Embedded right on the edge of an enormous footprint.

Dave nudged Oscar and pointed at the same time calmly saying, "Pete, don't move a muscle; don't back up."

Pete was standing in the back half of the footprint. "Oscar, can you make out what kind of animal makes that footprint?" Dave asked.

Oscar stepped closer to examine the impression in the muck. "I'm not sure; it's very distorted from the rain, maybe a large bear; the toes looked dug in deep like it was running," Oscar reported.

The large footprint was about three feet behind the last footprints that Dan Simmons had left in the mud which Dave was now examining. "Look here, Oscar, the toes of Dan's prints look thrust ahead, like he was drug forward and lifted off the ground."

Excitedly Oscar yelled out, "Look, Dave, another large footprint!"

Another fifteen feet ahead of Dan's footprints, there was another larger skid in the mud. It was at the end of a deep impression with the toes of the print deep in the mud. It was as if an animal had been running at top speed, leaping into the air, grabbing Dan off his feet and landing on the other foot on a slide and jumping again, making a stride of almost twenty feet.

Oscar said, "Seems like a bear took old Dan out."

Dave was looking up, shook his head and remarked, "You may be right, Oscar, but something isn't quite right for bear tracks; do you see what I mean?"

Oscar looked closer at the series of tracks. Oscar rubbed his chin with his forefinger and thumb, and said, "Yes, Dave, I see what you mean; a bear would have left two sets of tracks and not one. Whatever it was, was walking upright."

Chapter 2

Hats Off

Dave agreed with Oscar that he should continue to search the area while he returned to town and filed a missing person report at the sheriff's office. He said he would also inform Bill and Sue that they could return to town as they would no longer be needed to search in the afternoon.

Chief Ranger Dave Notworst made his way back down the hillside, cautiously pausing between steps so he wouldn't roll headfirst down the steep hill. Laboriously watching his actions, slowly lifting the foot behind and carefully placing it in front of the other as it sank into the soft soil; the slippery pine needles didn't help. Dave was headed to meet Sue and Bill waiting for him at the bottom. They were no longer needed for the afternoon search since the trail had hit a dead-end.

Oscar decided to head in the direction the last footprints pointed, hopefully, to find more clues. Tommy was on his right, and Joe was on his left, again spaced 15 feet apart. They also descended the ridge as it tapered down to the main road far below them. Oscar sent Pete on around the horseshoe ridge to the other side of the gulch to survey from that side of the draw for any signs.

Dave was feeling at a loss for explanations about Dan

Simmons. He had no other option but to file a missing person's report at the Sheriff's office.

When Dave arrived at the truck, Sue and Bill were waiting nearby. Before they could speak, Dave reached in through the truck window, grabbed the 2-way mic and radioed for a chopper to search for anything they could spot.

Dave spoke into the mic, "Calling Sky Adventures; come in, Mitch." Mitch Cochran was a decorated vet; he learned to fly choppers during the Vietnam war.

Mitch came back, "Go ahead; this is Mitch."

Dave explained the situation to Mitch and told him the coordinates to search. Mitch had been made aware of the situation by Oscar who had called him the night before. Oscar had filled him in about the lost traveler up Cedar Creek Watershed and ZT 145.

Dave turned his attention back to Sue and Bill. Sue was a mountain woman through and through. She wore men's boots and pants. The only thing that distinguished her from one of the boys was her red bandana. She wore it to keep her hair out of her face, and she had a small knot tied in the front at the top of her forehead; she looked a bit like "Rosie the Riveter."

Sue squinted her eyes from the sun and said, "Dave, what's the story so far?"

Dave filled both Sue and Bill in on what they had found, and how the tracks just stopped. He did not include any details of the size of the prints or how it looked like some two-legged monster had grabbed Dan right out of his tracks.

Dave cleared his throat and then added, "Looks as if Dan Simmons may have had a run-in with a bear. All we found of him was this bloody torn piece of a flannel shirt" Which Dave held up for them to see.

Dave looked at Bill and requested, "Bill, can you have one of your guys at the car lot come up and tow Dan's Cherokee? Could you store it in your sales lot? We don't need to take it to the impound lot; there is no crime yet."

Bill nodded, "Sure can, Dave. I'll keep it safe until he returns."

Dave summed it up, "Well there is nothing to track up there; I'm headed to the sheriff's office to fill out a report; you two might as well head back to town and business as usual." Dave got an okay from Bill; Sue and Bill got into Bill's CJ5 and backed it down the road.

Dave spun around and opened the door of the truck, and then unburdened himself of the .45 and then his pack onto the passenger side of the seat. He wiggled his body around to a comfortable position, fastened his seatbelt and started the engine. Dave carefully backed the truck to maneuver it around Tommy's vehicle and then Pete's 1948 Willys-Overland pickup truck. Going past Pete's rig, Dave thought to himself, "For being such a crusty character, he sure keeps his old Willys in nice condition. He was always asked to drive it in the 4th of July Day Parade." Dave backed into the turnaround, shifted the truck into second gear and headed his government green truck back down ZT 145 toward the main gravel road. Once on the main road, Dave was deep in thought, trying to work out the events in his head; the two hikers, maybe they were still camped in the park, and he decided he needed to talk with them after he spoke with the Sheriff.

Dave went over the events of the day, considering what he planned to share with the Sheriff. He didn't want to leave any details open to misinterpretation. Two years ago, the town got overrun by Bigfoot idiots. Dave thought to himself, "We don't need those hare-brained look-e-loos up in the woods again. All that nonsense turned into a lot of overtime trying to keep the peace, which all ended with a melee inside Murphy's Pub." That summer kept both Chief Ranger Dave Notworst and Sherriff Spencer Harrington busy, to say the least. Dave recalled not getting more than 2 hours sleep at any one time that summer. When fall finally came, the woods filled with hunters and the Bigfoot sightings came to an end. Which also included the hounding by that damned reporter lady, Wendy Storms. Dave thought, "I could live as a happy man my whole life without ever seeing that prodding, invasive, sensationalistic witch ever again." Dave couldn't even stand to watch Channel 12 News because he couldn't stand the sight of her and that whiney voice of contention. And who the hell but Wendy would go out into the woods in high heels?" Dave secretly hoped she would twist an ankle and be sent back to Seattle for treatment.

Dave reached the North Bend Sheriff's Office and turned into the parking lot that was also shared by the courthouse. Dave parked in the fire hydrant NO PARKING area, and all painted in diagonally striped yellow. Dave did this on purpose, just to get under Deputy Higgins' skin. Higgins always gave Dave a parking ticket for the violation, and the sheriff always tore it up. Dave walked up the five granite steps and opened one of the aluminum cased glass doors as a small ding went off alerting anyone inside the sheriff's office that the door had opened.

Higgins looked up from his paperwork and boldly stated, "Well, looky here, if it isn't Chief Ranger Notworst." Higgins added gleefully, "What can we do you for today Notworst?"

Dave looked at the skinny Barney Fife look-a-like and said, "Howdy, Higgins, I need to talk to the sheriff."

Higgins looked over the top of his glasses and came back with, "You might as well have a seat; Sheriff is taking a report over the phone; they found the old Swede's truck nosed into the creek just outside of town. Looks like he had his fill at Murphy's last night."

Still thinking about what he was going to tell the sheriff, Dave said, "I can wait; got any coffee on?"

Higgins nodded his head towards the table with the coffee maker and a tray of clean cups on it. Higgins said, "Help yourself."

Dave walked over to the table and up-righted a cup and pulled the coffee pot out of the Mister Coffee and filled the cup.

Higgins spoke up, clearing his throat first, "Notworst, what is that? Is that German, Italian or Polish?" Dave frowned, tired of the game with Higgins. Then Higgins added,

"Just what kind of sausage is a Notworst?" Higgins continued, "Tell me Dave, is Notworst made out of head cheese or pork belly?"

Dave had heard it all many times before, growing up with the last name of Notworst, he was teased from the first grade through High school. Higgins' mentality, had been stunted somewhere around Junior high school and his humor was non-existent.

Dave blew on his coffee to cool it, and then calmly spoke, "Tell me, Higgins, is your girlfriend still dating two guys?"

Higgin's grin turned to a tight-lipped glare. Marylou, Higgins' girlfriend was a well-known barfly down at Murphy's. Higgins stood up sharply, sending the old wooden-castered chair zipping across the floor striking the watercooler.

"Hey!" said Higgins, "You had better watch what you say."

Dave looked Higgins in the eye and said, "Why don't you go out into the parking lot and write some tickets?"

Higgins picked up his ticket book and headed for the door, and as he walked through the door, he said, "Damned good idea."

Sheriff Spencer Harrington was not a tall man and a bit heavy-set, but he had a way about him that commanded people's attention. When the situation arose, Sheriff Harrington had a way of talking that he could not only calm and subdue someone but also could persuade them to cease whatever they were doing. This talent alone had gotten him re-elected four times; also folks get comfortable with how things are and don't want change. Besides that, Sherriff Harrington had a well-proven track record for a job well-done. Dave Notworst had a good relationship with Sherriff Harrington and relied on him when things got sticky, and they both shared the same opinion of Wendy Storms. That alone made points with Chief Ranger Dave Notworst. Dave heard Spencer say goodbye on the phone and hang up the receiver.

Spencer walked out of his office, looked at Dave and said, "Where's Higgins?"

Dave smiled and said, "He's in the parking lot writing me a thank you note for my excellent parking skills."

Spencer smiled and told Dave, "Come into my office." Dave walked into the office followed by Spencer; then there was the sound of the door swinging and rattling shut.

"What can I do you for, Dave?" asked Spencer.

Dave paused and then said, "Looks as if Dan Simmons is missing and I need to file a missing person's report with you."

"Oh, Son of a Biscuit!" said Spencer, "Give me the details."

Spencer slid open the bottom drawer of his desk and pulled out a folder with forms in it. He pulled a pen from the cup of pens on his desk and started to write the date on one of the forms. Dave detailed the whole scenario from the hikers' story the night before and then the Search and Rescue mission and what they had found. Dave left out all the details about the enormous footprints, and the speculation of a creature walking upright. But he did give his professional opinion on the possibility of a bear attack. Mentioning that he thought it might have been another black bear attack, especially with the news of a record 700-pound black bear being shot by a hunter just a few months before.

Spencer asked, "What kind of tracks did you see?"

Dave looked Spencer in the eyes and said, "I took some pictures with my phone; maybe you can tell me." Dave pulled his phone out of his pocket and thumbed his way through the pictures and then handed the phone to Spencer. Spencer flipped back and forth through the photos, stopping and studying each one and then returned to first of them.

Spencer looked up at Dave and said, "Not very clear pictures or tracks, but I would guess that it wasn't a bear."

Dave stared at Spencer, "Whatdaya mean?"

"Dave, you know, those are not any bear tracks either of us have ever seen," Spencer stated with a bit of irritation in his voice. He added, "Can you sit there with a straight face and tell me those are bear tracks?"

Dave looked down at his hands, then out the window behind Spencer. He then returned his focus to Spencer's face. Dave said quietly, "Spencer, what are we going to call it? Do you want those Bigfoot kooks back up here again this year? I might as well quit being a ranger right now! I'm just not going through that again."

Spencer got Dave's drift, and slightly changing the subject, he said, "What do you know about Dan Simmons anyway? Where the hell did he come from and mostly, what the hell was he doing up there?"

Dave took a long deep breath and paused before he began. "Well, Dan Simmons came over the mountain here two years ago, when all the hubbub about Bigfoot was in full swing." Dave continued, "I was down at Murphy's having a cold one when Dan Simmons came up to me. He asked if I was Park Ranger Notworst."

Dave continued to tell Spencer Dan Simmons' story about how he had come over the mountain from Spokane. He was a student at Gonzaga University and studying anthropology. Dave continued about how Dan was writing a paper on Darwinism for his doctoral thesis, and the media buzz about Bigfoot sparked his interest.

Dave recommenced his explanation, "He went on to tell me something about GMO, you know Genetically Modified Organisms; you know the scuttlebutt that tree huggers have been upset about, what chemical companies are doing to corn, right? Then something about species cleansing through a cloning process. Something about making monkeys less like monkeys." Dave was rubbing the back of his neck.

Spencer looked as if he were starting to fall asleep, and said, "Yes, I know what GMO is, but what the hell does that have to do with what Dan Simmons was doing over here on this side of the Cascades."

Dave smiled and said, "Your guess is as good as mine; I'm just telling you what he was saying."

Spencer smiled at Dave and said, "Okay, Dave, we won't go down that road again."

"Good then," added Spencer, "I think that I have enough to go on; I'll file the report and send out a missing person on the APB wire, and we can all hope that Dan Simmons shows up sometime soon."

Dave agreed and stated, "I'm headed over to Mitch Cochran's chopper pad to find out what he saw from the sky this afternoon."

Spencer opened the door for Dave. As Dave walked out of the office, he could see Higgins smiling, sitting in his chair with his feet on the desk and the fingers of his hands intertwined behind his head.

Higgins commented, "I left you a present on your windshield, Notworst."

Dave responded with a "Good, I'm out of toilet paper."

With that, Dave walked out of the sheriff's office, down the steps and headed for his truck. Dave opened the door of the truck ignoring the flapping pink piece of paper pinned down by the driver's side windshield wiper. Shaking his head, Dave thought to himself; North Bend must have more jackasses per capita than any other city in the United States. Pressing the pedal down as he turned out of the parking lot, he caused a rear tire to hit a wet patch of pavement making it spin, then chirping and squealing when it hit the dry asphalt. In the rear-view mirror, Dave could see Higgins throwing the door of the sheriff's office open and running down the steps. Dave smiled.

On his way to Mitch Cochran's airfield, Dave decided to stop for a late lunch at the Double D Diner. Betsy would be working the afternoon shift, and Dave always enjoyed her brassy conversation. No one could keep Dave on his toes as Betsy could. She had a quick sense of humor, and sometimes it was a little extra sharp. Dave was a bit sweet on Betsy, and if there were a gal in North Bend that put up with Dave, it would be her. Dave pulled into the small parking lot, squeezed his truck into what looked like a compact car parking space, jumped out of the truck and headed for the door. Dave scanned the place and spotted an open stool at the counter. Dave sat down and pulled the menu from the rack in front of him. Betsy walked up just as Dave was checking out the sandwiches.

Betsy pulled the pencil out of her hair and the order pad from her apron pocket. She said, "What will it be today, Dave?"

Dave looked up from the menu and said, "What's the special today, Betsy?"

Betsy cocked her head in a matter-a-fact manner and said, "Honey, I'm the only thing special in this place, but you already knew that, Dave."

Dave smiled and said, "I think I'll have the Paul Bunyan burger, with everything on it; oh, yes, vanilla shake too."

Betsy said, "You got it, Big Dave." Betsy was the only one that could get away with calling Dave Notworst, Big Dave. Betsy sent in Dave's order in her own special way, "One full Bunyan with cheese and leave it on the hoof." Translation, meant everything on Dave's burger and rare, just the way Dave liked it.

It was slow in the Double D Diner, having just finished the lunch crowd and before the dinner surge started.

Dave used the downtime to strike up a conversation with Betsy, "What's new in town today?"

Betsy answered, "The Darcie twins are having a double wedding next month." Then she added, "All the hoopla about your Search and Rescue mission up Cedar Creek. How is that going?"

Dave frowned, "Not so good."

Betsy went on, "Well, you missed all the lively conversation about it at lunchtime."

Dave asked, "What did you hear?"

Betsy, raising her eyebrows, said, "A lot of folks had a lot to say about that Dan Simmons; everything from what was he doing in the woods, to buying him a bus ticket back to Spokane." She added, "Seems, that for a fella that doesn't talk much, people have lots to say about him."

Dave nodded in agreement, "Anything else?"

Betsy shook her head back and forth, "Dave if you have to ask --- your favorite subject came up, Bigfoot."

Dave looked down at the glass of sweating ice water and said, "I was afraid everyone would start talking about Bigfoot again."

Betsy sighed, "Well, that's why Dan Simmons showed up here in the first place." Betsy said, "Look, hon, you enjoy your lunch; I have to go and give that dishwasher a lesson in cleaning silverware."

Dave looked back up, "Thanks, Betsy." Dave picks up the fork on the counter, looked over both sides then scoured it with the paper napkin.

Since he was a big man, Betsy always gave Dave extra fries and a vanilla shake and a half. The big meal just barely puts a dent in Dave's appetite, so he always buys an apple pie turnover to go. Paying his tab, Dave made his way out of the diner and into his truck. Carefully backing his vehicle out of the tiny space and pulling out into traffic, Dave drove up East North Bend Avenue towards Mitch Cochran's airfield. As Dave got close to the airfield, he could see that Mitch was back because all three of the choppers were there. Dave pulled into the gravel parking lot and spotted Mitch checking the fuel in one of the choppers. He parked the truck and walked over to where Mitch was.

Dave spoke before he reached Mitch, "Afternoon, Mitch, how's business?"

Mitch was tall and skinny; he seemed to always be in a good or optimistic mood. "Hello, Dave, good to see you." Mitch came back, "Business is slow; I appreciate the Search and Rescue jobs you throw my way," he added.

Dave said, "I'm gonna cut to the chase; tell me, what did you see up there? I'm hoping you saw more than what we found."

Mitch got quiet, "Well, Dave, I saw your tracks --- well, the tracks from the four-wheeler and I saw Oscar and the two guys with him but not much else, except ---."

Dave spoke up anxiously, "Hey, Mitch, anything is better than what we got; whadidya see?" Dave was excited to get some new lead he could work with, anything.

Mitch nervously went on, "The next ridge over; I spotted something out of the corner of my eye. I quickly pushed the stick down and to the right and banked the chopper in that direction." Mitch fidgeted but continued, "I got low, as low as I could get, just above the treetops."

Dave prompted, "Okay, go slow and give me all the details; don't leave anything out."

Mitch swallowed and said, "Dave, I don't know how you are going to take this; I don't want the community talking trash about me. This business is my livelihood. You know, all that agent orange garbage and the onset of dementia; you know I'm not a crazy Viet Nam Vet, right?"

Dave came back with, "Mitch, you're a solid guy; I have no reservations about you."

Mitch looked at Dave, "Well, you may change that opinion after I tell you what I saw."

Dave tried to calm Mitch down, "Look, Mitch, I have known you for --- what --- 25 years give or take, right?"

Mitch, clearly shaken after he started to tell Dave what he had seen, his voice faltered just a bit. "Dave, I have seen some crazy messed-up shit in my day; you know I was in Nam, and some of those guys came back off-center, then I spent two years on the L.A.P.D. bomb squad. That's what pushed me into starting a business way out here. I saw some grotesque mutilations from the poor bastards we couldn't save."

Dave interrupted, "Okay, Mitch, take it slow; it's only you and me here; tell me what you saw."

Mitch started again, "Anyway, I come over the top of this big cedar tree and in the clearing below, I see, what I think is this huge reddish-brown bear running."

Dave tried to sooth Mitch, "Okay, take your time; what happened next?"

Mitch's voice changed, "As I looked closer at this running bear, it is running on its hind legs and at top speed. Dave, on its hind legs." Beads of sweat formed on Mitch's forehead, and he continued, "But that's not the crazy part."

Dave felt a little embarrassed to see a marine acting this way, "Mitch, come on, spill it."

Mitch, straightened up and continued, "Right, well, the crazy thing about this bear is he's not only walking upright but, he's, get this, he's also wearing a camo jungle hat, with it strapped around his chin."

Dave's eyes bugged open, "What!?"

Mitch continued, "Yaw, and about that time he hears my chopper, he turns to look up, and the bear has a face, and the damned thing is smiling at me!" Mitch continued, "At just that moment, I have to pull back on the stick to clear this fast-approaching cliff. I quickly circled back around, but by the time I got back, the thing was gone."

Dave consolingly smiled at Mitch and said, "Okay, Mitch, okay, let's just keep this between us for now, agreed?"

Mitch nodded his head in agreement, "Dave, it was hard enough to tell you; I don't want to have to tell anyone else."

Back in his truck, he headed towards Ranger Station 5; Dave got a call from Sheriff Harrington.

Dave answered, "Ranger Notworst here."

Dave could hear Spencer through the receiver. "Hey, Dave, just a heads-up; after I sent out the APB on Simmons, I got a call from Channel 12 News." Spencer continued, "Our favorite news reporter wanted to know the status."

Dave felt a depressed, sinking feeling in his gut, or maybe it was the loaded Bunyan on the hoof kicking in. At any rate, it was the last thing he wanted to hear. Dave came back with a, "What the hell was she asking?"

Spencer went on to tell Dave that she wanted as much background on Dan Simmons as she could get, and the status of anything on the search. He also told Dave that the Dean at Gonzaga called; he was also looking for Dan Simmons; it seems that some grant money went missing about the time

Dan made his trip over the Cascades, to spend time running in the woods around North Bend. Spencer let the Dean know that if they ever found Dan, he would be sure to call him back.

Spencer concluded with, "Dave, you better watch Channel 12 News tonight to see what dirt Wendy Storms has under her sharp little fingernails. She was digging pretty deep."

Dave concluded the conversation with, "Thanks, Spencer, I will tune in and catch the BS."

Dave did a quick run-through of the campground to police the area; everything looked normal. He then headed over to Ranger Willkie's house; he was the other ranger that collected camping and day park fees. Dave pulled up in front of Tom Willkie's house just as Tom was lighting the briquettes on the BBQ. Dave could see Tom from his truck as he pulled in, so Dave just walked around the garage and into the backyard. There was at least one thing that irritated Dave about Tom, that was, he liked to talk like a Canadian, eh?

Dave walked up to Tom, smiled and said, "Hello, Tom, did you have any trouble today?"

Tom smiled back at Dave and said, "Piece of cake," pause, "eh?"

Dave cringed. Dave asked, "Any trouble down by the day parking at the lake?"

Tom started his wind up with, "Yah, well, we had a couple of hosers down there wanting to drink some suds and sipping on a Micky, but I put a quick stop to that one." Tom added, "I let 'em know, no open containers, eh?" Once Tom started, it was almost impossible to turn him off. Tom continued, "Dave, stay for dinner; were havin' burgers with back-bacon. Eh."

Dave answered, "Thank you so much, Tom, but, I had a late lunch, and I need to get back to write up a report."

Tom asked, "Any luck finding Dan Simmons?"

Dave answered a disappointing, "No."

"Well, ya know what I think Dave," said Tom.

Dave emotionally braced himself, and asked, "What?"

Tom went on with, "Ya know, when he comes down out of the woods, we should all pitch in and buy him a one-way, back to Spokane, eh? That guy has caused a real kerfuffle with the town, eh?"

Dave genuinely smiled at Tom and said, "I'd be willing to pitch in on that one too. Good night, Tom." With that, Dave headed back to his truck.

Dave got back home just in time for the K-RAP, Channel 12 News at 5. He walked into the house dropping his .45 and backpack on the kitchen table. Reaching into the icebox, retrieving a frozen Hungry Man for dinner, and set it on the counter. He walked over and picked up the remote and switched on the TV and surfed the channels until he got to Channel 12 News. They were talking about the traffic on I-5 and expected delays, then on to Ronald McDonald House and then more of the same old, same old. Then came on Wendy Storms, high heels, tight fitting pantsuit and all that troweled on make-up.

Slick Willie, or whatever the news anchor's name was, started out by saying, "It looks as if we have a lost hiker in the Cedar River Watershed area just east of Seattle; now with that story is Wendy Storms."

Slick Willie asked, "Wendy, can you give us details of what is going on up there?"

Wendy came back, "Sure, William, it seems that an abandoned vehicle was found by two hikers yesterday afternoon; here is an interview with those two."

The screen switched over to a video of Wendy interviewing the two hikers. Wendy asked, "What did you find?"

The one on the right, spoke first, "We were like hiking really deep in the woods and came out on a trail. We walked about a mile and found this blue Jeep."

The second one broke in, "Dude, it was abandoned, and the keys were still in it." He continued, "The door was left open and up against a tree and these footprints were headed up the hill."

Wendy tilted her head and raised one eyebrow and inquired, "Did you see anything else?"

The first hiker said, "That's about all we seen, but there was this outrageous stench, Dude, it was unbelievable."

The second hiker continued with, "Dude, then there was that howling sound; it gives me the shivers, Man."

The two hikers continued talking to each other in the background, saying over and over Dude, Man, awesome, outrageous, totally. Wendy faced the camera and stated, "That's not all, William; it seems that the North Bend Sheriff's Office filed a missing person report this afternoon when the park rangers came up empty with their Search and Rescue mission."

William asked, "Wendy, didn't you cover a story a couple of years ago, something similar up in the Cedar River Watershed area?"

Dave flopped down in his Lazyboy forcing out a big exasperated sigh. He put his hands on each side of his face and said, "And it hits the fan."

Wendy Storms, shyly grinning stated, "You are so right, William, it seems that two years ago, some hikers photographed Bigfoot up there."

"Really," came back William, "Wendy, tell us more. Do we have that photo archived?"

Wendy went on to say, "The hikers that took the picture never released it to the media; they felt it was of great value and they still have not released it as of today; the picture, however, was shown to a Dr. Ferndyke Finkelstein from the University of Colorado who debunked it." Wendy continued, "Dr. Finkelstein stated the picture was too grainy to determine what the creature was but added if it were a bear standing on its hind legs, it would be the tallest damned bear he had ever seen."

William went on, "Thank you, Wendy, for that chilling report; well, there you have it folks; Bigfoot in our own backyard; coming up next, coffee colonics --- Can they make you younger?"

Dave picked up the remote and shut off the TV; he was

no longer hungry. He got up, picked up the frozen Hungry Man dinner and threw it back into the freezer. Instead, Dave reached for a glass and the bottle of Old Bushbuck Irish Whisky. Dave poured two fingers of whiskey into the glass, sat back down in the Lazyboy and before he could take a drink he was fast asleep. The next morning Dave woke up with drool running down his chin, slumped over in the easy chair. As he got up, he could feel the hike from the day before in his back, buttock and down each calf. Dave walked over to the stove, lit the burner and prepared the coffee pot. Then headed into the bathroom and started to shave; he could hear the percolation of the coffee pot starting. He shaved off the day-old growth and undressed and showered. When he was done, so was the coffee; he poured a large cup and headed to the bedroom for a fresh uniform for the day. He thought to himself, "A shower, a cup of coffee and fresh clothes can make a guy feel great."

Dave was ready to greet the day at full force, ready to tackle whatever the day had to offer. No challenge was too surmountable compared to the way he was feeling. He topped off his uniform with his hat, reached for the door-knob and with gusto, pulled open the door and stepped into the sunshine. As he stepped onto the porch, he looked out in front of his cabin; immediately Dave's knees went weak; his breath shortened; his heart-rate went up, and his head became dizzy. Sitting outside his house was a Channel 12 News van, and in a bold regatta outfit stood Wendy Storms, ready to rain on his parade. Dave quickly mustered all his strength, stepped off the porch with confidence, walked up to Wendy Storms, tilted his head down, and as a true gentleman, touched the brim of his hat with his right index finger, smiling. He spoke in a clear and confident voice, "Good morning, Ma'am, how may I be of service?"

Wendy smiled; a man in uniform always made her feel a little giddy. Her quickly switched-on smile turned into a tight-lipped interrogating smirk. Wendy asked, "May I ask you a few questions about the missing hiker?"

Dave was wearing his best persona, thankful that he had put on a fresh uniform for the surprise attack. No introductions were needed; she knew Dave, and everyone knew her. Wendy had a way of cutting to the heart of any situation; call it a knack, but Dave thought it was more of a character flaw.

Wendy started by looking at the camera. Dave was standing to her right. She spoke clearly, "We are standing just inside Iron Horse State Park with Chief Ranger Dave Notworst. Ranger, can you tell our viewers what you found yesterday during your Search and Rescue attempt?"

Dave smiled at the camera and laid out the sequences of the search, "We received a report of an abandoned vehicle up Cedar Creek Watershed Road. I drove up to see the sight myself and immediately ordered a Search and Rescue mission at first light."

Wendy looked puzzled, "What do you mean, Cedar Creek? I thought this was Cedar River Watershed?"

Dave smiled again, "Yes, it is but service road ZT 145 follows Cedar Creek which turns into the Cedar River Watershed."

Wendy nodded, "Well, tell me Ranger Notworst, what did you find?"

Dave's smile waned, and he continued, "We found an abandoned Jeep, searched the area for clues and followed a trail to the top of the ridge where it ended."

Wendy looked seriously at Dave, "Have you given up the search?"

Dave looked at the camera and stated, "We have an ongoing investigation, and I have sent out more men today policing that mountain range in a large grid. I also have choppers flying the area from daylight till dusk. All the lost hiker would have to do is make some type of signal, and we would spot him."

Wendy then asked, "Is the missing hiker Dan Simmons?"

Dave stated, "I am not at liberty to release any names; I would suggest you talk with the Sheriff's department."

Wendy pressed Dave, "We have an eyewitness account that there were unusually sized footprints at the scene. Can you comment on that, Ranger Notworst?"

Dave shook his head, "Again, you will have to get answers to that from the sheriff's department."

Wendy thanked Dave politely for his explanation of the search; then she turned to the camera as the cameraman shot a close up cutting out Dave. Wendy continued, "As the search continues for the missing hiker, we will have updates as the day goes on; this is Wendy Storms, KayRAP 12's 'Knows in the Air.'" That was Wendy's moniker, KayRAP 12's "Knows in the Air." You could just about read anything you like into that, and most people did.

One of the film crew yelled, "Cut!"

Wendy turned to her producer and said to him, "Let's head over to Murphy's Pub and see if we can catch any of the rummy's coming out of the bar; that young kid, Tommy Wells, maybe he has more to say about those big footprints."

Wendy's producer, Phil, came back with a, "You got it."

The cameraman slid the door of the van shut. Wendy sat in the passenger seat, and Phil drove. The engine roared, and off they went. Dave watched their cloud of dust follow them down the road, thinking to himself, "If it is ten years before I see that woman again, it will be too soon."

Murphy's Pub was opened in 1969 by then owner Norm Prickett. Norm had invested in many businesses, but all had failed, so he decided to start a business that, if it failed, he could enjoy it as it went under. So, he sold everything he owned. A logging truck, a gold dredge, two pack mules, he had when he operated a hunting guide service, and bought a rundown shack on the main drag of North Bend. Now Norm wasn't even Irish. Neither were any relatives in his lineage. The name Murphy came from Murphy's Law. Norm figured, if there were anything he could do to be a success, it would be to do just the opposite of what his propensity told him to do. Norm named the bar Murphy's Pub, not Murphy's Law, because, that name would have jinxed him. Norm passed on some years ago. His daughter Josie Wildflower now runs the pub. The name was her mother's and the legal name on her birth certificate. Norm had married May after Josie was born. May Wildflower was from the Snoqualmie Tribe; she made it clear to Norm, she needed no man to raise a child. Norm started clean living after he married May, became a respectable Christian, quit drinking, and became an honored businessman of the North Bend community. Murphy's Pub, on the other hand, is still a pretty rough place on a Saturday night.

The K-RAP 12 News van pulled up in front of Murphy's Pub. The parking lot had just three trucks parked in it, and one of them belonged to Tommy Wells.

Wendy Storms had a glint of success in her eye when she saw the pickup with the silver cowgirl mud flaps. "Bingo!" she said.

Wendy jumped down out of the van and walked towards the smoky bar with high-heeled determination and a lot of backfield in motion. Phil was on a dead run to keep up with Wendy, and the cameraman was a close third. Wendy hurled the steel barred door open and stepped into the bar. The first thing that would hit you was the smell of stale cigarettes, then the smell from the men's room, kind of urine mixed with a cheap urinal cake smell. Just behind Wendy stepped Phil and then the cameraman.

The old Swede, sitting at the end of the bar, laughed at the sight coming through the door and said, "I didn't know the circus was in town," then followed it by a cigarette-induced wheezing laugh.

Josie Wildflower was behind the bar and yelled, "Hey, no cameras in here; take it outside."

The cameraman quickly about-faced and went back out the door. Wendy spotted whom she guessed was Tommy Wells sitting hunched over at the far end of the bar; Wendy walked right to him.

Wendy said, "Hello, Tommy, do you remember talking to me on the phone last night?"

Tommy looked like someone had just run over his dog, teary-eyed and somber and a good two sheets to the wind. Tommy kind of slurred, "Who the hell are you?"

"I am Wendy Storms, KayRAP Channel 12 News; we talked on the phone last night," she stated as a fact.

Tommy came back with, "So, what do you want from me?"

Josie interrupted, "Are you going to order a drink? If not stop harassing my customers and get out."

Wendy turned her attention to Josie with a here comes the catfight look; slowly running her tongue across her bottom lip and squinting as she turned her head toward Josie and leaning into the bar. "What have you got that isn't poisoned?" came back Wendy.

Josie smiled and said, "Not anything that you'd order."

Wendy snapped, "Give me a whatever."

Josie set a shot glass on the bar, grabbed a bottle of Mudnyereye Whisky and poured half of it on the bar and half in the shot glass, and she said, "Five bucks."

Phil paid her and Josie headed to the other end of the bar to get the old Swede some pull tabs.

Wendy turned her attention back to Tommy and said, "Tommy, you told me last night that you had pictures on your phone of some unusual tracks that you saw when you were on the Search and Rescue yesterday. May I see them?"

Tommy said, "Hey, I was pretty drunk last night; I'm not sure what I said. Lady, to tell you the truth, I signed an oath when I joined Search and Rescue, and I can't tell you anything, or I'll lose my job." Tommy pushed himself away from the bar and standing up the best he could. He added, "I'm taking the fifth on this one; isn't that what they say in the movies? I gotta take a whiz." With that said, Tommy staggered toward the men's room. When Tommy was gone, Wendy looked at his coat draped over the bar stool.

Phil said, "Wendy, don't do it." Phil knew what Wendy had in mind.

Wendy slipped her hand into one of the pockets of the

jean jacket, then the other pocket, pulling out a cell phone. "Bingo!" said Wendy.

Chapter 3

Rattlesnake Lake

Dave thought to himself, "If Wendy Storms is the worst I have to deal with today, then it is still a good day."

Dave grabbed the 2-way radio and spoke into the mic, "Search and Rescue, come in, Oscar." Dave waited for the answer; it didn't return. Dave said again, "Search and Rescue, come in, Oscar."

A buzz and a snap, Oscar spoke from the small speaker in Dave's dash, "This is Oscar, go ahead, Dave."

Dave asked, "How is the search going, Oscar? Any clues?"

Oscar came back, "We have found a clue, Dave; it's not much, but anything may help at this point."

Dave questioned excitedly, "Oscar, what have you found?"

Oscar came back with, "We found a camo jungle hat; do you think it's Dan Simmons'?" The communications went silent; Oscar said, "Dave, do you read me?"

Dave sat in the truck with his head in his hands for a few seconds. Dave keyed the mic, "Great, Oscar, what else have you got?"

Oscar replied, "We are up against a cliff here; I sent up

climbers to have a look around. They will radio me if they see anything."

Dave said, "Thanks, Oscar, keep me posted. Ranger Station 5 clear."

With all the media in town, Dave decided to play everything by the book. After all, the radio band used by the Parks Department could be picked up by anyone.

Dave headed to the Double D Diner for an early lunch in town and then to check in with Spencer to see if there were any new developments at his end or if Wendy Storms had visited him too. Dave pulled into the Double D Diner, and the only spot that was left was the compact car parking space. Dave did his best to pull in straight and leave everyone space to ingress and egress their vehicles. Dave opened the door to his truck and hit the mirror of the truck next to him. Dave squeezed out of the cab, popping a button off his shirt. "Crrrap!" cursed Dave. Dave got past the truck and into the parking lot. Looking down, he could see his shirt was opened up exposing his tee-shirt. Dave sighed out loud, "Thank you St. John for a clean tee-shirt." That made Dave smile and chuckle just a little bit. He then headed into the Double D and sat down at the counter.

Betsy walked by smiling and said, "The usual, Hon?"

Dave smiled and nodded in agreement. Betsy had no more than set down a glass of ice water in front of Dave when the blare of a cop car siren came from down the street. Dave stood up, and looking out the window; he could see the patrol car with Higgins in it roaring up the street, squealing around the corner and headed in a southern direction. Dave shook his head, pulled his cell phone out of his uniform pocket and called Spencer.

"Sheriff's office, Sheriff Spencer Harrington speaking. How can I help you?" said Spencer.

Dave said, "I just saw Higgins go by the Double D Diner

setting a new land speed record; what's going on?'"

Spencer sighed, "Dave, I'm glad you called; we got a call that there are some bikers up at Rattlesnake Lake raising a ruckus; you better head up there and make sure Higgins doesn't shoot somebody. I've got to stay here; I'm the only one to answer the phone and keep the office open; dammed Higgins."

Dave stated, "On my way, Spencer," and he hung up.

Dave looked at Betsy and said, "Better put a hold on that burger." And with an awful Arnold Schwarzenegger imitation, Dave commented, "I'll be back." Betsy smiled politely.

Dave had even more trouble squeezing back into his truck, mostly because he was in a hurry. He pulled his vehicle onto the highway and headed for Rattlesnake Lake. As Dave passed under I-90 and through the roundabout for the off- and on- ramps to the south of the interstate, a dozen bikers passed him and thundered around his truck, the last one flipping him off. Dave took a second look at the last biker; he kind-of looked like a skeleton with inked skin stretched over the top. The skinny biker, dressed in a sleeveless denim jacket, with boney arms protruding the gaping armpit holes. A colorful flap of excess skin waved in the breeze.

Dave thought to himself, "I didn't think Hells Angels lived to a ripe old age," shaking his head.

Dave was glad he had put on his .45 for the second day in a row. As Dave pulled into the parking lot at Rattlesnake Lake, he could see people loading coolers and beach chairs into their cars while the mothers held their children close and covered their ears. "What the hell?" Dave thought.

Then he saw it, "Jesus, Mary and Joseph!" Dave blurted out.

It was an awful, disgusting sight of human devolution. It looked like a Haight-Ashbury retirement facility---wrinkled old bikers and their sagging old-ladies. It was a sea of stretch-marked tattoos that one could not distinguish what the tattoos had once illustrated. All that was left was a blurred version of what it once was. Dave consciously had to make an effort to close his mouth. He thought, "Somebody should call Ripley's Believe it or Not; this has got to be a record. The largest collection of sideshow freaks ever assembled." Right in the middle of them was Higgins, waving his gun, screaming at the top of his lungs, and thoroughly entertaining everyone within 30 feet of him. Dave said out loud, "I'd better put a stop to this." He looked into his rear-view mirror and pulling in just behind him was, of course, the Channel 12 News crew. Dave stepped out of his truck, donned his military-style ranger hat and walked toward the crowd of bikers. Just behind the crowd was a large banner advertising BIGFOOT BALL. Dave said under his breath sarcastically, "Thank you, Wendy Storms." A boom box was blaring an old biker song....

Bitchin' motor runnin',
Head out on the freeway
Hair blowin' in the wind
Tats showin' what we got to say
Yeah, My Baby's smokin lightin
See it in her face
Revin engines, soundin frightin
We're beatin' the Rat Race.
Born to be...

... and the music stopped. Dave stood next to the boom box with the cord dangling in his hand, and everyone was now staring at him.

Dave took this opportunity to speak, "Now that I have your attention, I need you to disperse and leave the campground."

A skinny biker with a long gray beard spoke, "Hey, Man, what gives; we're just havin' some fun; don't come down on us, Man."

Dave leaned over and looked the little guy directly in the eyes and said, "This is an alcohol-free park; that means that sidecar over there with the keg in it, is not allowed." Straightening back up and addressing the whole crowd, Dave added, "I think you, gentlemen," Dave clears his throat, " and ladies need to find a different location for your Bigfoot Ball; so, move it on down the road." Dave smiled and said, "Get your motors running."

One of the bigger, more seasoned bikers, Bad Billy (that was what the patch on his leather vest stated). Dave assumed that was his name, and by more seasoned, he was just aromatic from a distance. Bad Billy walked up to Dave and didn't stop until his protruding belly bumped into Dave.

Bad Billy asserted his position, "Look, Ranger Rick, this is a public facility, and we are the public. So, I think you better back off and let us have our day in the sun."

Dave replied, "Well, Mr. Bad Billy, that is not going to happen today or any day for the next millennia. So, get on your Moped and find another place in the sun to play."

Bad Billy came back with, "Hey, Ranger Rick, you're not a cop, you're just Smokey the Bear's little buddy, so if you're not going to back up your threat, we're not going anyplace."

Some of the other old bikers started to pick up Bad Billy's cue and were yelling in the background, "Hey, Ranger Rick, whatcha gonna do? Yah, Man, whataya gonna do?"

Bad Billy was taking a fighting stance and clenching a fist with his right hand which hung by his side. Dave looked down and spotted that Bad Billy had Bad Feet. He had on a pair of orthopedic shoes and, on one foot, there was this colossal bump sticking out to the side. Bad Billy pushed his belly back into Dave and started his wind up. Dave stepped forward, just a little, just enough to step on Bad Billy's bad bunion. Bad Billy let out a loud scream, and a dog ran and cowered under the picnic table. Bad Billy limped toward the same table and sat down.

From behind Dave came a couple of Burripp, Burripp sounds. It was Spencer in his police car followed by two State Patrol cars. The old bikers were now taking down the BIG-FOOT BALL banner, and their engines were starting. One by one they began moving out; two of them were trying to get Bad Billy into a sidecar.

Dave turned to Spencer as he was approaching, "Thank you, Spencer; I wasn't sure how that was going to shake out."

Spencer smiled, "Dave I wouldn't leave you hanging; I was on the radio to the State Patrol as soon as you hung up. How is Higgins?"

Dave and Spencer looked over at Higgins' patrol car, and he was passed out in the front seat. Dave said, "Just too much excitement for him in one day, I guess."

Spencer looked at Dave and commented, "Don't look now."

By the time Wendy Storms had assembled her news crew, the banner was gone, and most of the geriatric Hells Angels were pulling out of the park. Wendy was furious that she hadn't been able to get a scoop of dirt here. However, she still tried to rattle Dave and Spencer.

Wendy cornered the two gentlemen between Spencer's patrol car and Dave's truck; Wendy politely asked, "Gentlemen, now that I have you together, can I finally get some answers to my questions?"

Wendy yelled to Phil, "Start the camera."

Wendy started by saying, "I am here with Sheriff Spencer Harrington and Chief Ranger Dave Notworst; can either of you tell me the name of the missing hiker?"

Wendy put the microphone toward Sheriff Harrington.

Spencer cleared his throat, then clearly stated, "Well, Wendy, you already know that; you or someone at your station somehow intercepted the missing person APB. But we have now contacted next of kin, and I can officially release the name as Dan Simmons."

Wendy then asked, "Have you any clues that could shed light on the case, say like any pertinent physical evidence, maybe footprints?"

Dave smiled at Spencer; Spencer then said, "We have an ongoing investigation here; other than that, any evidence we have will not be released at this time."

Wendy looked back at the camera, "That's the update from North Bend and the missing hiker; we will be releasing updates as they come in."

Wendy Storms was not satisfied with the answers she

got, and very unhappy that Phil was unable to get the news van parked fast enough to get the old bikers on video. Headed back to the Hyway Motel Wendy decided to go through the pictures on the cell phone she had lifted from Tommy Wells. She pulled the phone out of her pocket and turned it on; the screen just said, "Low Battery." Wendy griped, "Crap!" It's okay; she remembered that she had a charger back at the motel and sooner or later she would have the pictures and her audience would be seeing them tonight. She would deliver just what everyone had been dying to see, and she was going to have her day in the sun.

Back at Murphy's Pub, Tommy Wells was just waking up from being slumped over on the bar. He reached into his pocket to retrieve his cell phone and call his girlfriend. But, the cell phone was gone. He searched the floor around the stool, nothing. He then headed out to his truck to see if it could be in there. Tommy turned his truck inside out, but no phone. Then he remembered, that witch, Wendy Storms; she must have taken it out of his jacket when he went to the men's room. He started his truck and headed for the Hyway Motel.

Dave got back into his vehicle and waited for Spencer to pull out so he could back up his government green truck.

Then a buzz-snap came from the small speaker in the dash, "Calling Ranger Notworst; This is Oscar, Search and Rescue, come in, Dave."

Dave picked up the mic clipped to the dash and answered, "This is Dave, go ahead, Oscar."

Oscar responded, "Dave, I have some good news and some bad news."

Dave prompted, "Spill it, Oscar."

Oscar continued, "Well, the climbers scaled the cliff.

Two-thirds of the way to the top, they found a cave; inside the cave, they found Dan Simmons' notepad and a camera."

Dave said excitedly, "Camera, great; is it intact? Can we retrieve the pictures?"

Oscar said, "Well, it's an old-style film camera; the lens has been shattered and busted clear off, but I don't know if any of the film was exposed."

Dave, unable to stand the suspense forcibly prodded, "Okay, Oscar, what is the good news?"

Oscar's voice was tinny coming over the small speaker in the dash and sounded a bit eerie. Oscar came back with, "The last entry in his notebook says in big letters, DON'T FOLLOW ME!!!"

Dave started rubbing his forehead and queried, "Oscar, did you see anything else?"

Oscar continued, "Well, the climbers walked back into the cave and found lots of small animal bones like a cougar had been living in there. But the crazy thing is..." The 2-way radio went dead.

Dave panicked, "Oscar, come in Oscar; can you read me, Oscar?"

After a few seconds, a fuzzy message came back, "I'm here Dave, the reception is bad, I guess."

Dave asked again, "What was the crazy thing they saw, Oscar?"

Oscar answered with, "Dave, the cave, the climbers walked back into the cave. Well, the thing is, the cave goes all the way through the mountain and comes out the other side." Oscar continued, "It's just the craziest thing; the climbers said it looks like the cave was dug clear through to the other side, man-made so to speak."

Dave told Oscar, "When you get back into town, bring the notebook to the sheriff's office, and I will go over it with Sheriff Harrington."

Oscar replied, "Will do, we are wrapping it up for the day; by the time we get down off the mountain, it may be near dusk. Over and out."

Dave said, "Channel clear."

Dave pushed the shifter to the right and up into reverse, backed out of the parking spot and then shifted down, to the left, then down again into second gear. Dumping the clutch, spinning gravel, he caused the truck to lurch forward. Dave headed back to the Double D Diner for a late lunch. This time there was an accessible parking space on the street. Dave eased into it and turned off the engine. "Boy, I worked up an appetite brawling with those bikers," he said under his breath. Walking through the door, Dave caught Betsy smiling through the crowd at him; she waved him toward an empty booth; this was code meaning she wanted to sit with him and chat between orders. Dave slid into the booth the .45-grip jabbing him in the side; he rotated the gun belt to ease the pain.

Betsy sat down across from him. Bubbling and gushing, she said, "So tell me, Big Dave, what happened? I heard you took care of a whole bunch of dirty bikers all by your strong, handsome self?"

Dave smiled and blushed, "Well, I just talked them into moving out of the campground and on down the road." Feeling a little surge of ego, he continued, "They were a bit of a rough bunch, scaring off the family campers."

Betsy smiled, "Ranger Dave, you are my hero, so lunch is on me. And if you can find your way over to my trailer tonight, I'll have some ice-cold beers in the fridge with your name on them." With that Betsy slid out of the booth, smiling and gave Dave Notworst one of her flirtatious winks. Dave was so excited, he could barely eat his burger when it came, and he could hardly wait until the sun went down.

Tommy Wells pulled into the parking lot of the Hyway Motel; slowly he drove through looking for the Channel 12 News van. He made his way to the back of the motel and parked his truck behind the dumpster. Tommy reached under his seat and pulled out a .38 special he had purchased from a pawn shop on his last trip to Seattle. He hopped down out of the truck cab, reached behind his back and up under his jean jacket slipping the .38 into the top of his jeans. Tommy walked with his back to the wall of the motel. Reaching the end of the building, he looked around the corner toward room 26. The Channel 12 News van was parked outside. The door of room 26 flew open as Wendy Storms walked toward the van with a suitcase rolling along behind her. Tommy ran to a nearby car and hid behind the front fender. He quickly moved up to the next car, and then the next, until he is only two parking spaces away from the Channel 12 van. There were just two empty parking spaces between Wendy Storms and Tommy's .38 special. Phil started the engine, and dropped the van in reverse, one rear wheel spitting gravel under the van. Tommy then panicked and ran toward the van with the pistol gripped in both hands ready to unload into the side of it. Phil dropped the shifter into D and stomped the pedal. The van launched gravel and rocks into the air. A fist-sized rock shot from the rear tire headed right at Tommy Wells, sweet innocent Tommy Wells, like a cannon's projectile from the gates of hell. Tommy started to drop his two-handed grip on the .38 special just as the rocket hit him right where his unborn children live. Tommy dropped to his hands and knees, vomiting the meager contents of his stomach. The Channel 12 van took off toward I-90 and headed back to Seattle for Live at Five.

After lunch, Dave headed straight to the sheriff's office; he had received a call from Oscar. Oscar had left the search early to get home for a small emergency. On his way, he dropped off the camera and notebook with Spencer. Dave parked in his usual NO PARKING spot just reserved for him and walked into the sheriff's office. Something was wrong; some little annoyance seemed to be missing.

Spencer came out of his office, "Come on in, Dave," he called, waving him towards his office.

Dave walked in and sat down and said, "Where's Higgins?"

Spencer smiled and said, "I sent him down to the hospital; his blood pressure was going through the ceiling."

Dave nodded and said, "So, let me look at the notebook."

Spencer tossed it on the desk in front of Dave. Dave picked it up and started thumbing through it. Dave moved his head in a yes motion as he read, flipping page by page, uttering an occasional Hm and Aha or Aah.

When Dave had finished, he looked up at Spencer, and Spencer was looking back, tilting his head to the left he said, "Reads like a stereo manual, a whole lot of nothing."

Dave nodded his head in agreement and added, "Well, Dan Simmons is some sort of a scientist and has a tendency for writing that way, but they are his notes, and they make sense to him; we need to try and decipher it or break the code."

Spencer raised his eyebrows and added, "There is one thing for sure; he doesn't want us poking around in the woods looking for him; that much was clear."

Dave smiled and said, "Yes, there's not much to decode or read between the lines in, DON'T FOLLOW ME!!"

The chair squeaked as Spencer leaned back with fingers interlaced behind his head. Spencer then added, "Later today, I'm going to send Higgins to Seattle to the police photo lab to try to retrieve the pictures from Dan Simmons' 35mm camera."

Dave agreed to the photo developing decision and said, "Mind if I take this notebook home with me tonight and read over it again?"

Spencer said, "Sorry, Dave, it's evidence; I have to keep it in the safe. You're welcome to read it as much as you want here."

Dave, "How about photocopies?"

Spencer responded, "Knock yourself out; just make sure you fill up the paper tray before you leave; that empty tray just drives Higgins nuts."

Dave smiled, "Okay."

When Dave had finished copying the notebook, he placed it back in Spencer's safe, said goodnight to Spencer and headed home.

Walking in the front door, he stripped himself of his .45, feeling released of the extra weight and the belt cinch poking him in the belly. He pulled a Coke out of the fridge and sat down in his easy chair and started going over the notebook copies. Page 15 seemed to call to him. Dan Simmons wrote; "This is the fifth day of sitting in the cold from dawn till dusk. I have set up a natural blind of pine branches and the mossy material that hangs from the trees. I am deep in the Cedar Creek Watershed. I sit all day in silence with my camera on a tripod waiting motionless to catch a glimpse of the creature. It is 3:45 p.m. It is like time has stopped. I cannot hear a thing; there is no movement in the woods --- no birds, no deer, no squirrels. I can feel my blood surging through the veins in my neck and pulsing in my temples. As I sit quietly, I can hear my slowed breath go in and out. It is like I am in a vacuum of time. I look down at my digital watch; frozen at 3:45; it has been 3:45 for too long. I think it has stopped. But that's impossible; if my watch were dead, there would be no display. Just ahead of me up the hill, I notice movement. The creature appears as if out of thin air; it takes a few steps and stops; it tilts his head back like it is smelling the air. The creature turns and looks up the hill and then cries out in a screeching howl like it is calling to others; this is my chance. My thumb pushes the plunger of the shutter release. Click, click, click, the creature turns and looked me directly in the eyes and disappeared, back into thin air."

Dave let out a big sigh, threw the copies onto the table next to the easy chair and got up and walked into the bathroom to shower before heading off to Betsy's place. It will be great to relax and have a couple of beers. Dave had wanted to ask Betsy out for some time now. Dave smiled. Guess she made it happen.

Dave, showered, shaved and dressed in his Saturday night's best and slapped on some aftershave just to spice things up. He cupped his hand over his mouth and his nose just to check to see if the mouthwash had done its job. Dave smiled into the mirror and said, "Perfect!" Dave headed out to his government green truck as if his feet were not even touching the ground. Everything in the world is right tonight. Dave started his truck and headed down the road to paradise. He pulled into the driveway of the best-groomed trailer in the whole darn trailer park. Every picket in the fence is perfectly straight and pearly white. All the roses are red, and the white Christmas lights around the awning was illuminated in a crystal champagne glow. Dave's blue lustrous eyes reflected the dots of the white lights from the awning over the front door. He made his way from the gate to the front door of the single-wide trailer; he softly knocked on the aluminum door with a porthole window. Betsy opened the door slowly revealing her meticulously groomed hair, make-up and well-chosen dress that revealed just enough cleavage, but left the desires of the imagination. Betsy smiled in a euphoric welcoming manner, "Come in, Big Dave." Dave smiled and stepped over the threshold not knowing that this night would change his life forever.

Betsy's mother told her that the way to a man's heart is through his stomach. Tonight, she meant to lay it on as thick as she could --- marinated baked pork chops, mashed potatoes, corn on the cob. The smell made Dave's stomach growl and mouth water. Betsy walked over to the fridge and pulled out two beers; she put one on each side of her mouth then bit down and opened both bottles at the same time, just something that she had learned at finishing school. Not at the school, but it was extra-curricular, behind the gym, you know

--- street smarts. Dave was impressed; he had seen this done before, but it was in his days spent in the service, from a guy named Biff, but that guy lost his teeth early on. Dave thought, "Hell, I could break-wind, and I wouldn't even have to try and squeeze it out, just let'er rip, and Betsy wouldn't even bat an eye. Wow! What a gal." He was hooked; the honeymoon had already begun---so to speak. The conversation became engaging and carried throughout dinner; the connections were sparking, and both drawn like moths to a flame. It was kismet, destiny, the heavens opened up, and the angels sang. As the evening progressed, they sat on the porch under the crystal champagne lit awning in a swinging chair for two. Betsy's head lay on Dave's broad shoulder. As they looked out towards the night, a shooting star shot across the sky.

Betsy looked at Dave and said, "What was your wish?"

Dave smiled and said, "Same as yours."

Chapter 4

SasQuatched

The sun warmed the feathers on his back; the wind pushed against his wings. As the gusts would hit him; he could feel the pressure flex and the stretching of the muscles and tendons in his wings. The feathers on the tips of his wings would bend, like fingertips flexing under the weight of something stronger than himself. Tucking in his tail feathers, he could advantageously increase the power of the updraft and soar higher above the clouds. The oneness, the freedom, to tilt a wing and twist his body and change direction, to dive into the endless clouds, then pitch his body and rise again into the blue sky. This was the physical sensation of flight, the wind pushing against his body, and his body pushing back defying and resisting its power. The ability to ascend high into the sky and witness the curvature of the earth was exhilarating.

The dream dissipated quickly, and it pixelated into small squares, breaking and flying apart only to reveal the stark, painful reality. The first thing he felt as reality returned was the sore, over-worked muscles of his back and legs; he felt a painful stiffness on his face. He reached and felt something dried from his forehead down to his cheek and on down his neck. It was blood, dried blood, coagulated and stuck to his face and shirt. He could only see out of his right eye, and he felt the damp of the ground beneath him. He could see that he must be inside a cave; he could look out from the entrance and see some bright light; was it dawn, or dusk, or maybe a bright full moon? He couldn't tell; he tried to lift himself up but the pain was intense. He looked about the cave, but he couldn't see anything in the dark; then he saw it. Like a dog's glistening eyes in the night, glowing back at him. "What the hell was in this cave with him?" he thought. The eyes were staring back through the darkness; does it see him? The thoughts continued. "Don't move; play dead; oh my God, there is another set of eyes staring back at me. Two sets of glowing eyes." He felt his mind fade and drift back into unconsciousness. As he did, he thought he heard a voice in his head, "You are safe...." And then he passed out into blackness.

Dan Simmons woke in pain, his belly ached from hunger, and his mouth was dry from thirst. He could see it was daylight outside of the cave. The damp smell within the cave blended with another familiar smell, the smell of the creature. Dan struggled to push himself up; the pain was intense, and he felt feeble; it took his whole spiritual and physical strength to raise himself from the cave floor. He closed his eyes and gathered all of his energies to push himself up and then he fell against the wall of the cave, sitting with one leg folded under the other. Breathing in and out forcibly to push more oxygen into his system, he slowly opened his right eye; an icy chill ran over his body, his heart raced, and his body trembled from the sight a few feet in front of him. He could not flee; his body did not function; he was at the mercy of the fearsome beast towering over him. It forced a muted grunt and blew air from its nostrils. It squatted, facing him; the enormous, magnificent creature in this position, was still almost as tall as Dan was when standing fully erect. Calming a bit, he started to notice the looks of the creature. Its nose was small compared to its face, not pointed but short like a chimpanzee's nose. The skin of the face was dark brownish, and matted reddish-brown hair surrounded the exposed parts of its face. Its head was twice the size of his. A pair of teeth or long, sharp fangs descended downwards from both sides of the upper mouth. Jutting up from the lower jaw was a pair of opposing fangs passing outside the upper canines. The creature, mostly covered in hair except for the dark skin of the chest and abdominal muscles which were framed in by the foot-long reddish hair. The inside of the fingers and palms were also bare. The fingertips did not possess nails, but only short round inch-long claw-like protrusions.

In the creature's hand, he held some roots; he tossed the tubers onto the top of Dan's bent leg. Again, the beast emitted a muted grunt. Followed by a motion of the creature's hand directed towards the roots and then upwards toward its mouth. Dan thought to himself, "It must want me to eat them; it may be some type of herbal medicine." He cautiously picked up one of the roots and tried suspiciously to bite into the dirt-covered, twisted vegetal. Again, came a muted grunt as the beast grabbed the root out of his hand, and with a quick slicing motion of its claw, split the bark from the root and peeled the rest exposing its white flesh. Then it handed the stripped morsel back to him and indicated again to eat. Dan bit down into the soft fiber and was surprised by the sweet flavor in his mouth. His stomach immediately desired more and longed for it to satiate his hunger pangs. He welcomed the simple sustenance. He bit again and chewed and swallowed it with savor. He could immediately sense the effects of eating it, so after his third or fourth bite, he could feel a slight euphoria filling his mind. His pain was subsiding. He bit again into the root and chewed, but this time he coughed and spit some of the repast out. The creature then handed him a clear bag-like container filled with what he assumed to be water.

The bag resembled a goatskin bag for carrying drink, but a bit unusual; it was all transparent including the strap for carrying it; there were no buckles or rivets to attach it to the bag. It was all one unit. The creature handed it to Dan, and he raised it to drink from it, but there was no opening. Again, the beast grunted at him and motioned with its hand. He once again lifted the bag to his mouth and, as though magically, an opening appeared in the bag as it came close to his mouth. He drank in the refreshing fluid. To Dan, it was like finding an oasis in the desert. He could feel the fluid flowing into his inner parts, something he had never felt before, a rejuvenation of muscle and tissue; his body felt light, and the pain was now quickly dissipating. He continued to drink; it was as though he couldn't get his fill. He drank until the bag was nearly empty. He was now starting to be able to open his left eye; he reached up and pulled the dried blood from his face in chunks; he pulled hair from his eyebrow in the process. He was now able to see out of his left eye; he could tell his eye was swollen and most likely blackened. The creature motioned with its hands for him to stand up. He looked around and picked up his camera and notebook, but the creature grabbed the camera from his hands and threw it across the cave, the lens breaking off when it smashed into a rock. He would no longer be able to take pictures.

From outside the cave, Dan could hear people talking from a distance. He stood and walked to what he concluded was the cave entrance. Dan looked out and down a sheer cliff. He saw below that there was a search party advancing up the hill. Knowing that he wanted to study the creature, he didn't want to be interfered with by anyone. From now on, all the observations would have to be kept in his head. He turned back toward the creature which was now standing, and what a magnificent creature it was! Dan's head came only to its waist. He sat down on a rock ledge with his notebook in hand, turned to a blank page just after his last entry and wrote in large all cap words. DON'T FOLLOW ME!!! The creature was anxious to leave and kept motioning for him to follow. He stood up and then dropped the notebook to the floor of the cave and followed the creature farther into the cave. The cave descended into the earth. The air moved past them and upwards toward the opening they had just left. The cave was becoming damper and cooler. He felt his way along by running his hand over the wall of the cave. The light diminished as they moved away from the entrance. His eyes started to adjust to the near-darkness, and he could barely see the outline of the creature in front of him. He could feel and hear crunching under his feet. Sometimes he stumbled on the debris-laden path. At one point, he reached down and picked up one of the objects under his foot; he felt it; it was long and flexible. He mentally examined the item as he turned it about in his hands. He realized he was holding a bony spine and its gristly connecting tissue which held it together. Bones! They were walking on the bones of animals. At least, he hoped they were animal bones.

They reached what seemed like a curve or corner of the cave and started down a steeper grade. Dan didn't realize this at first, and downward momentum forced him to stumble into the creature which turned and growled and blew hot air at him from its nostrils. He knew it had turned and faced him because he could feel the force of its exhale on his face and his hair also blew backward at the same time. Dan apologized out loud, not realizing that an apology meant nothing. They came to a more significant cavern-like room; he knew this because he could no longer touch the cave walls easily with both arms and with hands extended. This observation caused Dan to become disoriented because he no longer had a reference point. He reached forward to feel for the creature, and it was a good thing he did because it had stopped. He didn't want to anger the beast by stumbling into it again, and he certainly did not like to be breathed on from those large nostrils. The creature let out a muffled grunt. Then in response came other grunts from all around the room. Dan realized that probably four more massive creatures now outnumbered his minuscule form. Without thinking before speaking, he said aloud, "Toto, I don't think we're in Kansas anymore." His comment was quickly followed by more grunting and snorting, from all around him. "Oh, Dammit!" Dan thought, but this time he kept the comment to himself. As the old saying goes, "Only speak when spoken to," or in this case, "Only grunt when grunted at." He felt a push on his back indicating the direction he was to move. The group left the room and returned to the tunnel and continued onward. He was behind one creature and was now being followed by another; he made sure his steps were steady and sure. He didn't want to upset the beings any more than necessary and he sure as hell didn't want one of them stepping on him.

Dan started seeing the faint outlines of the three creatures ahead of him; this illumination of the area meant that they were getting close to another opening of the cave. As they walked, his visibility increased. He turned to look behind himself which annoyed one of the creatures to his rear. It snorted violently in his direction. Dan thought, "Okay then, keep eyes facing forward." He was just angering everyone today. Dan did curiously notice that the creatures behind him had tree boughs tied to their legs, which were dragging on the ground. They emerged from a smaller opening of the cave and stopped just outside on a level patch of land which allowed Dan to look out over an area he had never seen. He saw a trail stretching out ahead of them down the mountainside and into a valley below, surrounded by mountains. It was a hidden little pocket of wilderness. The view was beautiful. Waterfalls on three of the mountains which encircled the valley which displayed a small lake surrounded by gigantic trees. It was a lost paradise, unmolested and pristine; he drew in the air, and it was pure, like no air he had ever experienced before, or maybe it was just the residual effect from the root he had previously ingested. In any case, the scene captured his attention, a Sasquatch heaven.

They followed the mountain path toward the valley; the group had been walking for about 45 to 50 minutes when their attention was attracted to voices from far up the hill behind them. Dan turned around and saw two men standing at the exit of the cave from which he and the Sasquatch had just come. A commotion broke out among the beasts, with lots of snorting and grunting and arm waving. The most significant being, the one Dan had first followed through the cave, waved its arms at two other Sasquatch as in a command. The two creatures started running back up the hill toward the cave's exit.

Dan watched as the two men at the cave exit were looking around; he didn't think the two men had spotted the caravan of creatures and himself down below on the trail. The two men from Search and Rescue looked around for several minutes and then they must have decided there was nothing significant on this side of the cave. They turned around, left the flat area at the rear end of the tunnel, and re-entered the cave. With no tracks to follow, the two climbers headed back to the Search and Rescue team at the other end of the cave.

Dan moved along slowly and continued to watch as the group of Sasquatch continued down the trail; he would look up at the cave exit occasionally and then back down at the path making sure he didn't stumble. When Dan looked back up once more, he could see the two Sasquatch, which had been dispatched up the hill, standing at the cave exit. He now stopped to watch them. The creatures waved their arms as if trying to create some invisible force of energy or synchronicity with nature. To his surprise, the cave's exit immediately disappeared. All that remained were the two Sasquatch standing before what appeared to be a rock slide over the former cave exit. Dan concluded that they had done this to protect their sanctuary. He thought to himself, "Hm, I have just witnessed applied quantum mechanics."

Dave woke, a bit disoriented and foggy, and abruptly realized he had spent the night at Betsy's. A little embarrassed and slightly hungover, he could hear Betsy, clanking pots and pans, in the process of making breakfast in the kitchen.

Just as Dave rose from bed, Betsy walked in with a steaming coffee. "I thought you might like a cup of Joe to wake you up this beautiful summer morning," smiled Betsy.

Dave returned a smile trying to show great enthusiasm and said, "Why thank you, beautiful."

Betsy returned to the kitchen. Dave quickly dressed; he wanted to make his excuses to her so that he could leave because he needed to meet with Spencer to debrief Oscar about the previous day's search. Betsy had a full plate of hash browns, four eggs over-easy and five strips of thick cut bacon. If that couldn't fill Dave up, there was more on the stove. Betsy liked big men and knew it took a lot of fuel to keep them happy.

Dave sat down at the table, smiled at Betsy and said, "My, my, this does look good." He had worked up an appetite for whatever Betsy was serving.

Betsy told him, "Go ahead and eat your fill; there is plenty more on the stove. I know you have a full day ahead of you, so eat up and be on your way. Maybe I'll see you at the diner for lunch."

Dave appreciated that Betsy was understanding of his position and his dedication to his job.

He asked her, "How would you like to go down to Unky Rays for a banana split tonight?"

She smiled saying, "Sounds great, Dave; it's a date." He smiled and took his last bite of hash browns and eggs.

Unky Rays was a small ice cream parlor on North Bend Way, owned and operated by Ray and Jenny Foyt. It was best-known for their homemade ice cream, processed in the little kitchen in the back of the store. Many people thought it was the best ice cream in the Pacific Northwest. One of the favorites was Huckleberry ice cream with fresh huckleberries picked in the mountains around North Bend. Because of the short season which only lasted through August, the ice cream was only available for a few weeks. And one thing about Ray, he made sure everything was fresh. He was an artist when it came to ice cream --- fresh cream from the local dairy, pure sugar from Moses Lake sugar beets and some local honey; then there was his special ingredient that no one knew but him. Everyone had their opinion of what goes in, but only Unky Ray knew the truth. Some of his ice cream had won awards, and word-of-mouth had brought some high rollers in the ice cream business to town. One of Unky Ray's best recipes was a combination of chocolate chunks and Bing cherries, which he named after Jerry Garcia, the Grateful Dead lead singer. But one day there were a couple of scoundrels who went by the fictitious names of Jen and Berry who came to town with plans to steal his recipe. The next year the culprits came out with their version, and they didn't even change the name of the flavor. No shame in the ice cream game.

Dave finished his breakfast, thanked and kissed Betsy goodbye and headed for the sheriff's office. He pulled into the parking lot and parked in his designated NO PARKING space, next to the fire hydrant. As he walked through the door of the sheriff's office, there sat Higgins watching his every move. Higgins said, "Do I need to write you a parking ticket, Notworst?"

Dave smiled and said, "Do what you do best, Higgins." Higgins hoisted his belt and headed for the door, ticket book in hand.

Spencer was on the phone and Oscar was already there. Spencer motioned for Dave to come in. As Dave walked through the door, Spencer motioned him to shut the door behind him. He sat down next to Oscar and waited for Spencer to get off the phone.

Spencer hung up the phone and said, "That was Dan Simmons' mother; she is putting up a hundred-thousand-dollar reward for his safe return. I guess she had reward posters plastered all over town yesterday. She also called Wendy Storms. The reward money was a highlight on last night's Channel 12 News."

Dave said, "Well, that should bring 'em out of the woodwork, and make everyone's job a little bit harder."

Oscar shook his head, "Well, there goes my best tracker. Pete Davis will go after that easy money."

Dave asked, "Pete Davis?" Oscar nodded his head in

confirmation. Dave added, "Let Pete go; you'd be better off without him; he's more of a pain in the tuchus than he is a help."

Oscar smiled, "I guess you're right, Dave."

Spencer cleared his throat and said, "Okay, let's get down to it, Oscar; when you sent your climbers into the cave, did they take any photos?"

Oscar said, "No, all they had were phones and the cave was just too dark to get any clear shots."

Spencer asked, "Did they see any tracks?"

Oscar answered, "No, it looked to them that the place had been wiped clean with a tree branch."

Spencer continued, "Do we have more skilled climbers we can send back up there. I would like them to go through the cave and scout the other side."

Oscar replied, "We do. I have two more that have been to Everest; highly skilled and now very motivated to join in."

Spencer commented, "Great. Dave, you can join in here at any time."

Dave cleared his throat, "Oscar, is there a faster way we can get to the cliff, instead of hiking all morning?"

Oscar replied, "Yes, we can have Mitch Cochran drop us and our gear very close to the cliff with his Bell; he can carry six of us."

Dave asked, "What do you think, Spencer, can we send up five guys including Oscar to climb back up and go to the other side of that cave?"

Spencer agreed, "We have plenty of money in the rescue fund from the past couple of years; I'd say pull the trigger."

All three were in agreement to launch a full assault on the cliff the next day.

Spencer told Dave, "Dave, we need to keep this notebook under wraps; this kind of stuff will just ignite the media, and we will have more knot-heads up here than we can count. Wendy Storms is just getting everyone stirred up. If she were to get her hands on a copy of that notebook, we would have every kook in the country up here camping out."

Dave thought to himself, "Hell, I hope I locked my door last night before I left. The copies were lying on the table next to my chair." Dave acknowledging agreement with Spencer said, "Yes, I have my copies safe and sound."

Spencer looked at Oscar, "Did you read any of Dan's notebook?"

Oscar replied, "Not much, mostly the last page."

Spencer asked, "Anyone else read it?"

Oscar continued, "No, my guys just picked up the evidence and put it in a bag, no leaks with them."

Dave was now nervous, thinking to himself, "I have got to get back to my place to make sure the copies are safe."

Spencer said, "Okay, Gentlemen, let's get set up for tomorrow's assault on the cave."

Oscar and Dave nodded in agreement.

Oscar added, "I will talk with my guys and stop and see Mitch and get things set up early tomorrow at 0500 hours."

Oscar got up and left the meeting to get organized; Dave continued with Spencer.

Dave asked, "Spencer, did you get any pictures developed from Dan's camera?"

Spencer answered with a disappointing," No, some of the pictures were of things that were unrecognizable, but they did develop."

Dave asked, "Can I see them?"

Spencer came back with, "Sure, here you go." Spencer pulled the envelope of pictures from his top drawer and tossed them across the table to Dave. Dave opened the pouch of photographs and examined them one at a time.

Dave asked, "Can I have them?"

Spencer came back with, "Dave, I know that they don't show anything, but it's still evidence, and I have to keep control of everything. Make copies if you want; the copier does color, and a damn nice job too. Ask Higgins; I think he has some copies of his girlfriend's derriere." Dave looked at Spencer with a frown of disgust. Spencer added, "There was some ruckus about it after last year's Christmas party."

Dave looked up with a squinted smile and said, "I'll take your word for it." Dave added, "I'll be right back with these,"

He got up and headed for the copier. As he was making copies of the distorted pictures, Higgins walked back in the door.

Higgins addressed Dave, "Hey, that's city property; is that authorized business?"

Dave smiled and said, "Would that include unauthorized photos of last year's Christmas party? Higgins, are you saving those for next year's Christmas cards?"

Higgins face turned red as he came back with a poorly executed, "Well, up yours, Notworst."

Dave finished the copies and returned the originals to Spencer's safe. He excused himself, "Thank you, Spencer, I need to make my rounds."

Spencer said, "See ya, Dave."

Dave hurried to get to his truck and make a beeline to his house to see if he had locked his door. He drove just over the speed limit by 5 miles an hour all the way home. Dave pulled into the drive at Iron Horse Park and pushed hard on the brake pedal. Campers with children were crossing the road; "How would it look if the Chief Ranger ran down campers," he thought. He stopped and smiled as each of them took their time getting across the road. After they had all crossed safely to the other side, Dave dumped the clutch, spun gravel and pointed the government green truck up the road to his house. He pulled into the driveway in front of his home and gasped; the door to his house was standing half open.

Dave shouted out loud, "Hells bells!"

Dave shut off the truck and not waiting for the engine to stop, released the clutch and the truck lurched forward and died. Beads of sweat rolled off of Dave's forehead as he took long strides toward the front door. Forcibly pushing the door the rest of the way open, he walked through. The super-energized door hit the coat rack and stopped. Dave walked toward his easy-chair and with total horror saw that all the copies of Dan Simmons' notebook were gone.

"Who the hell?" Dave called out loud.

But it was far worse than he first realized; Dave's government issued .45 was gone too.

Chapter 5

Papers, and other Missing Things

Rebecca Love came to North Bend a month earlier, rented a small home in a rural area at the end of a dirt road, far away from the town and unnoticed by most people. She kept a low profile but missed nothing. Anything that had happened in North Bend, Miss Love knew as if a resident for years. She could tell you who was sick, who was dating whom, most of the families, where to shop and all the functions of the infrastructure of the community. Rebecca was very adept at mining information without being noticed, being just another face in the crowd. This behavior was reasonably easy to maintain because of North Bend's location. Built near the I-90 interstate; many travelers flowed in and out of town daily. No one noticed her, but she absorbed facts and information like a sponge. Listening carefully at stores, coffee shops, and of course the Double D Diner. She read all the bulletin boards that were in most businesses; she knew who was selling what and who was looking for lost animals. Most people do not realize the wealth of information posted for anyone to see. She could even tell you about a recent posting at the Post Office, that there was a missing hiker and a reward of $100,000.00 for his safe return. Rebecca came to North Bend from Seattle where she was a student at the University of Washington; she had read a published paper by Dan Simmons about Charles Darwin's evolution theory and Carl Jung's theory of disambiguation. The one comment in his article that stuck in her mind was, "We are all a product of survival, not only in the physical but also spiritual. The cord between the two creates an evolution of both." She was so obsessed with this excerpt, she followed or had been stalking Dan Simmons right up until he disappeared.

Rebecca was up Cedar Creek Watershed road the night Dan Simmons disappeared; she also searched through his Jeep after he had gone missing. She was in the area the night Dave Notworst came to check on the abandoned vehicle report. Rebecca was still up there the next morning when the Search and Rescue team showed up at dawn. Rebecca thought Dan Simmons would return, but he never did; she hiked up the hill after Search and Rescue did. She knew every detail of what happened, but no one realized she did; Rebecca seemed to be able to blend into the forest. She had extensive survival experience; she had a natural attraction to the wilderness and was well-educated in survival skills. Rebecca was an avid reader of anything related to survival. Her curiosity all started with a reality TV show. The show challenged people by dropping them into a wilderness without knowing where they were. So, Rebecca wanted to know all the skills that other survivalists knew. She read, and when she could, she would go to training camps. One that Miss Love attended every year was Wilderness Awareness in Duvall. Rebecca always had in the back of her mind that if the apocalypse happened, she would move to higher ground, and get away from the mayhem in the urban areas. With her Bug-Out pack, Rebecca had everything needed to survive for an unlimited amount of time. But she was unable to save Dan Simmons, even though she had hiked most of the area searching for him. Now that there was a reward offered, she was far more determined to find him before the money grubbers did.

Dave realized he needed to swallow his pride and call the sheriff and report the missing firearm. He reached into his pocket and retrieved his cell phone, opened the screen to the quick dial favorites, and pushed the sheriff's number.

A greeting came over the phone, "Sheriff's office, Deputy Higgins speaking; what's your emergency?" Higgins asked.

Dave reluctantly said, "Hello, Higgins, can I speak with Spencer?"

Higgins came back, "One moment."

The phone went on hold, and Dave was listening to a recording of emergency numbers and what help you could get at each number.

Soon, Spencer answered the phone, "Sheriff Harrington here; what is your emergency?"

Dave spoke quietly and precisely, "Spencer, I have had a break-in at my cabin; can I get you to come over and take a report?"

Spencer said, "What's missing, Dave?"

Dave replied slowly, "My .45 for one thing."

Spencer said, "Okay, Dave, I'm on my way."

It was approximately twenty minutes before Spencer arrived; the patrol car slowed as it approached Dave's cabin. Dave was inside the cabin making an inventory of what was missing. Spencer knocked and walked through the open door. Dave was in the bedroom and walked out into the living room.

Dave spoke, "I have been through the whole house, and not much is missing, just the .45, the copied notes and five cans of Prince Oscar sardines.

Spencer frowned, "What do you mean, the copied notes?"

Dave nodded his head and answered with lips pressed tightly together, "Yes, they took the copies of Dan Simmons' notes."

Spencer replied, "Well, we can only hope that they don't get into the wrong hands; who would be able to understand much of what he was talking about anyway?"

Dave responded with, "I never had anyone bother anything in my house before."

Spencer said, "Well, we have a lot of strange people in town doing a lot of strange things; better keep things locked up tight."

Dave conceded, "I have learned my lesson; I just hope the .45 turns up at the pawn shop instead of at a crime scene."

Spencer replied, "I think I can poke around a bit; I may be able to scare up some leads. It is still a small community, and not much goes on around here without notice. I think I will make a trip over to Ranger Willkie's; maybe he saw or heard something."

Dave agreed and said, "Well, I have rounds to get to, and I have been neglecting my duties with all this Search and Rescue business."

The two parted. Spencer went to Tom's house, and Dave went back to Ranger Station 5 to check in.

When Spencer got to Tom Willkie's house, he could see Tom at the storage building loading canoes onto a trailer. Spencer pulled up next to Tom's truck and trailer. Tom spotted Spencer and waved as Spencer walked up.

"How's it going, eh?" greeted Tom.

Spencer returned, "Good, good; say, Tom, when you made your rounds last night and locked up gates, did you happen to see anything strange?"

Tom rubbed his chin with his thumb and index finger, thinking and said, "Not out of the ordinary; everything looked pretty snuff."

Spencer asked, "How about up in Iron Horse park?"

Tom stood there shaking his head back and forth, "I did notice a car parked in front of Chief Ranger Notworst's cabin; it seemed a bit out of place, eh."

Spencer asked, "Tom, did you happen to get a license plate number?"

Tom frowned and said, "No, it did have Washington plates though; it was a silver station wagon, a Subaru, eh.

There was a young gal picking up some papers off the ground, eh."

Spencer questioned further, "What did it look like, anything out of the ordinary or special?"

Tom, rubbing his chin and looking off into space, "Well, it had a dent in the driver's door, and let's see, there were some stickers on the back window, a torn peace sign, white and black. There was another sticker; what did it say? Oh, yah, Lilith Fair, whatever that is, eh."

Spencer asked, "Have you ever seen this car before?"

Tom, shaking his head back and forth, "Nope." Tom asked, "We got someone else missing?"

Spencer smiled and said, "God, I hope not; see you later, Tom." Tom waved goodbye and continued to load the canoes onto the trailer.

Spencer made some notes on his little palm-sized pad that he kept in his shirt pocket; he then started the patrol car and made his way slowly down the road. Every proper peace officer knows his community and who the degenerates are and what they do and where they hang out. Spencer thought he would drive around town and see if he could spot the silver Subaru on his way to Pete Davis' house. Cruising through town, he kept just under the speed limit, which usually made a few people nervous, thinking they were doing something wrong. Just that aura of authority caused people to be extra law-abiding citizens. Spencer headed out past the gravel pit and pulled onto a dirt road and headed up to a small unmaintained driveway which led up to a double-wide trailer. Spencer noticed that Pete's Willys truck was gone. Spencer thought out loud, "He must be out trying to claim that reward." Spencer then made a tight turn around in what must have been a front yard at one time, running over a few tin cans scattered in his way. Looking in his rear-view mirror, he could see the flattened tins. He then headed back to the office to check in and file a report on the missing .45.

Earlier in the morning Oscar, Mitch, and the climbing crew had made their assault on the cliff. The chopper set down just after 0600 hours, dropped off Oscar and his other four climbers, and all their gear. James and Tillman were Oscar's Search and Rescue teammates; assisted by Edgar and Alan, the two experienced climbers that had made it to the summit of Everest. Mitch was instructed to pick them back up by chopper when they radioed him to return. The four climbers headed up the face of the cliff; Tillman stayed behind to man the ropes on the ground, so they could later descend by rappelling. Oscar reached the top first; he stood at the opening of the cave and swung his backpack off and set it on the ground. He opened it up and started pulling out gear; mostly he wanted his flashlight, gun, and knife. The other climbers reached the cave, each one retrieving his desired apparatus. They all took a moment to eat protein bars and drink water. The two climbers that had made it to the summit of Everest talked about the Sherpas and the superstitious legend of the Yeti. As they rested and nourished themselves, they told the tale of a group that was at Camp 4 known as the Death-zone.

Edgar started to tell the story, "They never found anyone from that party; when they didn't contact the base camp, another party went out to search for them. What they found were ripped up tents and gear strung all over and lots and lots of crimson blood on the stark white snow."

Alan added, "After that, the Sherpas started making offerings of food and beer to the Yeti each time before they ascended to the summit."

The group then became quiet; all needed a short rest period before going into the dark, foreboding tomb of prey and the unknown.

Each of the group equipment and strapped on knives, guns, and gear. Before they stepped out of the light and into the darkness, the sound of clicking flashlights echoed in the cave. It switched to darkness quickly, and Oscar noticed a breeze coming up from the cave as they moved downwardly into the earth. Soon, everyone was stepping on bones or kicking them as they walked. It was almost impossible not to because the bones were everywhere. The flashlights made the journey move along more quickly. When they reached a corner in the tunnel, the descent into the earth became steeper making walking more difficult. They entered the large chamber, and they all started looking around inside the large room. Then Oscar noticed that the walls had images on them, covered with hieroglyphics or pictograms.

Oscar spoke out loud, "What the heck?" And he pointed to a picture of what looked like tall hairy beasts; they were all holding hands and ranged from tallest to smallest. He blurted out, "That looks like one of those stickers you see on a soccer mom's van; you know of the whole family, only these are beasts."

One of the climbers added, "What is that above them that looks like a spaceship?"

Oscar spoke, "Maybe, but let's keep going; we need time to explore the other side of the mountain."

As Oscar started moving, he kicked against something under the dust. Looking down, he saw a black stone caked with mud; strangely attracted to it, he picked it up, looked at it and decided to toss it into the large side-pocket in his cargo pants. Oscar wasn't a rock hound, but this small stone looked interesting; the object's weight was substantial and pulled downward in his pants pocket as he walked.

The four men passed through the large room to the opposite side and on into the last part of the cave toward the exit. The team sauntered along until they heard a low growl which startled them. As they were turning the final corner, Oscar froze in his tracks. And just like in a Three Stooge's movie, the men following him piled into his back. Oscar was shining his flashlight toward what once was the cave opening. The cave was now a dead end, but in its place, was a giant male mountain lion, growling and showing his massive teeth. The mountain lion backed against the wall.

Oscar whispered, "Okay, Everyone, keep your flashlights aimed at his eyes and slowly back away. Pull your pistols but don't fire unless he attacks."

The four men backed up slowly, the cougar snarling and growling. The animal's eyes followed the men's movements. When they reached the large room, they spread out and did not remain in a single file. Oscar tried to control the formation and head everyone toward the other side of the large room and back to the entrance of the tunnel. The men, frightened and not thinking clearly, scattered into the cavernous room and up against the walls. The cougar had now moved to the center of the room.

Oscar thought, "This is not an optimal situation; if one of us shoots at the lion, we will most likely shoot someone else in the team."

———

Spencer was heading back to the office when he received a call over the radio.

Higgins alerted, "Sheriff, we have a 211 at the General Store; George says the back door has been jimmied, maybe last night."

Spencer picked up the mic and answered, "10-4, Higgins, on my way."

Spencer turned the corner and headed toward the General Store. Spencer pulled up in front of the General Store; he parked on the street, just behind a silver Subaru station wagon --- a silver Subaru with a torn peace sign and a Lilith Fair sticker in the back window.

Spencer picked up the mic and radioed Higgins, "Code-1, Higgins; I'm going to need some backup; lock up the office and head over to the General Store."

Higgins responded, "On my way."

Spencer exited his patrol car, reached down to his gun and flipped off the safety strap holding it in his holster. He walked toward the General store and cautiously through the double doors. The bell on the front door chimed. George Wallis, the owner of the store, was standing next to merchandise shelves gripping a clipboard, going through an inventory list, checking for missing items. Spencer walked over as George changed his focus from the clipboard to Spencer's entrance.

Spencer spoke, "What have you got, George?"

George's lips pursed tightly, his head bobbing up and down, and sadly said, "Looks like someone pried open the back door. All that I have found missing so far is three cases of Old Milwaukee beer, all my beef jerky and a case of Slim Jims." George made a quick look around and added, "I think it was some of those potheads with the munchies. Since the state legalized that stuff, the fabric of society has been unraveling."

From out in the street came the sound of blaring sirens and the screech of tires; a few seconds later Higgins pushed open one of the double doors of the store. He moved in with his back against the door as he entered; both hands were on his firearm pointed at the sky, in his best Starsky and Hutch imitation.

Spencer yelled, "Higgins, put that thing away before you shoot somebody!"

Higgins straightened up and reluctantly holstered the gun. Spencer ordered Higgins to stand guard over the silver Subaru station wagon and detain anyone who tried to drive off in it.

Higgins answered, "Yes sir." And he headed back out the door.

Spencer then asked George to show him where the break-in had occurred. George took Spencer to the back of the store and showed him the claw marks from the pry-bar and the bent steel door of the rear entrance. Spencer could tell that the robber had taken his or her time during the break-in because the perpetrator had finished off three of Old Milwaukee beers. Leaving the spent bent cans lying on the ground. Spencer asked George for a large zip bag. George quickly returned with the request. Spencer took out his pen and lifted one of the cans and placed it into the bag and zipped it shut.

Spencer said to George, "I'll take this and dust it for prints."

Spencer only did this for George's reassurance, because even if he could lift a fingerprint, most likely he wouldn't be able to trace a transient perp anyway. Spencer told George he would go back to the office and file a report and check the bulletins to see if any other reported break-ins could lead to an arrest. George thanked him, and Spencer went out through the double doors.

Spencer looked out into the street. He spotted Higgins leaning against the silver Subaru flirting with a young lady dressed in camo cargo pants and a gray tank top. Higgins had both thumbs in his gun belt, and his chest was pushed out. Spencer thought he looked just like a little rooster coming on to a hen twice his size.

Spencer walked up to the two and cleared his throat and asked, "Higgins, what is going on here?"

Higgins stood up straight and said, "This is Rebecca Love, and this is her car."

Spencer smiled, "Miss Love, I am truly pleased to meet you; in fact, I am so pleased I am going to have to ask you to accompany me to the sheriff's office to ask you some questions. Please get into the back of the patrol car."

Rebecca resisted, "I have business to take care of right now."

Spencer firmly insisted, "That is going to have to wait; I need you to come with me now."

Higgins held the back door of his patrol car open for Rebecca, and she reluctantly complied and got into the back seat.

Chapter 6

Making it to the Top, Doesn't Make the Man

All four men had their backs against the wall as the lion shifted his weight from one front paw to the other; he held his mouth half open and made a breathing sound through his nose. Testing the air for scents, and trying to size up the situation. Knowing that the circumstances had changed, the lion was no longer the one with its back against the wall.

Oscar said calmly, slowly and distinctly "Keep your flashlights in his eyes so he can't see what he is facing."

One of the Everest climbers, Edgar, started losing self-control and started babbling, "What are we going to do? Shoot him, shoot the damn thing. I don't want to end up as bones left on the cave floor."

Oscar continued to talk calmly, "Okay, stay calm, don't get excited or the cougar will smell the fear."

Oscar thought, "Gees, this guy risked his life to climb Mount Everest, with all odds against him. I hope he doesn't lose it or something."

Oscar said reassuringly, "Stay calm; don't start becoming fearful; let him know you're in control."

Edgar said, "Hell, I'll shoot the damn thing," and started to raise his pistol.

Oscar again said softly but firmly, "Put that gun down; for God's sake, man, we are in a cave; if you fire that gun off in here, we could all be crushed by a cave-in, or killed from a stray bullet ricocheting off the walls. The gun should be just a last resort if the cougar charges."

Edgar was sweating; his shirt soaked. Panicked and desperate, he was fast becoming a loose cannon. Oscar had to think of something quickly, or they all could be dead. Oscar shifted to his left side so he would not be in direct line with Edgar; he raised his pistol and started aiming for the cougar's enormous head. Oscar steadied himself for what he was about to do and hoped that only the cougar would perish and that the roof would not come down on their heads. Oscar pointed the flashlight at the cougar's head. In the other hand, he held the pistol, pointed in the same direction. Unable to see the end of the pistol site, Oscar was genuinely shooting in the dark. He could feel the pressure of the trigger on his index finger as he began to squeeze. At that very moment, the nervous Edgar let out an explosive sneeze. In doing so, he simultaneously soiled himself. The sneeze caused the cougar to bolt through the tunnel, heading back in the direction of the cave's entrance. One climber shined his flashlight down the length of the shaft catching the cougar's tail disappearing into the darkness.

Everyone took a well-deserved sigh of relief; the tension had created a ridge of stiffened muscle in Oscar's neck, or rather a spasm that ran from behind his right ear to somewhere on his upper spine. Oscar pushed back the pain and checked with everyone and to see how they were holding up.

After they had all taken a brief rest, Oscar said, "Okay, I will head back toward the tunnel entrance first; the rest of you follow behind me."

Oscar led the way followed by the other Everest climber, Alan; then his Search and Rescue team member, James; the rear was followed up by the nervous Edgar, mostly because of his odor; and nobody wanted to follow him. Oscar cautiously advanced up the tunnel, shining his light as far as he could, expecting the cougar at every bend. Oscar saw the sunlight from the entrance of the cave, and no cougar was in sight. They slowly moved ahead. Oscar walked to the mouth of the cave and looked down the sheer cliff to the valley below.

From below the cliff, an excited Tillman yelled up to him, "Hey, there is a cougar just above you on the cliff, above the opening of the cave!"

Oscar spun around and looked. Sure enough, there was the cougar perched on an outcropping about ten feet above them. At that moment the cougar let out a blood-curdling scream, directed right at Oscar's head.

Quickly stepping out of the cougar's view, Oscar turned to face the team behind him and said, "Okay, we are going to rappel, one at a time; the cougar is just above us; don't look up; just focus on getting down the mountain safely without falling."

They were all in agreement. James went first; he made it down in record time and unclipped from the rope. Tillman signaled for the next to come down. Alan went next; he also rappelled quickly dropping several feet at a time as he descended. Once again, Tillman signaled for the next climber. Edgar grabbed the rope with both hands, swinging himself over the edge, then started down the cliff face. Halfway down, he lost his footing and spun out away from the cliff. Edgar slammed back into the sharp rocky cliff. Letting out an agonizing scream as he stopped descending. This outburst caused the cougar just above Oscar's head to let out another blood-curdling cry, as he exposed his long fangs. Edgar regained his footing and continued downward. He reached the ground and fell backward into the dirt. Tillman unhooked him and signaled to Oscar to hook up and come down. Oscar clipped onto the line, and as he started to make his way over the edge, the cougar jumped down from above the entrance of the cave and took a mighty swat at him; all of the cougar's claws exposed as they passed within inches of his face. Oscar rapidly dropped about 20 feet, placing himself out of harm's way.

When Oscar reached the ground, before he unhooked from the rope, he looked up to see the cougar turn around and head back into the cave, his tail slowly whipping back and forth.

Oscar sighed loudly, "What a day." He saw Edgar leaning up against a tree, an ice pack on his knee while he drank from a water bottle with his other hand.

Oscar asked, "Everyone okay?"

Everyone sounded off that they were all well; Edgar less enthusiastically indicated he was alright. Tillman was on the radio calling for Mitch to return with the chopper to pick them up. Oscar tended to Edgar to make sure he would not slip into shock. Edgar had calmed down, and his knee severely swollen but apparently, nothing seemed broken. Oscar walked over to James who was standing next to Tillman, the two guys that had been on the earlier search. They were the two climbers that first went into the cave.

Oscar said, "James, you said that the cave was a dead end; there weren't any other tunnels to follow, right?"

James nodded a yes. Tillman spoke up, "Whaddaya mean, dead end?"

Oscar looked at Tillman, then at James and said, "Tell him, James."

James looked at Tillman, shaking his head back and forth, said, "That's right, Tillman, the cave ended in a dead end."

Tillman angrily said, "Come on, James, we stood on the other side of that mountain. Don't tell me that it dead-headed."

James said, "Tillman is right, we both stood on the other side of the mountain; that cave went all the way through."

Oscar, still fuming, asked, "Is this Fantasy Island? Should I be looking for Ricardo Montalbán and his sidekick Tattoo?"

"Easy, Oscar, you're going to blow a valve; there has got to be a reasonable explanation for this," Tillman responded.

Oscar, realizing that it had been a long day and he was feeling the strain of the day, and the muscle spasm in his neck was not easing up, let the conversation drop. Just then, they heard the sound of the chopper coming over the hill. It was soon hovering over the top of the climbing team. The helicopter sat down, and everyone began grabbing his gear. Edgar limped toward the chopper; a large stain showed on the back of his pants; he sat in the opening of the chopper door and swung his stiff leg onto the platform. The rest of the men threw their gear into the chopper and, one by one climbed aboard. Mitch pushed the throttle, revving the RPMs and the craft lifted off the ground. It tilted to one side and made a sharp curve as it ascended and headed back to the airport.

Spencer escorted Rebecca Love into the sheriff's office and right into his office, then set her down in a chair; only then did he release her arm. "Miss Love, I have a few questions for you."

Rebecca looked at the office file cabinet and asked curiously, "Where did you get my hat?"

Spencer turned and looked at her, "What do you mean?"

Rebecca exclaimed loudly, "My hat; that's my hat!"

Spencer looked in the direction Rebecca was pointing. On top of the file cabinet sat the camo jungle hat that Oscar had found at the clearing below the cliff.

Spencer asked, "How do you know that is your hat?"

Rebecca said, "It has my survival camp patch on it, Wilderness Awareness camp, in Duvall, Washington.

Spencer leaned over his desk and asked, "Miss Love, how did your hat get in the middle of an investigation of a missing person?"

Rebecca asked, "What do you mean?"

Spencer was getting impatient with her asking the questions, said, "How did your hat get way out in the wilderness above Cedar Creek Watershed Road?"

Rebecca straightened up, accentuating her chest through the tank top shirt, "I was following a trail."

Spencer, "Really! And what trail was that? Let's just save some time here; we are searching for a lost hiker in that area; were you up there for the same reason?"

Rebecca, leaned back in the chair and looked out the window and snidely spoke, "Do I need a lawyer or something?"

Spencer smiled, "Well, I could lock you in a cell until you can find one to drive from Seattle, or you can answer a few questions. Okay?"

Rebecca responded, "Okay, I was following Dan Simmons; I parked out of sight in the underbrush. I fell asleep, and when I woke, he was gone." Rebecca shifted uneasily in her chair and went on, "When I woke up it was early morning, and there were some other trucks parked behind his Jeep, so I waited until the search team left, I then hiked up the hill."

Spencer prompted, "Keep going."

Rebecca continued, "I got to the top of the hill and down a draw and up the next hill; I hiked up that until I came to a clearing and there was this big cliff."

Spencer nodded, "Go ahead. Then what happened?"

Rebecca continued, "I was tired, and I sat down to have a drink; it was hot, so I took off my hat; I must have left it laying on the ground."

Spencer then asked, "Okay, that explains the hat, but what were you doing watching Dan Simmons?"

Rebecca explained that she had read an article he had written and wanted to talk with him. When she called Gonzaga University looking for him, they said that they had no idea where he had gone and that they wanted to speak with him if she found him. Rebeca stated that she finally got hold of a research partner of his and discovered that he was in North Bend doing some fieldwork. That was when she decided to come to see him and see if she could join in his research.

Spencer listened to the story and asked, "Did you talk with him?"

Rebecca's shoulders drooped, and she answered, "Yes, I did talk with him; he told me he did his field research alone, and that it was dangerous work and that I should go back to school."

Spencer concluded, "So you decided to stay and follow him around, right?"

Rebecca nodded her head in agreement.

Spencer changed gears, "What were you doing up at Iron Horse Park last night?"

Rebecca said, "I went up there because someone told me that there were some free Forest Service road maps, so I went to see."

Spencer wasn't buying looking for maps, but without any other evidence, he would have to let her go.

Spencer had Rebecca's Subaru towed to the impound lot and had Higgins search it. Higgins came back from thoroughly scrutinizing the vehicle; he walked through the front door of the sheriff's office, then walked up to Spencer's closed office door and knocked.

Higgins said, "Sheriff, can I talk with you?"

Spencer looked at Rebecca and said, "I will be right back."

Spencer left the room and shut the door behind him. Spencer walked over to Higgins desk and said, "What did you find?"

Higgins said, "Nothing much except a backpack with food and hiking gear in it, some maps and a tent, a sleeping bag, and some books. That's about it; oh yes, a notebook with several pages of notes about the area and the town."

Spencer asked, "What did the notes say? Did you bring it back with you?"

Higgins smiled and said, "It mostly named some town's people and what they did; there was something that had times and dates and some notes after that. Yes, I have it right here."

Spencer instructed Higgins to make copies of the notebook, and he went back to his office.

Spencer walked into his office, shutting the door behind

him; he smiled at Rebecca, "What were you doing outside of the General Store?"

Rebecca looked at him blankly for a while and then said, "I was across the street having a coffee and breakfast."

Spencer had hit a dead-end in his investigation. He asked Rebecca for the address where she was staying and insisted that she stay in North Bend for a few more days and maybe a week or two. If and when she plans to leave North Bend, she should let him know beforehand. Rebecca agreed, and Spencer had Higgins drive her to her car at the impound lot.

Finally, Dave was able to get a great deal of paperwork done without distractions, then he made some phone calls to vendors for needed campground supplies and even answered some hiking questions from passing park visitors. This kind of interaction was what Dave Notworst had signed up for; this was the life he loved, living in nature and helping visitors enjoy the experience. And he was feeling pretty good now that Wendy Storms had left town. Then to top things off, Betsy was coming over tonight to make lasagna --- one of Dave's favorites. Hopefully, she would clean his house while she was there. A woman's touch is just what Dave needed; what he didn't know was that it would come with a price tag.

Dave's cell phone rang. It was Spencer. Dave answered, "Hello, Ranger Dave Notworst here."

Spencer said, "Hello, Dave, I did some looking around and thought I had a suspect, but it didn't pan out; we also had a break-in at the General Store."

Dave asked, "Do you think it was related?"

Spencer said, "I am not sure at this point. Let me know if you see Pete Davis or his Willys up in the woods."

Dave said, "I will keep my eyes peeled."

Spencer answered, "Okay, I will let you know if anything develops, don't worry, I will find your .45."

Dave knew and trusted Spencer's ability to solve issues.

Spencer said, "Talk to you later."

Dave returned with, "Thanks, Spencer, goodbye."

Spencer had just set the phone down, not even releasing the headset when it rang. The vibration startled him. Like a knee-jerk reaction, Spencer squeezed the phone in his hand so tightly; he thought he could crush it.

Lifting the receiver to his ear, Spencer said, "sheriff's office."

From the other end of the phone came the soft, meek voice of Hillary Upshaw, "Hello, this is Hillary Upshaw over at, 'It Lives Again' second-hand store." A short pause then, "I've been robbed!"

Spencer gritted his teeth and calmly said, "Yes, Mrs. Upshaw, I will be over right away and take a report."

Hillary barked, "I don't want a report! I want someone arrested!"

Spencer stayed calm and explained to Hillary that a report was part of the process and that she should not touch anything until he arrives. With that, Spencer hung up and headed for his patrol car, explaining to Higgins on his way out the door. Spencer pulled up in front of "It Lives Again" second-hand store, parked his car and took a deep breath. He walked up to the front of the store and tried to turn the handle, but the door was locked. He tapped on the window and spotted Hillary in the back of the store; she saw him and came to the front. She stopped at the front door and smiled at Spencer.

Spencer asked, "Can you open the door and let me in?"

Hillary said, "You told me not to touch anything."

Spencer now losing composure said, "Mrs. Upshaw, did they break-in through the front door?"

Hillary responded, "Why, no, Dearie, they broke in the back door."

Spencer said, "Well, I don't think you are going to destroy any evidence then, besides how am I going to file a report if you don't let me in?"

Hillary cheerfully replied, "Okay, but only because you

told me to."

Spencer asked, "Mrs. Upshaw, can you show me where they broke in, please?"

Hillary shaking her head back and forth said, "This way; follow me; now don't knock anything over; be careful of the tear in the carpet there; don't trip."

They wandered past the semi-precious junk, antiquities and just plain odd novelties; the smell of dust and mold filled the air. Spencer started sneezing.

Hillary stopped, turned and looked at Spencer with a frown on her face and said, "Bless you, Dearie, are you getting sick?"

Spencer replied, "It is entirely possible."

When they finally arrived at the back door, Spencer looked it over carefully, but he was not impressed with the safety gadgetry of the hodgepodge old, rusty-locking devices. The wood on the frame split from the forced leverage. Spencer looked carefully and took a few photographs to compare with the break-in at the General Store. But by looking at the marks, he mentally made an educated guess that it was the same person. He took out his hand-sized notebook from his left shirt pocket.

Spencer asked, "Mrs. Upshaw, can you tell me what is missing?"

A tear appeared in Hillary's eye, and she said, "The only thing I could find that was missing was my late husband's banjo."

Spencer asked, "Where was that located?"

Hillary turned and walked to the front of the store. When she reached the counter, she stopped and pointed at the wall behind it. Hillary forcefully stated, "Right there, Dearie."

Spencer looked up and there behind the counter was a faded outline of a banjo.

Hillary started to cry more loudly, emitting sniffles, "That was just about all I have left of Johnny."

Spencer gave her a sideways hug to comfort her; she just

cried a little bit more and then stopped; then to show her internal fortitude, she straightened up and backed away from Spencer.

Hillary said, "He was a good man and devoted husband."

Spencer could see that she loved Johnny and still had a sparkle in her eye for him.

He looked about the store for any other evidence of disturbance, but it was hard to tell; his best chance of a clue was to look for smears in the accumulated dust or torn cobwebs. How could he tell if anything was missing without an outline? Sitting on an end table was a stuffed skunk with its mouth wide open exposing its fangs with its back hunched for a fight. There was a large armadillo hassock next to a female manikin with only one arm; dressed in a 1920s flapper dress with most of the tassels missing. The store was a converted old Victorian style home, and Spencer thought it was an appropriate setting for a second-hand store. As he walked around looking at all the lost treasures, one-of-a-kinds and even disturbing looking macabre items, he spotted it. There on the table, in the dust, a clear handprint. He walked closer to examine it. Clear as day, a full handprint was visible. He quickly started taking pictures, trying to be as accurate as possible. He placed a small cardboard ruler next to the handprint as he photographed. He knew he could not lift a print from the dust, but maybe he could from the smudge under the soot and on top of the table. What good would it do? Who was he kidding; he wasn't going to run a fingerprint for a missing banjo. But one clue stood out significantly. Other than the silhouette of the absent banjo on the wall. There in the dust on the table was something unmistakable. Spencer thought, "How could I have missed that?" Distinctly in the smut was the handprint. But clearly, whoever it belonged to, he or she was also missing the ring finger. Not the entire finger. There was just a stub of a ring finger left, not even enough left to hold a ring; severed just shy of the second knuckle. Now, Spencer had something to go on, a clue he could use.

Spencer finished his report, comforted Mrs. Upshaw and headed back to the office to write up his findings. When he arrived, he could see Higgins out in front of the sheriff's office. Higgins had a young J-walker stopped on the curb. He was giving him the full lecture of the dangers of the offense. Spencer was sure he would be writing a citation. Spencer ignored the confrontation and went into the office to fill out his report. He pulled out his notebook and looked at the digital pictures on the evidence camera. Selecting one from the break-in at the General Store, Spencer hit the print button and wirelessly sent it to the color printer. He then went through the pictures and selected one of the door jamb at the second-hand store and printed that too. He went through the handprint images and printed one of those. Spencer went to the printer and gathered his copies. Sitting down at his desk, he examined the pictures of the two break-ins. The scrape against the door jamb of the General Store looked the same as one on the wood door jamb at the second-hand store. Spencer now convinced it was the same perpetrator.

"Now," thought Spencer, "who in town was missing the ring finger on the left hand."

The silhouetted mountains appeared to have been placed over the vibrant sky, taking on a red-pink hue as the sun was setting for the day. Dan Simmons joined in a circle with the Sasquatch; all were flat-footed, knees bent and in a sitting position with thighs against their chests. The shorter Sasquatch, three of them, served berries, debarked roots, and water from clear bags. Dan had concluded that the shorter creatures were the females of the species who did most of the daily tasks. Dan decided that sexism had a direct correlation with evolution. After Dan and the larger members served their daily sustenance, the females joined the rest in the squatted position facing the circle and eating. The largest of the creatures, Dan assumed him to be the leader, who started grunting, a low soft grunt. The others joined in, emitting the same pitch; it had a very melodious tone. The most significant creature looked at Dan Simmons and motioned to him with his head. Dan understood that he was to join into the chanting. He tried to get the right pitch of the grunting, but it took a bit of trying to tune his vocal cords. With a bit more effort, Dan tuned into the rhythm, and the pitch and the whole group started to resonate on the same level. It sounded like a kind of mystic Tibetan chant and soon began to vibrate in his head. The chanting changed his awareness, altering his consciousness; a mellow, comforting warmth filled Dan's body. He felt a light floating feeling as though he could rise right off the ground. In the very center of the circle, a small flame ignited, rising about two feet off the ground. As the chanting increased, so did the height of the fire. It became brighter with feather-like flames of orange, red, and gold flickering in the approaching night. When the flames reached approximately six feet in height and five feet in diameter the chanting stopped, and there was an eerie silence. All of the creatures sat motionless, staring into the flames. They were fire-gazing as they quietly consumed the nourishing victuals set before them. Dan too sat and gazed into the fire and ate. As he chewed, he looked deep into the flames; Dan could tell that he had entered an altered state. He started to see images --- faces; he could see Rebecca Love. She seemed to be preparing herself for a journey. In that instant, he, Dan Simmons, knew that she was coming to find him.

Chapter 7

The Black Orb of Passion

Dan Simmons once again found himself dreaming of flying high above the clouds. He drifted upon the air currents as a red-tailed hawk. Dan visualized peaceful valleys below that would alternate and change dramatically. As he soared through the heavens, his body began shifting from the bird back into a man; the metamorphosis was painful and, mentally, it was profoundly disturbing. As he began to change, he also started falling. His twisting, tumbling naked body plummeted toward uncertainty. The fear of falling to his death caused intense anxieties. As he descended, the speed increased causing a burning sensation on his flesh. He looked below again; there was nothing visible below him; he was falling into emptiness. Dan quickly took intentional control; he realized that this was merely a dream. He thought that if he could control the circumstances, he could change the outcome of his destiny within this unpleasant revere. With this one thought, Dan began to be cognizant of his surroundings. Yes, he was falling, but the clouds and sky were absent. He was now falling through clear space, surrounded by a dark blue backdrop; against this blue background was a slowly-changing light show of soft pastel tints, similar to the Aurora Borealis. Dan noticed that his descent had slowed. Possibly because there was no visible destination or place to where he was falling, maybe it was the light show surrounding him that made the velocity of falling seem slower. This slowed descent now felt as if Dan were moving in slow motion. Why was he here --- in this place between life and the existence beyond --- between reality and the unknown? He felt as if he were in limbo between life and death. From within his head, Dan Simmons heard a voice, a familiar voice; it spoke to him, "You enter this life alone; you leave this life alone; you must question everything." He continued to fall, but now with an understanding as to why he had passed through here. Then the descent became rapid again; he was once again gaining speed as he fell. In his path was a gathering fog or mist; he began to fall even faster into the cloud, disappearing into it.

Dan awoke with a jolt, sitting upright and gasping for air --- panicked from the dream that had finally shocked him back into reality. Regaining his mental equilibrium, he looked down and saw that he was levitating five to six inches above the ground. "What?" he exclaimed loudly. Suspended upon a cushion of air. As he gazed around at the group, he noticed that all the creatures were floating above the ground. The fire in the middle of the circle had died out. He sat up cross-legged, enjoying the cushion of air beneath him; he was pleased and amused at the same time. He watched the sun beginning to rise over the mountains; he closed his eyes, placing his palms face up on his knees. He began to breathe in and out slowly. He focused his thoughts, clarifying his intent to come to a full understanding of what had taken place. He began to realize that he was presently in a situation that could make his work extremely beneficial to humanity. He would need to keep clear, well-defined mental notes. "If I could only ask questions," he thought, "there is great knowledge I could gain from what these creatures know. How they have existed for so many years without being caught is amazing! Man is a wicked foe, torturous and vindictive. If man can find any-thing unusual, he will kill it, exploit it for body parts, and then seek someone to buy it. Man has a short memory and soon forgets his shame. If he can dominate and control beast or man, he surely will. These creatures have remained aloof, undetected, preserved, and secure from man in these primeval forests. What does this species know that keeps its presence unknown, concealed from the invasive nature of man? How have these huge ape-like beings eluded capture?"

As Dan opened his eyes, he could see the Sasquatch stirring, awaking from slumber. As he looked around the camp, his eyes met the largest one's eyes. Dan could tell that this, the leader of the group, was deep in thought. Most likely wondering what to do with Dan Simmons and this breach of their security. While staring at each other, a voice from inside Dan's head, that same voice penetrated his thoughts, the same one he had heard before. It spoke to him again, "What do you want?" It was loud and unmistakably clear. The voice repeated, "What do you want?" Dan had no idea where this voice was coming from, or who it was; maybe it was a hallucination. Many strange and unexplained phenomena have occurred since he had entered this valley. Dan realized that the voice was the same as in his dream, and also, he heard it in the cave before he passed out. This voice was becoming incredibly annoying, and Dan wished it would stop. He was beginning to think he was going crazy. He was feeling a little emotionally unstable, and he needed to keep a clear head in order to observe this new species.

The voice came again but with more force, "What do you want here?"

Dan looked back at the leader and could see it was still staring at him. Dan thought to himself, "Should I just answer this voice?"

The voice came again, "Yes, answer me; what do you want?"

This voice continued to disturb Dan emotionally, and he thought, "God, help me."

The voice entered his consciousness again, "There is no God here to help you, only me, Jarl."

Dan mentally questioned, "Who are you?"

The voice spoke in Dan's head again, "I am the one who saved you."

Dan saw the largest Sasquatch standing and walking in his direction. When the beast had reached him, it squatted, flat-footed with its thighs against its stomach. The creature stared directly into Dan's eyes. The voice repeated, "I am Jarl." With that, the beast thumped its chest with its hand.

With a gasp of excitement and astonishment, Dan realized that these creatures were able to communicate telepathically. He was ecstatic and elated; he would now be able to talk without having to learn or re-invent language through signs, drawings, or laborious types of charades. This new revelation was a dream come true, to be able to ask a new species how it came to be and what it knew. "What do I want to ask first?" Dan questioned.

But the answer came quickly; the voice spoke again, "What do you want?"

Dan's mind was racing; what did he want to ask; there was much he wanted to know, so many questions. Dan thought, "What do I ask, what do I want? Well, I want to study this new species for the betterment of humankind."

Now Jarl was frowning at Dan, and he spoke, "Clear your mind; when you speak to me, quiet your mind it is cluttered with random thoughts. Think of only one idea. Just one thought, do not clutter my mind with your disorganized, misguided thinking."

Dan, frustrated, blurted out loud, "I just want to understand your species." From all around the camp came loud snorting sounds of vexation, the other creatures were upset from the outburst. Dan thought to himself, "What did I do?"

Jarl answered Dan, inside his head, "Dan Simmons, you spoke aloud; this is forbidden; this disturbs the thoughts and communications of others. Noise is also forbidden because the sound is a way that man can track us. Do you understand?"

Dan smiled and communicated, "I understand, but how did you know my name?"

Jarl transfer-spoke, "I know many of your thoughts; I read your thoughts before you ever saw me in the forest." Jarl added, "Now tell me what you want?"

Dan cleared his mind and transfer-spoke, "I want to study your species, and then use that information to better mankind."

Jarl raised his chin and transfer-spoke, "I understand, but I am not sure there is much hope for your mankind; it is self-serving and destructive."

Dan continued, "But isn't knowledge the foundation for hope?"

Jarl transfer-spoke, "Yes, knowledge is the start, and that is why fire-gazing is so important to our tribe."

Dan asked, "Fire-gazing, does it show the truth?"

Jarl answered, "Fire-gazing is the path to knowledge. What you ask of the fire, it will reveal. It reveals knowledge, truth, and sometimes the future."

Jarl stood up as he transfer-spoke, "Come, we need to move; we never stay in an area more than one day. We keep moving so that those that seek cannot find us."

Dan nodded indicating that he understood; he tried to get up and noticed that he was now sitting on the ground, no longer levitating.

The caravan of five creatures and Dan Simmons moved away from the clearing next to the lake and began following a dry stream bed. Dan speculated their heading was in a north-easterly direction. This new ability to communicate was more than Dan could have hoped for; he needed to remember everything accurately and in sequence. Keeping information clear was going to be his most significant task. He would be able to reveal the nature and culture of a species that was a legend, a myth --- stories told late at night around campfires. This discovery would stun his professors back at Gonzaga, and turn their theories on their ears.

The creature walking directly in front of Dan was a smaller one, and he reasoned it was a female. She turned and snorted in his face. She transfer-spoke, "I am Saga, and I would like you to keep your thoughts to yourself; try to control your thoughts or think quietly."

Dan quickly returned his thought, "Yes, thank you, Saga: I will from now on." She turned and walked quickly to catch up with the creature she was following. Dan thought to himself, "This is not going to be an easy task."

———————

Dave showed up at the sheriff's office at 8 a.m. sharp; he was meeting Spencer and Oscar to go over the discoveries on the previous day. Detailing the mission of exploring the cave and what was on the other side of the mountain. Oscar's message left on Dave's answering machine said nothing about what had happened other than they didn't find Dan Simmons. Dave parked his truck in his reserved NO PARKING space, got out and slammed the door. Higgins was standing in the parking lot watching Dave park in the NO PARKING zone. When Dave spotted Higgins, Higgins threw his arms in the air out of frustration. Dave swung open the front door of the building and headed toward Spencer's office. Oscar was in Spencer's office when Dave walked through the door.

"Morning," said Spencer; Dave nodded his head as he took off his ranger's hat. Oscar smiled and nodded at Dave.

Spencer looked at Oscar and said, "Oscar, you have the floor; go ahead and tell us what you found; we can't wait any longer."

Oscar cleared his throat, "Well, we didn't find much; the cave turned out to be a dead end."

"Really?" said Spencer looking somewhat surprised, given the previous data.

Oscar went on, "That's right, a dead end. I questioned the fella's that first went into the cave and they both said the cave went through and out the other side. I don't know what to believe, but I could not see any other tunnels. We had to cut the trip short due to an upset cougar." Oscar continued, "We found no more signs of Dan Simmons or any clues to where he went."

Spencer asked, "Are you planning any other missions?"

Oscar answered in a restrained manner, "We have nothing to go on, so until we get a better lead, we have nothing to search. Mitch Cochran is still running daily chopper flights over the area until our funds start to run low. Maybe we can get some assistance from the state or some federal money."

Dave interjected, "The park has had a steady flow of fortune hunters filling the campground. The woods are full of people crawling all over each other. I don't think there is any evidence left that hasn't been trampled on." Oscar nodded his head in agreement.

Spencer asked, "Oscar, did you find anything at all while you were in the cave?"

Oscar said, "Yes, but I don't know if it was Dan Simmons' or left by someone else. Frankly, I don't think it has anything to do with this case."

Spencer asked, "We'll decide that; what did you find?"

Oscar reached into his cargo pants side pocket and pulled something from its depths. "Here, have a look for yourselves," said Oscar, opening his hand to reveal what lay in his palm. Dave tilted his head as he leaned in for a closer look.

Spencer walked around from behind his desk and stated, "I'm not sure if that thing has anything to do with this investigation."

Dave said, "What? You found a marble?"

Oscar defended his find by saying, "It may look like a marble. But it is quite different. Here, feel how heavy it is."

Spencer tried to pick up the black object from Oscar's hand, but it was dense and heavy, and Spencer had to squeeze hard to grasp the object firmly to lift it. There was a small indentation left in Oscar's hand where the black object had sat before Spencer had picked it up. As Spencer raised it to look at it, the orb slipped through his fingers. The black object hit the floor with a loud thud; it didn't bounce, or roll; it didn't move, but lay right where it had made contact with the floor.

Dave looked at Spencer and said, "I have never seen anything like that."

Oscar added, "That little marble is heavier than anything of its size that I have ever seen."

Dave still quite unimpressed reached down to pick it up. As he bent down and touched the black object, a warm flush or tingling sensation surged through his body. At the same moment, he was thinking of Betsy. Dave grasped it with his thumb and forefinger. His fat fingers bulged around it. As he picked it up to examine it, he could feel its density and placed it in the palm of his other hand. He peered into the center of the small black orb; as he did, the black hue seemed to have a great depth to it, and it emitted a shimmering silver glow around its edges. At that exact minute, Dave decided to drive into Seattle on his day off and buy a wedding ring for Betsy. Upon his return, he would ask her to marry him. Dave continued to stare into the black orb. Silence loomed over the entire group. Dave had plans unfolding in his head, but he didn't understand why. He decided he would submit.

Spencer broke the silence by saying, "Dave, Dave, earth to Dave; Dave, do I need to get the smelling salts out?"

Dave abruptly broke out of the spell the orb wielded over him. He seemed a little confused and distant; clearing his throat, he said, "Odd sort of material; I have seen some dense objects like this before; let me think, I believe it was a mineral called Osmium. It was shiny like this, but it was in crystal form, not round."

Spencer said, "I don't care what it is. or what it's molecular structure is, it's going in the evidence collection; the damn thing gives me the creeps." Spencer added, "Well, Gentlemen, if that is all, I have some follow-up work to attend to."

Oscar said, "That's all I have to offer."

Dave shrugged his shoulders and said, "I need to get going too; by the way, tomorrow is my day off, and I will be out of town, so call me only if you need something."

Spencer concluded the meeting and Dave and Oscar left the sheriff's office. The three men were unaware of what this little black marble portended for the small town of North Bend in the coming weeks.

If you are fortunate enough to own an amulet, charm, fetish, talisman, mojo, juju or whatever name you call it, you would most likely know the outcome of any wish and corollary. To wish for something, could have adverse side effects. The Black Orb of Passion belongs to no one; it exists only for its own sake and purpose. It will, however, fulfill the desired request of the wish-maker. When it grants a wish, it does so without the conscious awareness of the wish-maker. It may not even require an actual want; just an intense, passionate thought can trigger the Black Orb into action. So one should be careful of his or her desires; you may receive your aspiration.

Oscar had no idea what he had kicked up in the dust in that dark room deep in the cave. The Black Orb was not from this world, or the world as we know it. Because of its nature, it probably should have been dropped into the deepest ocean, or a fiery volcano. It should not have ended in possession of the people of North Bend. But fate must knock on all our doors one day or another. It was about to wreak havoc on the people of the town of North Bend. They had pulled the short straw this day.

———————————

Gretchen Carter, an elderly cleaning lady, was good at her job. Sheriff Harrington was happy to have her in his employ. Gretchen, a bitter 76-year-old woman, had never had children, and had never married; she was unhappy with her lot in life. Her cantankerous attitude made her hard to deal with and very pugnacious.

That day her landlord, Philbert Bottomdolr, had served her with a notice of a rent increase. Gretchen had lived in the studio apartment above the drug store for 20 years and only twice previously had her rent gone up. She was furious about this perceived injustice. Gretchen was overtly cursing Philbert's name, and using the most un-lady-like language. Although she was on her way to clean the sheriff's office, thankfully, it was Sunday, and the office was closed. She could take her time without bothering anyone. Gretchen slipped her key into the front door keyhole and opened it to a peacefully quiet office. Gretchen didn't even notice the silence; she deeply engrossed in her negative thinking. Angry, revengeful desires overcame her. Filled with hatred for that tightwad named Bottomdolr and his damned rent increase and the burden it had placed on her finances. She started to clean Spencer's office, dusting the furniture, the desk, and then the file cabinet. She was ruminating about Bottomdolr's greediness. Deep in her anguish, she mentally plotted ways to get revenge; she could probably run over his cat, or she might just knock over all the trash cans behind the drugstore. She could send his wife a letter declaring that he was involved in an affair. Maybe he should just be burned at the stake. Yes, the little worm should burn at the stake! As she dusted the top of the file cabinet, she heard a loud thud on the floor. She looked down and saw a black marble. She bent down and picked it up.

Meanwhile, at the Double D Diner, Philbert sat sipping a cup of tea and reading the Sunday paper. Betsy was standing behind the counter totaling receipts when she witnessed the most ghastly, supernatural, unbelievable, unexplainable phenomenon she or anyone else in North Bend had ever seen. Philbert, while reading the sports section, spontaneously combusted, leaving only his smoldering shoes on the floor and a scorched butt-mark on the seat of the chair where he had been sitting. Some black soot smudges were left on the table where his arms had rested. A cloud of smoke rose above the booth of Bottomdolr's last resting place.

Chapter 8

Boil Boil

Monday morning brought more bad news; pulled up in front of the Double D Diner was the KRAP Channel 12 News van carrying perky little Wendy Storms. She was standing in front of the diner, dressed in the highest heels known to women's fashion and a tight dark blue skirt with a fluffy white blouse. She was poised to broadcast a live feed to the airways. A hand wave from the cameraman signaled her live connection.

Wendy began, "Good morning, Seattle, this is Wendy Storms with a Kay-RAP, breaking news exclusive. We are live from North Bend, where it seems that in this diner behind me, just yesterday morning a man was burned to death. As I have it, the victim was a local businessman named Philbert Bottomdolr. Kay-RAP News has been notified that a terrorist group named The Preservation of Sasquatch Society is now claiming responsibility. But that is unconfirmed at this time. It seems that Mr. Bottomdolr, who was a regular patron of the Double D Diner was seated in a booth when he ignited. He burst into flames and turned to cinders as he read the Sunday paper. An eyewitness confirms that the victim was smoking a Cuban cigar at the time of the incident and that immolation could have been self-inflicted. The owner of the

Double D Diner denied this claim; stating that smoking is prohibited. The diner is closed until the investigation is concluded. Looking through the window (the cameraman took a close-up) you can see the booth where Mr. Bottomdolr had been sitting; it has since been cordoned off with yellow crime scene caution tape." The camera panned back to Wendy, "That is all we have at this point; please stay tuned for updated broadcasts on this tragic human auto-incineration story. This is Wendy Storms, Kay-RAP's 'Knows in the Air'. Back to you, William."

Higgins was standing guard at the entrance of the Double D Diner and watched the broadcast in its entirety. He was impressed with Wendy's appearance and professional mannerisms. But he mostly liked her looks; she was a smart and great-looking TV personality, just the kind of woman Higgins dreamed of taking home to mother. She was bold. Higgins liked that strong characteristic. She was a sexy-dresser, and he wondered if she smelled good too.

Wendy walked up to Higgins and looked at his name tag, then said, "Hello, officer Higgins."

Higgins stood up straight, puffed out his chest and pulled in his gut, trying to increase his height and improve his physique and replied, "How may I help you, Ma'am?"

Wendy returned her award-winning smile, a smile that had won her many broadcasting awards; she then asked so innocently, "What can you tell me about the burning man?"

Higgins firmly replied, "I'm sorry, Ma'am, I am not at liberty to discuss an ongoing investigation."

Wendy smiled, reached out and straightened Higgin's tie. Higgins felt his knees getting weak, and his breathing became labored.

Tilting her head and shyly smiling, she said in a soft cooing voice, "But Wendy wants to know."

At that point, Higgins turned to putty, pliable, submissive to that beckoning voice, plus she smelled delectable. In his state of swooning, he couldn't help but answer the siren's call. Wendy asked again, "What can you tell Wendy poo?"

Higgins took a deep breath and spilled his guts. To everything that Wendy asked, Higgins complied. After getting Higgins' cooperation, Wendy dug deep, filling her shovel full of North Bend's best dirt.

Wendy was back in North Bend; she had an agenda she needed to follow. Wendy's conversation with Higgins was most profitable; she decided to expand her web of intrigue. She still had Tommy Well's phone containing the pictures of the footprints that she couldn't access. The phone needed a password, and a determined Wendy Storms was going to get Tommy to give it to her.

She ordered Phil to drive the van. "First things first," she said, "I want to swing by Murphy's Pub to see if Tommy Wells is drinking his breakfast again."

Phil smiled and said, "Yes, Ma'am."

Phil spun a 180 in the middle of North Bend Way and headed toward Murphy's Pub. Pulling into the parking lot, they saw only one pickup truck. Wendy knew it wasn't Tommy's. "Damn," said Wendy. She decided to go to Tommy's house but had no idea where he lived. After thinking for a brief moment, she said, "Higgins, I'll call him; he will tell me where Tommy lives." Wendy smiled as she thought to herself, "Higgins is better than directory assistance and more reliable." Wendy retrieved Higgins' card from her clutch purse and dialed his cell. In just 2 minutes of sweet talk, she had the address. Wendy relayed the address to Phil, who entered it into the GPS, and down the road, they went. Twenty minutes later, Phil turned the van onto a narrow dirt road that meandered through the woods and eventually opened into a small cow pasture. In the middle of the pasture sat alone 28-foot Totem camp trailer, complete with a half-rusted, half-white 50-gallon propane tank. Next to it was Tommy's pickup truck. Wendy yelled, "Bingo!"

Wendy jumped out of the van and headed for the front door of the trailer, carefully stepping between the cow pies. She rapped her gold ring on the glass storm door. No answer. She then pounded on the door with her tiny insistent fists.

From inside the trailer came a moan, a clank of bottles and then a reply, "Hang on; just a sec, man." Tommy Wells flung open the door. He was standing there in only a cowboy hat and sagging gray underwear. Tommy squinting his eyes said, "Hey, do you know how early it is? How can a man get some shut-eye? What the hell do you want?" Rousing from his stupor, Tommy realized who was at the front door; he said slurring his words, "Hey, you're the bitch that stole my phone. What the hell do you want?"

Wendy said sternly, "I want the password to your phone."

Tommy replied, "And I want to meet the Pope, but we both know that ain't gonna happen."

Wendy sharply responded, "Living way out here must be pretty lonely without a phone; do you want your phone back?"

Tommy demanded, "Hell, yes."

Wendy again jockeyed for position, "Tell me the password and I will give you your phone."

Tommy said, "Up yours."

Wendy said, "That attitude is not going to get your phone back."

Tommy replied, "No, 'Up yours,' is the password."

Wendy went back to the van, pulled out the phone and typed in UPYOURS; the screen changed to the main menu. Wendy screeched, "Bingo!" She tagged all the photos on the phone and emailed them to her phone; she then checked her phone to make sure she received them. Wendy returned to the porch and handed the phone to Tommy, who quickly grabbed it out of her hand.

Wendy in her snottiest voice said, "You might want to take a trip to Walmart and buy some clean underwear unless those are purposely stained to identify the front from the back."

Tommy got the last laugh though; as Wendy turned and stepped off the porch, she plopped dead-center in a fresh green cow patty. So much for those very high heeled, satin white Manolo Blahnik shoes.

Back in the van, Wendy, so determined to get her program ready, didn't even think about her shoes; she had her next victim to take out. She looked at Phil and said, "Let's pay a visit to Chief Ranger Dave Notworst." Phil nodded at Wendy and spun a circle of brown tire tracks in the soft green pasture, and headed toward Iron Horse Park. Some thirty minutes later the KRAP News van pulled up to Ranger Station 5, but Dave's truck was not there. Wendy got out of the van and walked up to the station door, opened it and walked in. Looking around, she spotted all the maps and brochures, gift items, postcards, stuffed Smokey the Bear dolls, bumper stickers, but not Dave Notworst. She walked right up to the counter and tapped the round bell rapidly several times for service.

From the back office walked tall, slender Tom Willkie. Tom greeted her, "Good day; what can I do you for?"

Wendy stated, "I am looking for Ranger Dave Notworst."

Tom answered, "He booked off work yesterday and today; should be back late tonight; can I help ya, eh?" Then Tom added, "Oh, I know you; you're that news lady, a bit of a keener aren't ya?"

Wendy was not amused; she could tell an insult, even if she didn't understand Canadian slang. She responded with, "One does what one has to, to get to the truth."

Tom said, "True, but if you want to talk with Dave, you haveta come back tomorrow, eh."

Not happy, Wendy said, "I can do that." She abruptly spun about and marched out the door.

Tom thought to himself, "Funny looking shoes; wondering why was one green?"

Wendy, once back in the van, ordered Phil to return to the Hyway Motel and book some rooms. She wanted to go through the pictures from the phone before the five o'clock news broadcast. Halfway back to the motel, Wendy remembered that Higgins had told her about a Rebecca Love, that knew Dan Simmons, and that the sheriff had questioned her. Wendy looked on the back of the card where Higgins had written down her address. Wendy then ordered Phil to put the address into the GPS as she handed him the card. When they arrived at Rebecca's house, the silver Subaru was in the driveway. Walking out of the side door of the house came Rebecca with a backpack. Rebecca was in a hurry and didn't want to talk to anyone. Phil pulled in behind the Subaru, blocking it in.

This move irritated Rebecca, and she yelled, "Hey, I'm getting ready to leave."

Wendy jumped out of the van, one green shoe, and one white shoe, moving as fast as she could make them go. Coming face to face with Rebecca, Wendy said, "I just have a couple of questions, and we will leave."

Rebecca responded, "I know who you are and I have nothing to say to you or the media."

Wendy said, "I just want to know how you know Dan Simmons?" The cameraman was now out of the van and taping the conversation; Phil had a mic pointed in their direction.

Rebecca replied, "I know of him, and his work, and that he had gone missing."

Wendy continued, "What do you know about his work?"

Rebecca was getting irritated with Miss Wendy Storms, and about to unleash ten years of Tae Kwon Do on her puny little butt. Rebecca stated, "I have my problems, and I don't need you bugging me right now."

Wendy continued to probe, "Maybe I could help? I know lots of people, and a few at the University of Washington."

Rebecca started calming down now, almost in tears, "I think that his work is valid, and people don't understand; he is onto something, and he needs to get due recognition for it."

Wendy insistent, proceeded, "Well, I can get his story out there, and I can do it in a way that shines a light on what he is trying to do and the good it will accomplish for all of humanity. You would want that, right?"

Rebecca stood up straight, "Yes, that is what I want for him and his research, for him to be known, to be understood and not seen as some boogieman chaser."

Wendy went on, "Well, then, that is what we'll do; we will get it down on the record, and you can tell it like it is."

Rebecca was smiling now, "Ok, let's do it."

Phil and the cameraman were getting it all down on tape. After 2 hours of heavy questioning, Wendy thanked Rebecca for the detailed information and said her good-byes. Back in the van, Wendy told Phil to head back to the motel and get ready to edit the video they had just shot of Rebecca; the footage needed to be ready for the 5 o'clock news broadcast.

Soon after Wendy had left, Rebecca had everything packed. She started her Subaru and headed in the direction of Cedar Creek Watershed Road ZT 145. Rebecca had her bug-out pack and was determined to spend as long as needed to find Dan Simmons. She knew in the back of her mind that he had discovered the Sasquatch and that he could be in danger. From the rumors circulating Rebecca knew that the cave was a dead end, but also knew there was another way around. She had seen a pass that went between the mountains, hidden, and looked as if it hadn't been used for many years. She discovered it when she followed Dan's trail up to the cave. As she had wandered around and got lost, she was trying to find her way back to the clearing below the cave. She pushed aside some brush and there it was. She had followed it for a few klicks, but got tired and was out of supplies, so she marked the entrance with three sticks tied with a torn piece of her sleeve. Rebecca was now determined to find Dan Simmons and to help him with his work. When she arrived at ZT145, she drove all the way to the road's end; she found an overgrown trail and pulled the Subaru in under the canopy of tree boughs, almost hiding the car from sight. Pulling out her bug-out pack, water container and a fanny pack full of must-keep-dries, and hoisting them onto her back, she walked steadily into the night, not stopping, determined to find him, at all cost.

Wendy Storms was also determined --- to get her name on national television, maybe even internationally. This story could make her career. Phil and Wendy were cramped into the back of the van, cutting and editing every foot of video they had shot with Rebecca Love. They chopped and snipped and edited the footage until it resembled nothing of the truth. She was determined to invent pure, unmistakable, sensationalism, to rouse the attention of the masses. Wendy meant to stir up trouble, cast a dreaded spell, to magnify the idea of horrific beasts descending on the little town of North Bend. She was intent on bringing suspicion to the authorities who, she would claim, covered up the facts. Like a witch tending her caldron, cackling and giggling as she stirred, she added gnarled bits of this and severed pieces of that, concocting a gaseous creative literary mixture and boiling it down into a nasty, venomous porridge. The only thing smaller, more vicious than Wendy Storms, that could possess more evil, was the Black Orb.

Chapter 9

Say It, And They Will Come

The KRAP Channel 12 News van was parked in front of the North Bend Courthouse. Wendy was ready to broadcast another breaking news exclusive. William Ditlisquatt, the KRAP news anchor, was sitting at the news desk when the red light on the top of camera 2 came on.

"Good evening, Seattle," said William. "Tonight, we have an exclusive, live news story from North Bend. Hello, Wendy, are you there?"

"Hello, William, yes, we have some breaking news here in North Bend; as I broadcasted this morning, there was a horrific murder at the Double D Diner yesterday. A local businessman burst into flames as he sat reading the paper. We don't have any more details on that incident, but we are awaiting a coroner's report. However, relating to other news of the area, we do have an exclusive interview with a local woman who personally knows the missing hiker, Dan Simmons. Here is that interview." The live feed switched to a recorded tape.

Wendy asks, "Do you know Dan Simmons?"

Rebecca answered, "Yes, I know Dan Simmons (There is an obvious jog in the video where there is a missing portion.) very well."

Wendy asked another question, "Do you know why he was here in North Bend?"

Rebecca responded, "He was doing field research, (There is another obvious cut in the tape.) Bigfoot or Sasquatch."

Wendy asked once more, "Do you know where Dan Simmons is now?"

Rebecca replied, "The boogieman (Another cut in the tape.) has him."

Wendy questioned further, "Do you feel that Dan Simmons is in danger?"

Rebecca, "Most likely."

The feed cut back to Wendy, "There you have it, William, proof that there is something unknown lurking in the woods surrounding North Bend.

William broke in, "Uncanny and chilling reporting, Wendy; do you have any other evidence?"

Wendy responded, "Yes, William, I have some photos shot from the first Search and Rescue mission that went out looking for Dan Simmons."

The screen then flashed to a photograph of an enormous footprint; in the photo is a ruler showing the massive size of the impression. Then the next picture came on the screen, of a different impression and a man's hand pointing into the footprint. A third photo showed a goofy Pete Davis standing next to one of the footprints, looking like a big game hunter out of Africa, with his rifle sitting on his hip and pointed to the sky. The only difference was that Pete was smiling with that missing tooth exposed and outfitted in his green rubber waders.

The camera cut back to Wendy Storms, glowing, radiant, smiling, standing in front of the North Bend Courthouse. Wendy concluded, "That is all we have at this point, but as more facts become available, we will be updating you; this is Kay-RAP's 'Knows in the Air' Wendy Storms."

The camera cut back to William, "What a supernatural and chilling story from North Bend tonight; mothers, tuck your children in securely tonight and lock all your doors; you heard it, the Boogieman lives. Coming up after this commercial break, we have a clinical psychologist who explains why doing "That Crazy Hand-Jibe" leads to early stages of senility. The broadcast cuts to a commercial while "hand-Jibe, hand-Jibe, doin that crazy hand-Jibe" plays in the background.

———————————

The night was robbing the daylight; Dan Simmons once again watched as the Sasquatch prepared for evening nourishment and fire-gazing. Saga, the one that had addressed Dan earlier in the day's travel, placed water, roots, and berries in front of him. He sensed great sadness in her. Dan transfer thought, "Why do you have such sadness?"

Saga looked Dan in the eyes, "I am not supposed to think about it."

Dan, "I don't know your species, and I just want to know more about why you would be sad."

Saga responded, "I lost my paired mate, many warm summers ago."

Dan was very interested to know more about this species and their mating habits; he continued, "Please share; I am interested."

Saga squatted in front of Dan and began to tell her story of woe. "The group had been traveling in the high parts of the mountains, a place where trees didn't grow, and the snow stayed all summer long. As we hiked, the ground shook, and a large boulder rolled down the mountain killing my beloved." She could hardly cope with the telling of her loss and has been overcome with loneliness ever since. Saga became anxious and said, "I must now go serve the others."

Dan commented gently, "Thank you for sharing."

With that, Saga continued, placing roots, berries, and water in front of the other creatures sitting around the circle. As the sun was setting, the group started their grunt-chanting, and Dan joined in; soon a small flame appeared in the center of the ring of Sasquatch. It grew as they were eating and they began fire-gazing. Dan looked across the top of the fire, enjoying the view of a magnificent mountain peak in the distance which reflected a red-orange hue from its snowcapped peak. It was the tallest of the mountains surrounding the valley, and it magnificently parted the red sky. Dan ate his roots and drank the water from the clear bag, saving the tasty berries for dessert later. As he gazed into the flames, he began to relax, the flames drawing him in, the dancing flames lulling him, beguiling his attention. Feeling warm and content, he willingly let the flames absorb his thoughts. Dan remembered what Jarl had told him; that fire-gazing can answer questions. So, Dan looked deep into the fire and asked a single question. "Why are these creatures here?" There was an explosion of sparks bursting from under the fire; Dan could see images zooming past him; gradually, he was starting to lose consciousness. Beams of light shot out from the fire and shot past Dan; presently, his body began to glow. The intensity of the moment was almost too much for him; Dan passed out.

Dan awoke, inside a dream, in a different reality or dimension; he found himself standing on hard white sand; there was no horizon. The hard sand blended into the sky above his head. It was as though he was standing on white sand in a thick fog. Only sand and fog were visible. He kept turning in a circular pattern, but he could distinguish no difference in the environment. White sand and white sky surrounded him. Deep inside his head, at the base of his skull, within the reptilian portion of his brain, he heard a small voice. Actually, it was more like a vibration, like an uncomfortable vibrating itch inside his brain. Someone or some dominant force was feeding him thoughts. They were ideas or communication beyond his comprehension. What did these thoughts mean? It must be some kind of message, possibly in a language that he could not decipher? The entity was unable to communicate with him in any way. No matter how hard it tried, Dan could not understand the message. Suddenly, the vibration ceased. From out of the fog above Dan, an object appeared; it was very flat, long and metallic; it did not have an end or beginning; from what he could determine, it was opaque, and was entirely symmetrical. It floated down from the ethereal white space and hovered above the ground. Dan was unable to determine its actual dimensions; there was no reference point, nor could he tell if it was close or far away.

In the center of the object an opening appeared, a dark opening in the perfectly smooth object. Dan saw a creature emerge from the object, but the entity seemed nearly invisible or somewhat translucent. It floated to a position just in front of him. He could only sense it, and he knew it was there. The vibration started again at the base of his skull. This time Dan could understand what the entity was telling him. The communication was not in any language he could recognize, but it came in the form of pure knowledge. He was able to understand it, even though it lacked sound; this was a knowledge transfer through both pictograms and emotions. He was now beginning to understand why the creatures were on this planet and what their definite purpose was. An entity, millions of years before this time had terraformed this planet. The creatures were incubated to be this planet's caretakers. The Sasquatch were highly-developed life-forms, genetically engineered to resist germs and bacteria. They had self-healing abilities. They were endowed with very long life-cycles and would breed only to replace their deceased members. These creatures possessed superhuman abilities. The entity reached out and touched Dan's forehead. His head jerked backward and everything when black.

Rebecca Love arrived at the clearing below the cliff and the cave; she headed for the hidden path that led between the mountains. She hurried because it was growing dark and she wanted to cover as much ground as possible under sunlight. She pushed her way through the thick brush and found her marker, the three sticks tied together with the flannel shirt sleeve. She moved through the last bit of brush and ended up on the trail that passed through the mountains. She had only walked about two klicks when the trail ended. She knew that she had gone farther up this trail before, but on this trip, the trail ended in a thick growth of lodgepole pines. Rebecca was confused; she must have made a wrong turn, but now she was mostly tired and dehydrated. The sun had set, and the temperature was dropping fast. She made camp under a cedar bough that was close to the ground, rolled out her sleeping bag and crawled inside to get warm. She ate a protein bar and then an apple to satisfy her hunger. The warmth made her sleepy, and soon she was asleep.

Secretly hiding in the dark was Pete Davis who had been following Rebecca for some time. Pete had once seen her and Dan Simmons together at Murphy's Pub. By what he could hear, he knew that Rebecca was attached to Dan, and if anyone were able to find him, it would be her. Pete had been parked down the road when the KRAP Channel 12 News van was at her house. He waited until they left, and then when Rebecca started out, he followed her. Pete kept a great distance between them because he knew she was on her way to ZT145. He concluded that from observing her backpack, sleeping bag, and camping essentials, she had prepared for an extended stay in the woods. Pete knew she was on her way to Cedar Creek Watershed Road. He was just biding his time until she made her move. Pete had his supplies ready, too. He had an advantage because he could move faster on his four-wheeler than Rebecca could walking.

Pete arrived at the clearing below the cliff, but it had taken him a bit of tracking to find Rebecca's hidden trail through the mountains. It wasn't too tricky, however; she had left her marker lying on the ground --- the three sticks with the strip of cloth. Pete settled in for the night. Building a fire to warm himself, he enjoyed several Old Milwaukee's to take the edge off of the night's cold.

Due to Miss Wendy Storms' report, the next day, things in North Bend started to take on a different life. There was no 'Business as Usual' because our country is so sensitive to trigger-words, the moment Wendy Storms broadcast the word, "Terrorist". A swarm of government agencies, NCIS, FBI, and CIA invaded North Bend. Since these agencies do not even attempt to communicate with each other, mostly out of fear that one will take credit for finding a nugget of espionage, they all showed up. It was a page out of a Tom Clancy novel. You couldn't swing a dead cat without hitting a black SUV. Agents in dark suits wearing sunglasses with curly wires coming out of their ears. They looked at everyone as a possible suspect. If there had been an evil element in North Bend, this sight would have tipped them off that Big Brother was watching. The oxymoron, "Government Intelligence", appropriately defined this influx of agents swarming into North Bend. This ostentatious demonstration would have sent any spies within fifty miles headed in opposite directions.

Even worse, everyone with the inclination to look for Bigfoot, and who had heard Wendy's broadcast was now headed in the direction of North Bend. Scientists, Bigfoot hunters, fringe reality TV camera crews, and looky-loos. Camp trailers towed by SUV's, all hungry to see the Bigfoot legend in real life. One camper was heard saying, "The kids wanted to see Disneyland, but this is better than Goofy." The congested traffic in the small town was beyond belief. What's the first thing people want or need to do when they stop? The gas station bathrooms were devoid of toilet paper and towels and were filthy and abused-looking. The stations were also out of gas, and the tanker trucks were somewhere on I-90 stuck in traffic. All the grocery store shelves were empty, or nearly empty; even the SPAM was gone.

Sheriff Harrington couldn't get his patrol car out of the courthouse parking lot. He called the state patrol, but they were busy tending to accidents; he was on his own. Higgins was having an anxiety attack, so Spencer needed some back-up, and quick. He phoned Dave Notworst, but Dave had problems too. Spencer just walked out into the packed street and calmly started resolving problems. The congestion problem was insurmountable. People were setting up lawn chairs, barbeques, and picnic tables which lined the sidewalk. North Bend had become the world's largest tailgate party. But it didn't end there; all exits from I-90 into North Bend were blocked with cars. And who was at the core of this dilemma, Wendy Storms. She was basking in the glow of the spotlight.

Chapter 10

All Roads Lead To

Dan Simmons woke the next morning feeling well rested, but he was concerned that his request during the fire-gazing might have disrupted the Sasquatch. He looked around the area where the fire had been, but there were no signs of an explosion. All the creatures were awake and moved about the camp. Dan spotted Jarl walking his direction. He thought, "Here it comes; the outsider has caused more trouble." Jarl walked up to Dan, bent his knees and squatted face to face with him. Dan was anxious to apologize and thought first, "I am sorry for the explosion and all the commotion at last night's fire-gazing."

Jarl replied, "There were no disruptions last night, just a quiet fire-gazing. You must understand that fire-gazing is a personal experience; what you experience does not affect others. It is just for you; what you see, what you hear, whatever you encounter, is because of what you ask of the fire. It is your truth."

Dan asked, "My truth or the truth?"

Jarl replied, "That depends on how you asked the fire, and what you saw, only you can tell."

Dan asked, "How do I tell the difference?"

Jarl responded, "Ask differently. If it is a truth, the answer will be the same, but in a different setting." Jarl told him that the males of the group were going out to scout; he was to stay with the women and help them gather. The males would be back to move camp later in the day.

Dan let Jarl know he understood and sat down to contemplate what had happened to him the night before. He slowly breathed in and out, holding his breath during each exhale and inhale. Thinking deeply within his mind, he closed his eyes and tried to relive the dream. He wanted to remember every detail, and discovered to his surprise that he was able to; it was as though he had stepped back into the dream. He began going over every segment, how it felt at the base of his skull, how he was able to know the invisible entity was there. It was as if the dream were somehow seared into his brain. After reliving every detail of the dream, Dan could still not unscramble the truth. Was this his self-manipulated imagination or the actual truth? He needed to ask the question again, but differently; but how? Dan spent the rest of the day contemplating the question. When he opened his eyes again, he looked up expecting to see the majestic mountain he had noticed the night before. To his astonishment, the mountain was no longer there. This realization made him feel disoriented and confused. He looked to the right and then to the left. And there it was on the left. During the night, he must have moved about in his sleep. He looked down, and there were the berries he had not eaten. He realized that he hadn't moved, but the mountains had moved. The mountains were rotating around the valley. "How could this be?" Dan thought, "I must ask the fire."

Spencer had slept at the office on the couch. He awoke to the loud sound of a gunshot. Jumping to attention, he charged out the door. An argument was in full swing; Spencer ran and split the two apart with his body. "What is the issue here?" Spencer demanded. At the same time, he jerked the pistol out of the hand of one of the men. There was a dispute over whose ice chest was whose. One filled with beer and the other was empty. The argument had escalated from whose cooler it was, to comments about the each other's mother. He finally de-escalated the fracas. After defusing the quarrel, Spencer noticed that his town had somehow invariably turned into a landfill overnight. There was trash collecting in the streets and piled up against buildings. What was he going to do? Spencer went back into the sheriff's office and called the State Patrol. They had been all night trying to deal with the congestion on I-90; the dispatcher told Spencer that traffic was backed up from Issaquah to Snoqualmie Pass and emergency helicopters were making trips back and forth from Seattle. This situation had now become a high-level disaster. Emergency phone calls were pouring in, and the chain of command was now being put to the test. At 10:00 a.m. the president of the United States had declared it a national disaster. The National Guard was now landing Chinook helicopters at the edge of town in empty fields. The Red Cross had joined them and were setting up in town with fresh water and were handling minor health concerns. The National Guard kept the peace with some of the militia dressed in riot gear, and Spencer was glad. During the night some shop windows had been smashed, and the looting had begun. Hell seemed to have broken out in North Bend, and Wendy Storms was in High-Heaven, broadcasting non-stop, giving updates on an hourly basis.

Rebecca woke to the sun rising. A chill was in the air, and she could see her breath in the frostiness outside her sleeping bag. She mustered the courage to emerge from her warm cocoon. She rolled up her sleeping bag, gobbled down a protein bar, consumed the rest of her dried fruit and finished breaking camp. She had to look for a different trail; the one she had taken was a dead end. She must have made a wrong turn and missed the right trail. She became more focused and looked for signs of a different path. As she reached the end of the trail where the lodgepole pines had hidden the trail's end; to her surprise, the pines were gone, and in their place, the trail she had walked before was again visible. Somewhat confused but pleased, she continued, following the path through the mountains. She was feeling invigorated, and the hiking warmed her chilled body.

Pete Davis woke hours later, with a headache and an urgency to abide by nature's call. After relieving himself and thoroughly scratching all of his morning itches, he indulged in breakfast which consisted of beef jerky and a couple of cans of Old Milwaukee beer. With his belly full, Pete threw his leg over the four-wheeler like mounting a horse; Pete started the engine and headed out. Making his way through the brush, he found the three-stick marker and pushed his way through the trees and onto the trail. Pete's plan was working well; he made fast time up the path until he reached a creek he needed to traverse. The front tires eased into the depths of the stream; then came the rear. This maneuver was where the weight of the heavily packed four-wheeler went awry. As Pete tilted the vehicle sharply to the right, one of the back tires found a deep void in the creek bed. Stuck and unable to advance, Pete revved the engine and rocked the vehicle back and forth violently. But the four-wheeler would not proceed. Cursing, Pete dismounted and looked around for something to pry it out of the creek. Prying the four-wheeler out of the stream turned into quite a feat for only one person, but Pete had a plan B at this point. He found a couple of broken limbs; the long one he wedged under the vehicle and set the center of the branch on a rock; the shorter one he shoved into the hole under the tire. Pete sat on the long branch and lifted the four-wheeler. As he did, he used his foot to guide the short log under the tire. To his amazement, the force of the water running down the mountain lodged the wood under the tire. As he stood up, relieving pressure on the long branch, the short log became trapped under the tire. Starting the engine, he throttled the four-wheeler to the other side of the creek.

When Pete had gotten stuck, the revving of the engine echoed through the mountain. Rebecca heard the noise of the engine. She looked down the trail from where she had come and then even farther down the mountain. She saw no one but was concerned that someone was most likely following her.

Dan Simmons was helping to gather the next evening's meal; the Sasquatch ate only once a day, but that didn't seem to bother him. He was becoming used to their routine. Feeling hungry only when they all sat down for the evening meal. He was instructed to look for berries, and soon he had wandered some distance from the females. He was starting to feel sore from doing this task; he noticed some berries farther down a small slope; he headed in that direction. As he walked, he felt his legs weaken. He stumbled and fell, rolling down the gradual hill. When he stopped rolling, Dan discovered that he was unable to move; his head ached, and his body was riddled with pain, so painful that he passed out. An hour or so had passed. One of the females had entered the tall grass headed for the same berry patch that Dan had spotted. On the edge just inside of the grass, she found Dan Simmons curled into a fetal position. He was still unconscious, so she picked him up and carried him back to the group. When Dan was back with the group of three females, he started to wake up. They fed him water and roots. Soon he was feeling better and able to stand.

Saga spoke to him, "You must not leave the group; you must stay near us."

Dan thought, "What had just happened to me?"

Saga explained to him, "When Gunnar took you from the forest, you were injured. Jarl feed you roots to quickly stop your pain. You must stay close to us until your body heals. We project an aura of protection."

Dan thought to her, "I don't understand."

Saga communicated, "We project an aura of protection; when you leave this protective area, you are exposed to the elements. Your pain of the injuries comes back."

Dan thought, "Do you mean I must stay near you?"

Saga responded, "Yes, as long as you are near us, you won't feel the pain of your injuries. As you heal, you won't feel hunger; you won't feel the cold, you won't get sick. But you must stay within our aura. To leave would mean death." Saga restated, "You must obey these rules. Do you understand?"

Dan acknowledged, "Yes. But how did I get injured, I don't remember."

Saga answered, "When Gunnarr first tried to capture you, you struggled when he shapeshifted, and he dropped you, and you fell. Gunnarr had to shapeshift into an eagle and use his talons to lift you off the ground."

Dan questioned, "Shapeshift? What is Shapeshifting?"

Saga, "Jarl will teach you."

Dan then understood what the entity had told him. These creatures possess extra-human abilities. That explained his quick recovery when he was in the cave and in a state of pain and unable to move. That part of his fire-gazing was correct. Dan was feeling well again, and just in time. The males of the group had returned and indicated that they had located a new place to camp for the night.

It was late afternoon when Rebecca reached the summit of the pass between the mountains. It was a breathtaking, majestic mountain range, with waterfalls, and lush forests. She could see a large lake, where she would head first, realizing all life needs water, but also, she could use a dip in the fresh water after a sweaty hike. She stood a while longer taking in the peacefulness and the beauty all around when the sound of a revving engine broke the silence. Now, Rebecca was confident that someone had followed her. Not knowing who it was, and what kind of danger she could be in, she took the knife out of her backpack and strapped it to her belt. It wasn't much but she had nothing else.

At the lower end of the trail, Pete was finding the climb difficult on the four-wheeler, and he wasn't making fitting progress. He was falling farther behind Rebecca and knew once she reached the other side of the pass, tracking her would become much more difficult. The four-wheeler pitched back and forth to negotiate the narrow trail. The stacked cases of beer mounted on the back were making the climb more difficult. Pete was sweating hard, and this was becoming too much work for him. He made it to a level place on the trail and stopped. Being very dehydrated and overheated, Pete peeled back the tab on a can of brew; even the warm beer tasted good. As he guzzled the beer, he stripped off the wrapper from one of the Slim-Jim's to ease his hunger. As he sat sideways on the four-wheeler, he looked down the steep hillside and spotted the creek in which he had gotten his four-wheeler stuck.

Rebecca was rested and ready to move on down the mountain. Before she did that, she took some compass readings to aid in navigating to get to the lake once she entered the woods. On the other side of the pass, Rebecca moved quickly; the downhill walk was easy and she could spend more time observing the lush forest. Rebecca noticed some wild Chanterelles, a mountain delicacy. They were the most sizable Chanterelles she had ever seen. Pulling a plastic shopping bag from her backpack, she quickly filled it. About a klick farther down, she found wild blackberries; pulling out another bag, she picked some of them. When it was half full and heavy, she stopped picking. "Wow!" she thought, "I don't even have to search for food." Eating the berries as she walked, she seemed revived and full of energy; however, she had earlier been feeling a bit tired; but now she began feeling great again. She picked up her pace and headed in the direction of the lake. Pete, however, was exhausted and loopy after downing three beers. He lay down on the uphill side of the trail and fell asleep. He didn't wake again until it was late afternoon, and discovered he had developed a little bladder accident as he slept; good thing he brought another pair of pants.

The male Sasquatch leading the caravan stopped walking; they had arrived at their new location. They were preparing the camp and getting ready for the sunset and the close of the day. Jarl came to where Dan was sitting; he squatted and looked Dan in the eyes. Jarl asked, "We know why you are here, but, do you wonder why we let you join us?"

Dan replied, "I'm not sure why that is; I have been wondering that."

Jarl continued, "Mankind is on the edge of extinction; the race will soon die out."

Dan responded, "How do you know that; are you sure? I know the environment is bad and wars continue, and we have the weapons to self-destruct, but tell me why you think so?"

Jarl explained, "The elders have foretold it."

Dan asked, "Who are the elders?"

Jarl continued, "You have talked with them, in your dreams."

Dan asked in surprise, "Will you tell me who the elders are; I don't trust my dreams lately."

Jarl said, "They are the ones that created Jarl, and the rest; we are descendants of the original ones that the elders created. The story has been passed down. The elders created this fertile living planet from barren cold stone. They then created us to tend to the planet. I have seen harmful things in my fire-gazing."

Dan commented, "And that is why I am here?"

Jarl answered, "Yes, we have watched you for a long time; we permitted you to see us."

Dan responded in amazement, "You mean that I didn't find you?"

Jarl nodded, "No, people cannot see us unless we let them; we are stronger than you; our brains are much larger and our thinking more powerful. Jarl can do things that you cannot."

Dan answered, "Yes, I am beginning to see that."

Jarl replied, "We have chosen you because you have purer thoughts, not like others of your kind. We chose you to take the words of truth back to them and make them see their destructive ways before it is too late."

Dan conceded, "I can tell that you are right, but words alone will not convince the powers that be, to rethink their ambitions."

Jarl said, "That is why you are here; I must teach you our ways, and with our powers, you will have the insight to know what to say and when. You will also need to use the power to fire-gaze for insight and intuition."

Dan responded, "You have my full attention and cooperation."

Jarl added, "Good, we must begin; for I have seen others of your kind and they are coming. We must be quick." Jarl stood up, turned and walked toward where the other male stood; Dan followed. Jarl looked at Dan and spoke, "We will teach you the first part of shapeshifting. First, you must learn to become invisible."

Dan, skeptical at first, watched as Jarl instantly vanished before his eyes. Dan was standing right next to him, but he could no longer see Jarl. Dan felt a sensation of a being or something next to him, and then Jarl appeared on the opposite side of him. Jarl instructed, "Watch closely; I will show you more slowly. Then Jarl's body began to change. At first, he looked flat, like two-dimensional cardboard cutout; then he turned sideways into a thin line and suddenly disappeared.

And just as quickly, the opposite happened, but ten feet away. A thin line appeared, then it opened to a flat image of Jarl. Finally, the image became three-dimensional, and Jarl once again was visible. Looking at Dan, Jarl said, "Now you."

Dan started laughing out loud, and the other male Sasquatch started snorting loudly. Dan regained his composure quickly and said, "Okay." And he began to clear his thoughts and to focus. As he quieted his thoughts, concentrating on vanishing, he could feel a chemical change taking place in his body. A warm rushing sensation pervaded his body, like the boiling of molecules inside his flesh. All of a sudden, he turned flat, then back to three-dimensional. Dan tried to focus again with more intensity, but he would just go back and forth between flat and three-dimensional. It seemed to him like holding one's breath and then having to release the air from the lungs. He gave up in despair.

Jarl growled, "You must let it take over your body, like the waters flowing from the mountains to the sea. Let nature have its way; do not force the action, become part of it, like the stream giving way to the river, and the river giving way to the ocean. Try again."

This time, Dan cleared his mind, and let the energy course through his body freely. He could see with an amazing clarity like never before. His body became light; he felt as if he were floating off the ground. The boiling feeling within his body returned; he flattened, becoming a line and then disappeared. It was a long time, perhaps 10 minutes he was gone. Jarl became concerned that he was struggling to return. Finally, a thin line appeared followed by a flat image, then the full life image of Dan re-appeared. With a release of enthusiasm, Dan said aloud, "Wow." The other male Sasquatch was once again snorting at the outburst. Jarl held up his hand toward the other male Sasquatch, and he stopped snorting.

Jarl spoke, "You must practice this for the rest of the day, understood?"

Dan agreed and continued to disappear and relocate to various places around the camp. As he practiced, he grew more adept at shapeshifting.

Rebecca spent the rest of the day trekking toward the lake, gathering more food along the way. Pete, regaining sobriety, moved the four-wheeler toward the summit of the pass, and struggled to make the vehicle fit the narrow path. Navigating a narrow trail, he drove the vehicle up to and around a large boulder to traverse the tight corner. He felt it pitch violently and he turned the four-wheeler onto its right side. Pete kept a tight grip on the handlebars while two cases of beer slid off the back and rolled into the deep ravine, breaking open the cases and puncturing the cans. They sprayed foaming beer down the hillside as they tumbled and tumbled and tumbled. Pete's grip on the handlebars kept his body from doing the same. Feeling weak, Pete barely pulled himself to safety but not before burning his arm on the hot exhaust. He sat down breathing excitedly, trying to regain his strength. Determined to move on, Pete unwound the winch on the front of the four-wheeler and pulled it up the hill and looped it around a tree. He hooked the other end of the cable to the rack mounted on the back of the four-wheeler. Pushing the button on the tethered control, Pete slowly righted the four-wheeler. Unfortunately, he was now down to only one case of beer. Pete continued his assault to the summit.

One of his worn heels scraped along the pavement, and the sole of each black shoe slapped down, alternating in rhythm as he walked along. A stray plastic bag blew across I-90 and up against his black pant leg. Billy Bob Compton didn't even notice the bag as he made his way from his abandoned car to the town of North Bend. After spending the night in his car, tired and thirsty, he needed to find food and water. Billy Bob or his given name William Robert Compton was a self-proclaimed minister. The truth be told, he received his title via mail from an ad in the back pages of a Rolling Stone magazine. This change transpired in his younger days back in the early seventies. For just ten dollars, he was transformed from hippy into an ordained minister. After that, he went by Reverend Billy Bob. Dressed all in black, except for the small white collar, along with a Bible he toted in his right hand. He headed for North Bend. Being tall and lanky, he towered over most people. Determined to save humankind single-handedly, he considered himself a spiritual force with which to be reckoned. Damnation or salvation, each man, woman, and child needed to make their choice in life. He was prepared to deal with either.

Chapter 11

Bad Moon Rising

Life is gritty, messy, and can be blatantly cruel at times. It's not where we have been, or what has happened to us; what matters is how these experiences mold us. We can choose to be hard and bitter, or pliable and kind. Billy Bob Compton was both, and when needed, he could alternate between them. He was not committed to either; he had not bought into any reality, but he was a master at manipulating situations, becoming chameleon-like, to fit any circumstance. As he walked toward North Bend, he passed other abandoned vehicles scattered along I-90; some campers and trailers were still occupied and he would stop to extend the hand of God, and in return request a donation to further his cause but mostly to sustain his life. Whether asked for spiritual guidance or not, Reverend Billy Bob would read scripture to console or encourage, then boldly ask for money. Sometimes, this tactic would work, but most times it was met with reluctance or outright hostility. In that case, Billy Bob would be compelled to push the issue. He would first use the fear of damnation or resort to describing the coming apocalypse. If not, he would move on to another negative motivator. Guilt could be a potent motivator to guarantee the extraction of some monetary nugget from his victim. He seemed to successfully eke out a paltry existence from his type of pandering. If the practice of "tarring and feathering" still existed in this day and age, Reverend Billy Bob would possibly have experienced it first-hand. Anyone still occupying their vehicle at this point was approached by Reverend Billy Bob Compton as he made his way up I-90 toward North Bend. The morning was not starting off well; donations were down and tithings were not forthcoming. Reverend Billy Bob was displeased and so were all those the Reverend left in his wake. Determined to be more productive for the day, he walked down the off-ramp and into North Bend.

The first person Reverend Billy Bob approached was a gas station owner cleaning his parking lot. Angered by not having any gas to sell and having empty shelves and refrigerators without goods, put the owner in a very resentful mood.

Reverend Billy Bob approached him; he started with, "May I share the word of the Lord with you this fine morning?"

The owner turned and replied with, "And I would be happy to share this broomstick with your backside. Get the hell off my property!"

Billy Bob knew that some people you just couldn't convert, so he kept on walking up the street to the diner. The sign in the window said, "Out of Food. Please come again." He turned the corner and headed toward the courthouse, trying to start conversations as he went. Just outside of the sheriff's office, he stood talking with a young man. The man was the owner of a traffic-locked SUV and trailer and a Bigfoot enthusiast. The enthusiast was inebriated and feeling quite depressed. His wife had left him behind and had gone up the street to a new-found friend's trailer to escape a marital quarrel. Reverend Billy Bob immediately sized up the situation and found a scripture that seemed to fit the occasion to a tee. He consoled the man by first reading the scripture and then praying with the distraught man. As the man's weeping subsided, Reverend Billy Bob without hesitation shoved out his hand and demanded compensation. The man refused and cursed Billy Bob's insensitivity, which caused a heated ruckus to erupt in front of the sheriff's office.

Sheriff Spencer Harrington was on the phone with the State Patrol confirming that one lane of eastbound traffic was now open and slowly moving when the shouting sounds entered the building. Spencer slammed down the phone and headed outside. He was short on sleep and out of patience. Walking up to the shouting men, Spencer shoved them apart. At first, Billy Bob wanted to confront Spencer for his rude interruption, then realized he was a peace officer. Worried that his reputation may have preceded his visit to North Bend, Billy Bob stopped resisting. The man that he had attempted to console was telling Spencer about his shakedown for money. Spencer gritted his teeth and held back his distaste for the situation and patiently heard both sides. Deciding to take Reverend Billy Bob into custody for further questioning, Spencer grabbed him by the arm and escorted him into his office. Once inside, Spencer calmed down and decided to have Reverend Billy Bob sit for a while in his office. Spencer asked for identification, for which Billy Bob produced a driver's license. Spencer asked him what his business was in North Bend. Billy Bob explained that he had just been passing through when he got stuck in traffic like everyone else. The Reverend added that he came into town to find some water and something to eat. Spencer then handed him a bottle of water and half of the sandwich he was having for lunch. After Billy Bob had eaten the sandwich and drank most of the water, Spencer continued to question him.

Spencer asked, "What were you doing with the man outside?"

Billy Bob shook his tilted head and stated, "I was helping a lost soul with the painful loss of his wife; she had left him because of his drunkenness."

Spencer then asked, "Did you ask for money for this service?"

Billy Bob supported his actions by saying, "The Lord's servant needs to be recompensed to continue his work and the relating of his word."

Spencer stated, "I don't care who you help, or God helps, you can't demand payment for reading out of the Bible or any spiritual guidance, not in my town."

Standing and raising his Bible, Billy Bob lit into a fire and brimstone recital of passages leading up to the damnation of man and the coming apocalypse and the Revelation and that man must pay the price with his soul. Spencer told Billy Bob to sit back down and shut his mouth. Spencer took Billy Bob's license and entered the ID into his computer to see if he had any priors.

Spencer told Billy Bob, "Relax, this is going to take some time to do a background check, so sit quietly and drink your water or maybe you would rather wait in the cell. Your choice." Billy Bob chose to sit quietly and avoid incarceration.

As the computer searched databases, Reverend Billy Bob sat nervously but quietly. Not knowing what may pop up, he stared straight ahead at Spencer's desk. Anger boiled inside, steam or perspiration was rising within the stiff white collar. Reverend Billy Bob felt he was being persecuted for his work by these ungrateful sinners, liars, and fornicators. What a blasphemous species! Humankind was damned to the fiery depths of hell, and Reverend Billy Bob was a witness to God's judgment. In his anger, looking straight ahead, he spotted it --- sitting on Spencer's desk, the Black Orb of Passion. Reaching, as if in slow motion, Reverend Billy Bob grasped it in his sweaty hand. Instantly, a chill ran through his body, as he saw a shift in life from what he knew into a new revelation. The Orb slipped from his hand and hit the floor with a thud, and just sat there motionless. Spencer heard the noise and turned to face Reverend Compton. Spotting the Orb on the floor, he bent over and grabbed it, and placed it in the top drawer of his desk. Reverend Billy Bob's eyes were now open; pupils dilated into black circles; the shining power of the Black Orb was reflecting in them.

Spencer demanded, "Keep your hands off my desk; better

yet, you can wait in the cell."

With that, Spencer took Billy Bob and locked him in the cell. But this act was too late; the powers of the Black Orb were already in motion. Reverend Billy Bob's warnings and predictions were now striking 12 o'clock, and darkness was descending on North Bend. Sitting in the cell, Reverend Billy Bob was permeated with a feeling of doom. He had used the word of God to justify his behavior and existence to provide himself with an income. Realizing he had helped no one with all his caterwauling about the foretold end of man. His heart was now filled with dread. "God would surely judge him most severely for his actions," he thought, "for his taking advantage of his fellow man." For Reverend Billy Bob Compton could now see the end of days, and his actions may have unlocked Pandora's Box so to speak. The battle of good against evil was approaching; the battle to end all battles was coming and he felt that Beelzebub had left his mark on him. A change had now come over him, like a light switch being flicked on. William Robert Compton dropped to his knees and prayed loudly for his salvation.

Wendy Storms needed to prepare an update for the quickly approaching five o'clock news. The station wanted something juicy; all the news channels had been covering the traffic snarl, and her story of the Bigfoot sighting was taking a backseat. Wendy's back was up against the wall. Another news reporter was eroding her account of the Bigfoot sighting as just another sensational hoax. He had intimated that Wendy Storms' facts had a lot of holes. Wendy needed to act quickly, she was desperate for something news-worthy and she only had one hour before she went live. Phil presented an idea; the old guy at Murphy's Pub, the one they called the old Swede. He had all kinds of stories about Bigfoot. Hell's Bells! He told the cameraman that he had once lived with Bigfoot for a while.

Wendy said, "Bingo! Phil."

They headed for Murphy's Pub and arrived just in time to go live. Sitting at the end of the bar near the door was the old Swede, well on his way to drunken oblivion. Wendy marched right over to him as Phil and the cameraman set up outside. Convincing the old man to an interview with her outside, in Murphy's parking lot. The attention indeed persuaded him, and Wendy's good looks enthused him. Wendy started right into the interview and quickly pieced together a story with a crudely assembled chain of events. She then escorted the old Swede out the door and positioned him in front of the camera. In seconds, the cameraman pointed at Wendy, and the feed went live.

At the station, anchorman William Ditlisquatt introduced Wendy Storms; Channel 12, Kay-RAP's "Knows in the Air" was live from North Bend with an eye-witness to Bigfoot's existence.

William said, "Wendy, what news do you have from North Bend --- where the President has just declared a national disaster?"

Wendy spoke swiftly, "It is true, the National Guard and the Red Cross have been deployed here to handle the problems arising from the traffic congestion. One lane of traffic is now moving in both directions, east and westbound and, as of this moment, the congestion in North Bend is easing a bit. Needed supplies have been coming in. Things seem to be getting back to normal."

William interjected, "That's great news; as I understand, you have a live interview with one of North Bend's longtime residents."

Wendy responded, "That's correct, William; I am here with a gentleman named Gilbert Eriksson, but everyone in the town calls him the old Swede. Gilbert, what can you tell me about the creature they call Bigfoot?"

Gilbert looked at the camera giving his toothless smile, "Well, Ma'am, it's this big hairy thing that lives deep in the woods, has a face like an ape, and it has these ugly teeth that stick up out of the bottom of its jaw and big fangs on the top. And it smelled purty bad too."

Wendy asked, "So you say that you have seen one?"

Gilbert growled out loudly, "Oh, sure I have, damn thing had me trapped inside its cave, some thirty years ago."

Wendy questioned further, "So you lived with Bigfoot then?"

Gilbert remarked, "Damn straight I did, and the thing kept feeding me these here roots."

Wendy queried, "Where did this happen?"

Gilbert replied, "I was up north of Roslyn, deep in the woods. I had been trapping beavers at that time; I ran out of food and passed out outdoors in the cold. When I woke up, I was deep in this here cave, and the Bigfoot saved my life."

Wendy beginning to realize this interview may have been a mistake asked again, "Can you tell me what Bigfoot looked like?"

Gilbert spoke out excitedly, "It was tall and big, double my size, covered in this reddish-brown hair, except for its face, hands, and chest. It smelled like hell too. It had a snout on it that looked like a monkey face."

Wendy coaxed more from him, "Have you see one after that?"

Gilbert said, "Hell yes, I sees them things all the time."

Wendy glanced at the camera, raising her eyebrows and asked, "When was the last time you saw one?"

Gilbert replied again, "Well, just yesterday; he was a using my outhouse. You know when nature's a callin you gotta answer."

Wendy began to look for a way out of the conversation, "Uh, well, uh, sure, I guess."

Gilbert continues, "Why don't you ask me about my younger days, when I was dating this young thing named Norma Jeane; she was a looker, went out to Hollywood and became a movie star, changed her name to Marilyn Mun Roe."

The camera quickly shifted to Wendy and cut out the old

Swede, but the old Swede moved in standing behind Wendy, smiling showing his one upper front tooth and waving to the camera.

Wendy quickly concluded, "Well, that's all I have, William. This is Wendy Storms, Kay-RAP's 'Knows in the Air' back to you." The feed went dead.

William said, "Thank you for that confusing interview Wendy; well, it is just a little early for Halloween and too late for April Fools. Coming up after this commercial message, President Trump's latest tweet that former president Obama may have been Osama bin Laden's twin brother, and neither of them had birth certificates to prove otherwise."

Wendy was crushed, shaken and speechless. Phil could see the impact that the interview had had on her and foresaw the following accusations of a hoax, and that Wendy was just building a sensationalistic uproar from a myth. "The other news channels are going to rip her apart," Phil surmised. Her credibility was waning, and now it was moving toward non-existence. The other news reporters soon would be jumping on the bandwagon. The next day some were showing lampooned versions of her interview; one journalist interviewed someone dressed in a Bigfoot costume sitting in an outhouse. More than likely, the only media job left for Wendy would be to become a game show hostess. She could still smile bravely and wave her arm and point. From this day on, she would be branded. Well, with her own true character.

Clearly distraught, Wendy began to develop a rash around her neck; it began to itch intensely, turned bright red, which was starting to concern Phil. A call came into Phil's phone; it was the station meteorologist; it seems that there is a doozy of a storm headed their way. It is going to dump some 12 plus inches of rain and hail, and oh, yes, lots of thunder. He explained to Phil that the station needed some footage in front of the North Bend courthouse for a breaking news update. Phil agreed, even though he was concerned that Wendy was not up for the job.

Phil informed Wendy, "We need to make a shoot outside

the courthouse; there is a huge storm headed our way."

Tears were running down Wendy's face. Black smudge marks from mascara streaked down her face, causing her look like a close cousin to Alice Cooper. Wendy sobbed, "Take me back to the motel; I need to fix myself." With that, Phil started the van, stomped on the gas and headed for the Hy-way Motel. Back in her room, Wendy changed her clothes and washed off the old gunk and plastered on a new face. Taking a pink scarf, she covered her reddened neck; looking in the mirror she mustered that in-charge face and took back her personal power. Smiling at herself, she said, "Bingo!"

They all piled back into the van and headed to the court-house. When they arrived, there was a 1962 red Cadillac con-vertible partially blocking the entrance to the courthouse parking lot. Phil had to drive over the curb to get into the parking lot. Phil and the cameraman soon were set up for the shot as the sun was setting. The wind was starting to pick up. The scarf around Wendy's neck was blowing to the east. Making the weather report look authentic; ironically, authen-ticity never happened in any of Wendy's previous broadcasts.

Higgins was watching from inside the sheriff's office; his heart swooned for Wendy Storms. From behind him, Spencer called to him. He wanted Higgins to retrieve the jail cell keys from his top drawer so he could let the Reverend out. Hig-gins went into the office, opened the drawer, still thinking about the beautiful Wendy Storms. Looking down, he spotted it, the Black Orb. Mesmerized, he could not take his eyes off it. Reaching down, with his index finger just above it; a spark jumped from the Black Orb making contact with his finger. His eyes turned to a glowing red, then back to blue. He turned and walked in a trance-like state out of the office; he walked over to the front door and just stood there. Spencer kept calling to him, but Higgins did not respond.

Out in the parking lot, Wendy was poised front and cen-ter, ready to broadcast a news update when her eyes turned red and then back to brown. Phil glanced at the cameraman and then again at Wendy. She was now also in a trance-like state. Wendy lifted her right arm, extending it fully and then dropped the microphone to the ground. She walked over to the red 1962 Cadillac, opened the driver's door and sat behind the wheel. Reaching out, Wendy grabbed the forgotten keys dangling from the ignition and started the engine, placed the car into drive and inched it forward stopping in front of the sheriff's office front door. Higgins stared back at her; she turned her head and looked into Higgins' eyes. Her scarf was gently flowing in the wind. Higgins unbuckled and dropped his gun belt to the floor, pushed open the door and walked to the Cadillac convertible. He opened the passenger door, got inside, and just as the door clicked shut, Wendy floor-boarded the gas pedal, swerving amongst the scattered vehicles, they disappeared up North Bend Way.

Spencer stood stunned, with his mouth wide open, not knowing what to make of the situation. He was unsure whether to be happy that Higgins was gone or to yield to the stress of having to run the sheriff's office alone. After a short contemplation of the situation, Spencer smiled and said, "God bless." And with that, he turned and went back inside and back to the business of the day.

Phil, being able to cope with high-stress situations, picked up the mic and signaled to the cameraman to start taping. Phil communicated an accurate and well-delivered newscast of the oncoming storm. He had just spawned a new career as a field reporter for the Kay-RAP News, Channel 12.

As the wind began to pick up, people were taking shelter wherever they could. The sky was turning dark, and the approaching black clouds were moving in rapidly. Spots of electrical discharges in bright flashes of light shot out between the clouds' dark folds. The animals were the first creatures to notice the changes in nature. The harsher the changes in the weather, the stranger wildlife behaves. As Mabel Fricke was pushing her walker up North Bend Way, an irate raccoon began chasing her. The faster she pushed her walker, the faster the raccoon pursued her. Having had enough of this tussle, Mabel pulled her cane from its hanging place on the walker and started jabbing the rubber tip into the face of the creature. The raccoon dodged the jabs in a serpentine manner until eventually, Mabel made contact. It stopped abruptly, stood on its hind legs and made an angry chattering sound as if it were cursing Mabel. The banded animal changed direction and began chasing a man in galoshes who was quickly walking in the opposite direction. In the middle of the intersection of Bendigo Boulevard, and North Bend Way stood a bull moose which had wandered into town. Standing in the middle of the intersection, it began directing traffic. Every time a motorist entered the intersection, the moose would tilt its head and point his antlers in the right or left direction. The nervous driver would oblige and turn that direction. The shocked drivers were more than happy to turn the direction the moose indicated just to avoid any confrontation. A large crack of thunder ended the interaction between beast and driver as the scared moose headed north on Bendigo Boulevard toward a forested area.

Loud thunder crashed as the rain droplets started quickly turning into a downpour. Rain fell so hard in thirty minutes that Ribery Creek was flooding the outlet stores' parking lot. Both the South Fork and the Middle Fork of the Snoqualmie Rivers soon passed flood stage and lapped at the bottoms of most of the old concrete bridges. An hour later, water started plunging over the bridge on the Issaquah-North Bend Road. The adjacent railroad bridge had collapsed just as an approaching freight train reached it. The first engine nosed into the river causing the trailing boxcars to derail in accordion fashion. The engineer and conductor dived into the swollen river at the moment of impact, thus saving themselves by clinging to a large tree branch jutting from the bank. A giant cedar tree that stood next to the courthouse was struck by lightning, splitting it in half vertically and catching fire. The falling half of the tree landed on the old courthouse roof setting it ablaze. The fire alarm sounded, and the fire department was quickly dispatched. When the fire truck arrived, the top story of the courthouse was engulfed in flames. As the fire crew manned the pumper truck and connected it to the hydrant, huge hailstones started falling. These were not normal-sized hailstones, but they resembled large fists or baseballs and were just as hard. Windows shattered and car alarms screeched for blocks. Unable to fight the fire, the firefighters stood and watched the courthouse, which became a blazing inferno. The hard-pelting hailstones broke the flimsy gas line attached to the meter going into the Double D Diner. The next bolt of lightning set off an explosion inside the diner, sending bricks, chairs and napkin holders catapulting sky-ward. Anything that wasn't bolted down was now going into orbit.

Spencer Harrington was standing outside the sheriff's office under the protection of the roof overhang in front of the doors to the office. Standing and watching in horror, in his transparent plastic raincoat, he saw the first piece of diner space-junk crash down. Ten feet away from Spencer, a coatrack embedded itself two feet into the concrete sidewalk; the base at the exposed end continued quivering from the impact for some time. Spencer stepped back against the doors. The second piece of space-junk, a 1956 Rock-ola juke-box, struck dead-center into North Bend Way, disintegrating on impact. Spencer, who started to step off the stoop to go and help the firemen, observed a toilet seat hit the ground and roll down the street, being thrust along by the gale-force wind. As the hail and falling space junk subsided, the fire crews got the fires at the courthouse and diner under control. The overflowing rivers were now rushing through the streets of North Bend, and fish wriggled their way upstream that flowed down the street. The storm finally seemed to be sub-siding. The dark clouds gradually parted, exposing a full moon and the smoke from the burning buildings turned the moon's color to blood red.

Chapter 12

The Other Side of the Mountain

As the sun was setting, Dan Simmons could see the black thunderclouds in the direction of North Bend. The clouds twisted into a funnel shape, lighting jumping between clouds and towards the ground. A bit concerned with this image, he still needed to focus on his training. Dan had been practicing disappearing and reappearing in various locations. Dan had proudly mastered this mental transformation to near-perfection. Jarl, noticing that Dan was obtaining the skill he had taught him, deciding on the next step in Dan's training. Jarl summoned Dan to join him and the other male Sasquatch in a field away from the females, who were now making camp.

Jarl told Dan, "This is Gunnarr; he will teach you the next step, to shapeshift, to change to different things, mainly animals or objects."

Gunnarr nodded to Dan and telepathically spoke, "Focus is most important in shapeshifting. To hold a shape takes mental strength, and there could be danger in losing focus. You may become lost and unable to return, unable to change back to your form and remain between life and death. Do you understand?"

Dan knew what/where Gunnarr spoke of, to remain forever

within the ethereal layers or the time/space dimensions. Dan had dreamt of this place between life and death.

Dan told Gunnarr that he understood. Gunnarr took a stance of one foot ahead of the other, raised his right arm and then swept his left arm up toward his right. Suddenly, he had changed himself into a mountain lion. The shape of the lion paced around Dan, snarling, showing its teeth. A fierce growl came from deep inside of the lion or Gunnarr. It lunged at Dan who hastily retreated. Then the lion changed, returning to being Gunnarr. Dan was amazed and very impressed as well as delighted with how the archetypical image of the mountain lion stunned and terrified him, even though he had just witnessed the transformation.

Gunnarr continued to explain, "Shapeshifting is similar to vanishing and then teleporting oneself as you have learned earlier, but shapeshifting needs a focal point for you to be successful, not only a mental one but in the physical realm also. To become something other, one must transform mentally first. To envision yourself as that object feel what it would be like to be that object. You must then become it, as you start to vanish, relax and feel your body change to that object on a molecular level. As you reappear, you realize you had become that object, the one you had focused. Be careful at that point because if you become distracted, your existence will become distorted. Hold your focus, clear your mind, mentally, becoming what you seek. The clearer your thinking, the faster your transformation will become. If you are changing for your protection, you must know your foe well and his fears. Become an object they might normally overlook."

As time passed, Dan had noticed that the longer he spent with the Sasquatch, the more his thoughts became more explicit and more intensely focused. He no longer needed his notebook; he remembered things as if seared into his memory. He understood every detail that Gunnarr had explained, and was ready to continue his training.

Dan said, "I am ready."

Gunnarr spoke, "Your technique is your own; as I

showed you how I move my body, yours must be unique to you. Think deeply inside yourself and find your flow; let your subconscious guide you; feel what is correct for you, then let it transform you."

Dan stood still with his eyes closed, letting the quietude enter his mind, thinking of just one thing. All else excluded and no longer existed in his mind. Transfixed with knees bent, he raised his fully outstretched arms. He uncoiled his legs as he left the ground and became a red-tailed hawk. He began soaring into the evening air, drifting higher, freely resisting earth's gravity. Higher, higher, up into the sky, looking down, he let his mind take on that characteristic demonstrated by the Sasquatch. Sharp focused and alert, he now could discern every detail of his new form. Involved in this flying pleasure, he could hear Jarl summoning him back. Dan turned and tilted his wings, shifting his tail and headed back toward Jarl and Gunnarr. He swooped in close, and spreading his wings wide to slow his approach; he drifted to a soft landing on the ground. First, the claws became feet and his wings arms. He slowly transformed back into himself; the transforming energy carried him forward. As he changed again, he swiftly walked forward in a few carefully decelerating strides, stopping just in front of Jarl and Gunnarr. At last, he felt confident that he had mastered the initial phases of shapeshifting.

With a warning, Gunnarr said, "That was very good, but you must learn to know your limits. Changing in mid-air would end your life; you have not completely mastered the technique yet. Be careful; shapeshifting has no mercy for ignorance or arrogance. It is to be used only as needed for honorable reasons ---for doing good. Do you understand?"

Dan nodded and said, "Yes."

Gunnarr spoke, "Honor the goodness within yourself, and use shapeshifting for only the good of mankind."

Dan answered, "I understand."

Pete had crossed over the summit, having driven through the narrow pass and arrived above the valley. He decided to set up camp here. Tired and consumed from an exhausting day, Pete spread out his sleeping bag and had a supper of a can of Old Milwaukee and a bag of Trapper Bill's beef jerky. He quickly got to bed and was soon fast asleep and snoring, sounding like a freight train coming through the woods.

Rebecca also prepared for the oncoming evening. She built a small fire and dined on mushrooms, blackberries and a dandelion and chickweed salad. She was in tune with her natural surroundings and adept at existing in the wild. She fell asleep soon after eating her gathered food and slept soundly in the crisp night air.

Standing in the dark away from the camp, Jarl could see the fire near the lake and knew that people were now in the valley. He returned to the camp, joined the group in a circle and started grunt-chanting. A small fire burst into flame above the ground and continued to grow more robust. The Sasquatch and Dan were staring into the fire and eating berries and roots and drinking water. Dan also gazed, thinking to himself, "I am still uncertain of the origin of these creatures. What do I know? I am not comfortable with the answers I have received from the dreams. I need reassurance." As he ate, he felt himself flow into the flames, being drawn by the dancing colors of the fire. He had to trust that the truth would eventually come. The flames were hypnotic, giving him a connectedness, a oneness with the fire.

Dan found himself enfolded inside his dream world once again. This time, he was on the north fork of the Clearwater River in northern Idaho. He was fly-fishing as a younger man. Dan, joined by a companion from a time when life's ambitions were not significant when time was plentiful, and life was carefree. He had stepped back in time. He felt the flow of joy. He timed the casting with the flick of his wrist; the line whipping out and back in following the movement of the pole, perfectly timed with the wind. He chose the right amount of line and the trajectory of the fly. The deep pool was concealing the Cutthroat Trout. His friend, Jonathan, yelled and held up a trophy which was thrashing and glistening in the sun. Dan called back, "Nice one." The two young men met at a location on the shore and opened their wicker fishing baskets to show their day's catch.

Jonathan smiled at Dan and said, "You know that it's true."

Dan asked, "What are you talking about? What is true?"

Jonathan said, "The creatures; they are the creation of the elders."

Dan asked again, "What creatures?"

Jonathan answered, "Come on, buddy, you know what I am talking about; you know you are dreaming, right? And you want to know the truth, where these creatures came from, geez, do I need to draw you a map?"

Dan replied, "Okay, tell me, my friend, what is it that you know?"

Jonathan spoke calmly, "The elders created, incubated, propagated the Sasquatch to be the caretakers of this planet. Comprende?"

Dan, smiling, responded, "I just wanted to hear it from you. A truthful source I could trust. That's all."

Jonathan nodded, "Well, there you have it; now let's get out the skillet; I'm hungry for some fresh trout; how about you?"

Dan smiled and answered, "You bet!"

Dan enjoyed the meal of fresh Cutthroat and the conversation and the company of his old friend, and the knowledge that time travel was attainable, if only in a dream and within the confines of the mind. But isn't that all that matters --- the realization of the truth?

Dan woke in the early morning. There was no noticeable sound, no birds singing or flying, no wind rustling the trees. He was alone with his thoughts. Those thoughts were excitedly active like the gears in a clock, turning and turning. They were like chocks and dogs falling into the teeth of the gears to keep them from rewinding. They were forward ticking and ticking, slowly working things out. The mind is a fleshly organ like a muscle, which if it becomes idle and it runs down from disuse; it shrinks and becomes atrophied. Dan could feel his brain, attempting to grow larger, accessing ideas like uncharted islands, expanding his capacity of understanding; his knowledge was tripling day by day. His newly attained clarity of thought was unlike anything he had ever experienced. Concepts and calculations were becoming easier. This clarity brought with it focused thinking. He had reached a higher level of understanding, a new plateau of consciousness. Evil plotting and brutalism were fear-based and grew out of ignorance. This new knowledge and understanding made way for harmony with the universe, and for acceptance and coexistence. He realized that he could now return to his world, his reality now was to seek ways to convince the leaders that there are means to change the destiny of humankind.

Looking up, Dan could see that the mountains again had shifted, and once again had rotated from where he had observed them the night before. He realized that these creatures were able to rearrange their environment.

He saw Jarl walking in his direction. Reaching Dan, he squatted in front of him, his thighs pressing against his stomach, flat-footed on the ground. Jarl picked up a flat, oval-shaped stone, waved his hand over it and an imprinted leaf image appeared on it. Jarl handed the stone to Dan. Dan turned it around in his hand; made of white quartz with gold strands or striations running through it and outlining the leaf.

Jarl spoke, "This is a Zemi; it has great powers, and you must protect it and not allow any other person to touch or possess it. Do you understand?"

Dan nodded and answered, "I think so."

Jarl said, "No, you must understand. Do you understand what I tell you? No other must touch or possess this Zemi."

Dan agreed, "Yes, I understand."

Jarl responded, "Good, this stone will protect you; it will show you the evil intent of others, so they don't harm you; it is a guide. Do you understand?"

Dan nodded, "Yes, I understand."

Jarl continued, "You can use it to contact me if you need. Do you understand?"

Dan nodded again, "Yes."

Jarl commented, "Good." With that said, Jarl stood and walked away.

Pete got up and stumbled about the camp, scratching his head and other body parts; he saw that the pass he had entered from the evening before was absent. All that remained was a trail leading down the mountain. Mornings were not kind to Pete; he had trouble waking and was very slow at getting motivated. He yawned widely. His breath was toxic --- so bad that it could wilt cactus. No woman on God's earth could stomach him in the morning and barely otherwise. No matter how attractively challenged a female was, she would see that Pete was no catch. He learned at an early age that love was not in his deck of cards. And that seemed just okay with Pete. By what he could tell, the opposite sex was fraught with perilous risk. He had seen many-a-man broken and laid waste from the agony of lost love. He was one for one, and one for one was what he would remain. To hell with the Three Musketeers; the buddy system was overrated anyway. The Big Cheese stands alone, and that was the way Pete Davis wanted to live his life. The only reason he was on this goose chase now was for the $100,000.00 pot of gold at the end of the "Lost Simmons" rainbow. If Pete had to hog-tie Dan Simmons and strap him over the back of his four-wheeler like a deer carcass, then that's the way it was going be. Pete headed into something that he was just not prepared for, but that was typical for Pete.

Rebecca woke refreshed. Feeling rested, she decided that she would take an early morning dip in the lake and wash off all the trail dust and sweat from yesterday's journey. A simple thing as a bath can create a renewed outlook on the situation at hand. Rebecca seemed tough on the outside and didn't take any crap from anyone; but what she really wanted, in her heart, was to be a kind and loving spouse to a good man she admired. Those men were few and far between. However, there was one who stood out in her mind, a few years older, but a man with integrity, adventurous spirit, and with unwavering strength; yes, true grit. Since John Wayne is no longer available, Dan Simmons fit that category to a "T," and she meant to win his affections. Now, what woman would not plot to capture her man? Adding the right bait to the snare, she could make the jaws of the trap snap shut. Rebecca reflected for a moment; no, that wasn't her way. She liked him very much but she reassured herself that she did not require a man after all; she only needed to rely on herself. Then again, she wasn't sure of that idea either, and she wondered, "Why am I here?" Love can be a funny thing though; sometimes, we find ourselves doing things we don't fully understand.

Rebecca broke camp and headed in a north-easterly direction. Call it a hunch, but she knew someone was behind her and she needed to put as much distance between them and herself as she could. Rebecca headed up a steep hilltop to her left with her instincts as her direction finder. She had her internal compass guide set to female hormones, and that is the direction her arrow pointed. And as it turned out, Rebecca was right; don't ever argue with woman's intuition, or you will lose. Rebecca got to the first flats at the mountaintop and looked around; there she found signs of a camp. There were mostly bark-food remnants and berry seeds; she could tell that it was a camp because the seeds and bark lay in a circle, as would be found around a campfire, but there was no sign of a fire. Locating some tracks leading due east, she followed in that direction. Walking all day, Rebecca began to think she may have lost the trail. Off to the right, she heard the sound of a breaking branch, and she listened to some snorting. She stealthily advanced, and in the clearing, she saw them --- Sasquatch. They were gathering blackberries; she quietly squatted and peered through the brush. She was astonished at what she saw --- "Bigfoot does exist!" she thought. She was amazed but her excitement was short-lived. From her rear, something grabbed her arm and spun her around. In shock, Rebecca let out a horrific scream. She was gasping for breath; her screams suddenly ceased. Terrified beyond belief. Jarl was holding her by one arm. She dangled from his right hand.

When Dan Simmons heard the first scream, he ran rapidly through the brush. He saw Rebecca flailing in Jarl's grip. Dan called out loud, "Jarl, Stop! Rebecca, what are you doing here?"

There was snorting coming from the other Sasquatch. Dan asked Jarl to let her go and, immediately, Dan put his arms around her to support her and reassure her she would be alright. She was in shock and panting uncontrollably, most likely from hyper-ventilating and being on the verge of passing out. Dan laid her on the grass and softly talked to her to get her to calm down. Rebecca tried to speak, but Dan placed his hand over her mouth so she couldn't. Dan thought intently and projected his thoughts into her mind. It was amazing, she could hear him on his first try. She was a natural; she could read his thoughts, and Dan was reading hers, very much to his surprise.

After she had calmed down and relaxed, Dan continued to communicate telepathically with her. He explained to her that it was unforgivable to shout or speak aloud near the Sasquatch. She needed to control her thoughts. As he told her this, he could see that she had become aware that her thoughts disturbed the Sasquatch. As a result, Dan found that he was less able to communicate with her. Dan had become acutely aware of her intentions toward him. He kept his thoughts buried deep in his subconscious. When she had sufficiently rested, he introduced her to Saga. Saga quickly took Rebecca into her confidence and asked her to help gather food in preparation for the night's meal and camp. Saga was able to communicate with Rebecca, and like two long-time friends, the two females became connected. First Saga told Rebecca of the loss of her beloved, and her ensuing sadness. Rebecca reciprocated by telling Saga of her longing for companionship and Dan filled the bill. They got to know each other intimately as they gathered the day's meal. The bond became strong, and soon they were chatting like long-lost companions. It amazed Dan how Rebecca acclimated to the situation, but he was glad because disruption would have destroyed his opportunity to communicate with the Sasquatch.

Pete, however, was not doing well. His four-wheeler gas tank had run dry, and he had drained his spare jerry can into the gas tank. Realizing that he had only a range of about twenty to thirty miles and would have to abandon the four-wheeler at some point. Pete tossed the empty can into the brush, cursing the situation. The trail had become much more comfortable for him now; also, the reduction in the extra weight would save fuel. Pete was not a smart man, and he became perplexed by simple problems, but he was one tough SOB, so what he couldn't figure out, he would force his way through. The thing was, Pete didn't learn from his mistakes and often made some doozies. But one thing he did know --- money was money and he aimed to fill his pockets with it. As he neared the lake, he saw where Rebecca had made her campfire. She had tried to conceal it, but Pete was an excellent tracker and knew where to look. He decided to camp at her old site for the night. Building a fire in the same spot and making an early dinner. He knew that she was not very far ahead, and hopefully had located Dan Simmons.

The carnage of North Bend did not look any better in the light of day. Spencer had reached his limit of resources and was now relying on the National Guard to keep the peace. Also, on the Red Cross to help with first aid and feeding the hungry, stranded families. The mop-up was not coming fast enough; most of the town still had no electricity and, for safety reasons, the gas company had shut off all service. The streets had strings of folks standing in soup lines, dirty and tired and with little hope in their hearts.

Reverend William Robert Compton was helping as many people as he could, giving aid to the Red Cross and dishing up soup to the masses. Apparently, His heart had found the right page of the good book to see his true self and scriptures were no longer needed.

A small fire smoldered in the Double D Diner, and a lone fireman sprayed water onto the flames whenever they flared up. Dave Notworst was taking care of his campers at the Iron Horse Park, giving food to those without and giving reassurance to those who needed it. Betsy was at his side, cooking meals and distributing clothing and canned goods. It was a case of a brother helping brother; sister helping sister; everyone was a soul receiving support from his fellowman.

Chapter 13

The Party

As another evening approached, Jarl came to communicate with Dan, "This woman has come for you; you must take care of her and be responsible for her. Because others have entered our valley, your time here is short. Learn what you can from the fire-gazing; ask your questions carefully. Your woman is unable to get answers from the fire; it has not been permitted; it's only for you. She will sleep next to you at the fire circle tonight; she must not speak, no matter what she may see. Do you understand?"

Dan agreed, "Yes, I understand."

Jarl added, "You will join us tomorrow. We must consult The Council; there has been a breach of our home community; we must ask guidance as to what to do."

Dan asked, "What do you mean by 'The Council'?"

Jarl concluded, "You will see tomorrow." Jarl stood and walked to his place in the circle.

Rebecca helped to serve the daily meal and then took her place to the left of Dan in the circle. The grunt-chanting started, and Rebecca quickly joined in. Soon the whole group was staring into the flames as they ate.

Dan wondered to himself, "What am I to do? I will be leaving soon; I am not sure where I am to go from here." He had no way to give proof of the Sasquatch existence. If Rebecca backed him up, then they would appear as a couple of kooks rather than only one. What was he to do after this encounter? Feeling that his pursuit of profiling a new or different species was no longer necessary, he had already found them. As an option, he could finish his education and teach at some college? Knowing what he knows now, how could he settle for doing that? He could not ignore everything he had discovered without wanting to reveal to all his students. A summer spent with the hairy Sasquatch in the mountains of the Pacific Northwest. This option would just drive him to near insanity. He would either end up being committed to an asylum from telling his story or be forced to become a recluse to keep it a secret. It was a lose-lose situation, a catch twenty-two, so to speak. He could move into the mountains and spend his time talking to woodland creatures. Well, wait a minute, that was what he was doing right now. That is what he wanted to do --- to become a kind of Jane Goodall, only not with chimpanzees, but with Bigfoot instead. That would add an interesting twist to being a primatologist. That choice would seem like reverting to becoming a Neanderthal, but that choice would be a wrong turn, and evolution might eventually have its way with him. All this negative thinking was making Dan tired and confused, so he just sat and ate as he stared into the fire.

Dan eventually lay back and fell asleep. Ghostly images swept through his mind; weird thoughts punctuated his dreams. White, nearly transparent apparitions, floated around him. Spectral faces stared back at him, taunting, mocking, tormenting him, seemingly flying through his body, gazing back at him and laughing. These were not ghosts, but fears that wished to control him; they were his insecurities, unfulfilled worries of future woes. Dan realized that only he was to be in control, not these mystical images. Clearing his thoughts in this dream sequence, he forced the images away and suddenly they were gone. His dream scene passed into scenes of forests, of thick dark woods, with tall cedar trees and giant ferns. Lush and dark, they became the setting for his next dream event --- he became aware of himself running through the shadowy forest along the soft earthen floor. He began running and trying to remain secluded, concealed, from something ominous chasing him, something villainous and menacing. He found a hiding place under a large uprooted cedar tree; he was breathing heavily from his relentless running and torturous fear. Looking down at the mossy earth below his feet, he could see that he had become covered with hair, a straggly, reddish-brown hair. Turning over his hands revealed his dark, leathery palms. Bringing his hands closer to his face, he saw the sharp claw-like fingernails that jutted straight out from his fingertips. Reaching upward, he felt his face; his nose was flattened and ape-like; his jaw was pushed forward from where it once was. His heart began pounding loudly; he heard approaching voices, men with flashlights. Suddenly, he heard the distinctive bolt-action of a rifle readied for firing, the loading of a live round. Panicked, unsure what was taking place, he shapeshifted just as a barrage of bullets ripped apart a small tree beside him. The rapid firing stopped, and the airborne dirt landed right next to him. There in the tree stump, poised and with tail raised was a scared skunk, paralyzed with fear, cornered unable to retreat. The rifle-toting men rounded the downed tree and exposed the sight with blaring flashlights. The approaching men, clumsily about-faced, withdrawing back around the tree nervously fleeing from the poised skunk.

Rebecca was having dreams of her own; standing at an altar, dressed all in white she stood in front of a priest; it was her wedding day. Glowing and smiling, she looked over her right shoulder and there dressed in a black tuxedo is a Sasquatch, smiling with glistening fangs exposed and snorting back at her.

The sky was clear and crispness was in the mountain air. It would be refreshing to some, but it was just plain painful to Pete, as he stood and drenched the remaining coals of the fire with a stale beer. He released his usual early morning flatulence. His entire morning ritual took five or six minutes to complete. The routine included brushing his teeth with his finger. Then unclogging his nose by pushing his thumb against one nostril, and giving a quick exhale, then the same process by pushing his other thumb against the opposing nostril. As he finished this process, he turned back to break camp. Pushing on a tooth with his tongue, he could feel it beginning to give way. Pinching it between his thumb and index finger, he wiggled it, gave it a forceful tug, and out it popped. Pete cursed and threw the tooth onto the ground. Guzzling the remainder of his beer, his usual breakfast, and belching upon completion; then he crushed the can against his forehead and Pete was ready for the day. Pointing his four-wheeler toward the next mountain, he gunned the throttle, spinning the back tires in a semicircle. Pete, happy to be closing in on Rebecca, started singing, "On the trail again."

Dan woke to Jarl's nudging him. Jarl thought-spoke, "We must go; it is a long walk to the top of the mountain."

Dan opened one eye and indicated, "I'm awake."

Dan got up and followed the two males; Jarl was in the lead. The others were still sleeping when Dan and the two male Sasquatch left the camp; the sun was not yet breaking over the mountain. They climbed a steady incline; it was difficult most of the journey. It was a narrow trail which was mostly rocky. They reached the tree-line. The mountain peak above them covered with snow. They climbed beyond most of the vegetation area and pushed into the snow; the wind was brisk and pushed forcefully against Dan as he walked.

When they had nearly reached the summit, they came to a flat area that was relatively large. Dan could see I-90 from this height as they rested.

Jarl produced a red stone, held it up to his mouth and blew across it. A yellow smoke rose from the stone as he blew. The smoke followed the direction of Jarl's breath. It continued to grow more massive as it moved farther away from Jarl. Even though the wind was strong, it didn't seem to affect the smoke. The smoke traveled to the far side of the surrounding level ground. It started to take on a form --- the form of a creature. At once, the yellow smoke transformed into a beast, a pure white beast. Its appearance and shape were of a Sasquatch, but it was pure white, similar in color to a polar bear. Dan assumed that this was an apparition of a Yeti. Jarl walked up to the Yeti and in a screeching high-pitched sound, began communicating with it. The screeching was horrible, and Dan cupped his hands over his ears. That helped a little, but his head ached from a sound which was not an audible sound. It was resonating in his head.

Dan could not understand the conversation or message, but the Yeti looked to be less than happy. Visibly upset during the whole discussion, the Yeti growled and shook his head from time to time. The screeching sound continued as Jarl merely listened. The two seemed to come to some agreement; then Jarl backed away, and the Yeti transformed back into yellow smoke, and the wind carried it off as a small cyclone; then he vanished completely.

As they descended the mountain, Dan inquired as to the purpose of the meeting. Jarl told Dan that he needed to report to the Yeti master that a human male and female had entered the valley and their home and that the Sasquatch was now at risk of invasion and discovery. Dan asked why he was permitted to attend the meeting and Jarl told him that he, Dan, was proof that humans indeed had entered the valley. Dan then asked about the Yeti, whether he was the creature that inhabited the Himalayas. Jarl told Dan that he was and that there were other tribes of Sasquatch-like beings, and white Yeti, all over the world, each created to adapt to their environment. Dan asked again why, Jarl needed to talk to this one. Jarl informed him that this was the eldest of all the species like Jarl himself and he was the ruler of the entire earthly species. He was responsible for making decisions that concerned all tribes. Even though Jarl had captured Dan and taught him of the specialized knowledge, and that they had made contact with the world of humankind, the Yeti had to sanction the process. Jarl was informed that he must now end the training and purge the valley of all humans. Dan was quiet the rest of the journey, wishing he had more time to learn from them.

———————

Rebecca and the females were gathering food near a trail that overlooked a plateau from which came an engine roar. The noise assaulted the ears of the creatures as it echoed out across the mountain range. As Pete's four-wheeler was roaring and getting closer, the female Sasquatch ducked down behind the dense brush, but not Rebecca. She found the biggest branch she could swing and stood in the middle of the trail, tired of being stalked and ready for a confrontation. Atop the four-wheeler was Pete straddling the machine and smiling his goofy smile. This time he had two holes from missing teeth, and he displayed that cockeyed evil Jack-o-lantern smile. That imposing smile warned of impending danger.

As he approached Rebecca, she yelled, "Stop right there, or I'll knock that hideous smile into next week."

Pete stopped and shut off the engine. Still smiling, he blustered, "There, there, little Rebecca girl, old Pete don't mean no harm. I'm just looking for the missing hiker."

Rebecca shouted back, "Well, instead, you found me, and my big stick!"

Pete, more calmly now said, "Let's just talk about this; I'm after that Simmons jerk! And wanting that $100,000.00.

You know it can be split say 80-20, odds in my favor. I'm willing to work something out."

Rebecca still wary, said, "Move away from that four-wheeler."

Pete swung his leg over the top of the handlebars, reaching down and pulling his rifle out of the scabbard as he did. He lifted it into the air to demonstrate that he was still in control of the situation. The three-female Sasquatch immediately shapeshifted into three large grizzly bears and came out from behind the brush.

Spotting the bears, Pete yelled, "Holy Jim and Tammy Faye!"

Pete started gradually backing away, tripping on a rock, and subsequently, falling backward, knocking himself unconscious. Rebecca dropped the branch, ran over to Pete and grabbed the rifle. She gave it a good heave over the edge of the ravine with the sound of it hitting bottom, breaking into pieces. The three females shapeshifted back into Sasquatch and stood over the limp, sprawled out body of Pete Davis. Rebecca managed to drag Pete over to a log and prop him up against it. There he sat, legs sticking out in a V-shape, head bent over his protruding belly, drool running out of his mouth. Rebecca examined the back of his head. There was no severe wound, but a big knot was forming. Rebecca asked the female Sasquatch for some water, which they produced in a clear bag. Rebecca poured half the contents on Pete's head.

Pete instantly revived and started yelling, "Okay, who's nextest! Which one you sumbeaches wants a piece of Petie?"

Slurring his words, Pete was reliving a bar fight somewhere in his jumbled memories. Rebecca poured the other half of the water over Pete's head. Pete came semi-awake, but having one eye open and one shut; he pulled his head up to see the three Sasquatch females standing over him. Pete slobbered out, "I don't like hairy womens." With that, Pete passed out again.

Rebecca, not knowing much about first aid, took a bandana out of her pocket and tied it around Pete's head. Thinking to herself, "It probably won't do any good," but she couldn't think of anything else to do for him.

About thirty minutes later, Pete came around again; this time he was thirsty. Rebecca gave him a drink out of one of the clear bags. Pete immediately spits the water into Rebecca's face. Pete blurted out, "Hey! That slop tastes like water!"

Rebecca responded, "It is, you stupid hick!"

Pete blubbered, "No, git me a beer outa there," pointing at the case strapped to the back of his four-wheeler.

Rebecca calmly said, "I don't think that's a good idea, Cowboy!"

Pete called out, "Who the hell asked ya?"

Rebecca pried open the cardboard case and retrieved a warm can of Old Milwaukee. She handed it to Pete. The three Sasquatch females were still standing there mesmerized. Pete paid no attention to them. Rebecca, on the other hand, was becoming quite concerned; the knot on Pete's head was turning purple and red. It was getting so big that it pushed the bandana down almost covering one of Pete's eyes. It started to look like Pete was growing a second head. Pete guzzled the beer, making sloppy, slurping sounds.

Then belched out a "yes, sir, that's more like it."

Finally, Pete glanced up at the Sasquatch females, somewhat cross-eyed, and said, "I want to buy these ladies a round," pointing at them with the hand holding his beer.

Rebecca challenged, "I don't think that's a good idea, and I don't think you should be either!"

Pete burbled out, "I want ta buy these ladies a goll-durned round of beer; give 'em a beer, damn it, Bar-keep!"

Reluctantly, Rebecca retrieved three beers, one at a time, pulling the tab, and handing the Sasquatch females one each. The three drank down the beer almost as fast as Pete had.

Pete slobbered out a command again, "Another round of suds, Wench!"

Rebecca shouted back, "Hey, You slimy piece of swamp scum..."

Pete interrupted, "Oh, sorry, My Fair Bar-tender-ness,

please another beverage for me and the ladies."

Halfway through the second beer, the female Sasquatch started to have a good time and were snorting hysterically at every vulgar word proceeding from Pete's mouth. Soon, Pete began feeling better and stood up.

Pete said, "I bet you ladies would like to hear some music."

He walked over to his four-wheeler and pulled a banjo from the second rifle sheath on the other side of the seat. He smiled and said, "Ladies, what would you like to hear? Any requests?"

Rebecca sarcastically requested, "How about, sit down and shut up?"

Pete answered naively, "I don't know that one, but here's one I learned from Unky Ray; it's called the Chicken Plucker Blues."

Pete displayed a missing a finger on his left hand, flipping the banjo upside down as he fingered the fretboard with his right hand. Then he could pluck the banjo with his left hand. The three Sasquatch females were jumping around to the music. Not being used to the intoxication they were having a great time. Pete stopped playing and started clapping his hands as he sang. The Sasquatch began mimicking him, and surprisingly they were keeping the beat to the music quite well. Rebecca was appalled at the scene and frustrated because there was nothing she could do. Saga was having the time of her life; this new experience was the best that she had felt since losing her beloved. Over-joyed, she was feeling alive again from the music. The beer had made her feel a little dizzy but in a good way. Pete played on, a blues rendition of an old Canned Heat song "Going' Up the Country." As Pete sang, the three Sasquatch tried to sing too, a kind of snorting of the words, trying to sing in the same way that Pete was doing. The three Sasquatch women started boisterously dancing to the music; the beer was kicking in, and they were jumping on one foot then the other. As they tried to snort-sing out the words, Saga was quite attracted to the music and the joyful feeling it gave her; it was exciting though very strange. One of the Sasquatch females was spinning around, and she lost her balance and fell. One of the other Sasquatch females started snorting loudly as if she were laughing at the one that fell. Pete had just started to play "Ain't got no home" by The Frogman when a piercing howl interrupted the raucous performance.

Jarl was standing about 20 feet away; his screeching howl showed his contempt for this unacceptable display. The three Sasquatch females ran and hid behind him. Pete stood gawking with his mouth wide open; he then realized that they weren't just hairy women, they were all Bigfoot. Jarl walked over, snatched the banjo out of his hands and smashed it against the four-wheeler. Next, he picked up one end of the four-wheeler, dragged it, and then pushed it into the ravine. There followed a crashing sound of it tumbling down the hill and finally landing upside down at the bottom. Everything Pete had brought with him was now smashed and lying in shambles at the bottom of the ravine. Pete became irate and shouted, "Hey, you hairy, stinking Mountain Monkey!"

Jarl waved his hand toward Pete and Pete was made unable to talk. Jarl ordered the females to go back to gathering food.

Jarl looked at Dan, "Do you finally understand? This is what man does. It is not our way." Jarl turned and walked away.

Dan accusingly looked at Rebecca. She told him that she tried to stop it, but Pete would not listen. Pete was sitting on the ground holding his aching head as if it were split open. Saga saw that Pete was in severe pain and she brought back some roots and water and convinced him to eat. Pete was unable to protest because he could not speak. Pete complied and ate the roots. Soon he was feeling better, and the swelling had gone down considerably.

Jarl walked away from the group and stood with his back toward them. Dan spotted him and went to him.

Dan tried to communicate with him, "That demonstration

of behavior is not a true representation of humankind. That man is an inferior example of what our kind is like."

Jarl turned around and replied, "That shows what mankind will become; it shows the selfish behavior and disrespect of others --- other creatures and other people."

Dan attempted to assuage his anger and disgust, "Yes, man can present a crude image, but, as a whole, man has produced great accomplishments and demonstrated amazing compassion toward others when he has the will to do so."

Jarl began to calm down, "You give me hope. If man destroys himself, our tribe will still be here to care for the earth, but without humanity. If that happened, our task of tending to this world would be easier. I brought you here because I think you may be their only hope for change."

Dan responded, "This challenge would be an enormous task. I promise to do my best, but I cannot make all the decisions required for change."

Jarl answered, "You must convince those who can. You must take up this challenge."

Little Annabelle walked down North Bend Way toward the burned-out courthouse. Her hair was windblown on one side; bits of twigs and a large dried leaf snagged in it. On the other side of her head was a swirl of hair precariously gathered by a nearly dislodged barrette. Dried, dusty tracks of tears streaked her innocent face. Her dress was untidy, and her white sweater was soiled, wrinkled and pulled up on one side. She was pulling a wagon behind. Her doll was propped up, riding in the back of the wagon. She made her way through the scattered bricks and other debris strewn about the sidewalk. She stopped just outside the sheriff's office and, facing the door; she stared inside. Seeming helpless, lost in deep thought, with only one shoe and a dirty sock on the other foot, the girl gazed forlornly. Spencer Harrington looked out the double doors while holding a cup of coffee. This tiny model of helplessness, this sweet, tender, vulnerable child was staring back at him. He set down his cup and hurried, pushing open the door, almost tripping down the steps. He stopped and knelt in front of the little child. He asked her who she was. The little girl told him she was Annabelle; she had lost her mommy and daddy. She was cold and hungry and wanted to go home. Spencer took her hand and walked her into the sheriff's office. He helped her into a chair, her short legs sticking straight out. Spencer went to the small office kitchen and made a cup of instant chicken soup in the microwave. While he was gone, Annabelle heard the top drawer in Spencer's desk slide open. This strange phenomenon piqued her curiosity.

As Annabelle quietly watched the desk, the Black Orb jumped out of the drawer, rolled across the desk and dropped to the floor. Then it rolled to the edge of a rug where Annabelle sat. She stared at the Black Orb sitting as if beckoning her. She asked, "Are you here to help me?" The Black Orb started turning slowly, then spinning in place. Annabelle asked again, "Can you help me find my mommy and daddy?" The Black Orb started spinning faster and faster. Annabelle started crying, "I want my home to be back to how it was. I want things to be nice again." The Black Orb rose and levitated above the desk and began to spin even faster. Annabelle's tears were running down her face, "I'm scared, please make things go back to where I was safe." The Black Orb began to smoke, spinning faster. It started to glow, turning a dull red, then brighter until it appeared to be red hot; then white smoke began surrounding it, and the smoke's volume grew to the size of a large beach ball. It began spinning even faster and emitted a humming sound. The orb, resembling a Van De Graff generator, began sending out small electrical charges scattered throughout the smoke. When the Black Orb changed to a bright white color, it immediately disappeared, leaving behind only the smoke. Spencer burst back into the room and shouted, "What happened?" Little Annabelle sat, tears running down her face, pointing in the direction of where the Black Orb had just been, and said, "It's gone."

Chapter 14

Now You See It; Now You Don't

The room began to shake, as if at the center of an earthquake. Pictures were falling off the walls, smashing onto the floor and glass shattering everywhere. The file cabinets were shaking back and forth, and drawers were sliding out. Spencer hung on to the corner of his desk. Dropping to his knees, he shuffled over to Annabelle, taking her into his arms. The office continued to shake; the cup of pens on Spencer's desk tipped over and rolled off, scattering pen and pencils all over the floor. A crash from the outer office sounded; it was the copy machine toppling to the floor, setting off its warning buzzer. A bookshelf full of forms and binders fell onto the floor. The shaking stopped abruptly, leaving the hanging office lights swinging back and forth. Spencer stood up holding Annabelle in his arms. He walked over to the double doors and looked out at the street. He stood at the door, mouth wide open. Annabelle pointed her small finger toward the street outside.

As they both looked on, they could see the overflowing river water had started to recede to where it had formerly been, taking the fish and frogs with it. Scraps of paper swirled above trashcans like cyclones and were sucked back down into the bins. Spencer walked out the door and stood at the end of the steps. There was no wind, just calm air; he saw the dark clouds part as the sun once again began to shine on North Bend. Bricks and debris from the gas explosion at the Double D Diner lifted and shot skyward as they reassembled themselves. A toilet seat rolled past Spencer and Annabelle, then lifted to the sky. Then from the middle of the street, little pieces of the jukebox started bouncing around like nuts and bolts bouncing in a blender. The pieces leaped up, and the once demolished 1956 Rock-ola jukebox reassembled into a whole, causing its neon lights to flicker on and off. An eerie sound of Rock Around the Clock started playing at a slowed speed as electrical sparks jumped about it. The jukebox shot into the sky like a rocket-ship headed into orbit. The embedded coat rack in the sidewalk, hummed and swayed back and forth and then it too ascended into space; the hole in the sidewalk healed itself, like water disappearing into a crack. The whole town was regenerating itself, returning to what it had been before the Black Orb came to town. The giant cedar tree next to the Courthouse, the one that split and set the courthouse on fire from the lightning strike, well, it pulled itself back together, and all the burned branches sprouted and were lush and green again. As Spencer and Annabelle watched the amazing transformation, the courthouse pulled the debris from the ground and began rebuilding itself until every brick and piece of lumber found its home. The skyward elements of the Double D Diner fell back to earth in slow motion; as each piece fell, they returned to where they had once been before the gas explosion. As the rivers subsided, the Northern Pacific Rail Road bridge over the South Fork of the Snoqualmie River rose and began to straighten itself. There was the sound of twisting steel girders uncoiling from the wreckage. Train boxcars straightened themselves, and the submerged locomotive engines sat once again firmly back on the tracks. All the destruction created by the Black Orb now reversed.

Betsy stood behind the counter of the Double D Diner and watched as Philbert Bottomdolr reappeared seated and reading the sports section of the Sunday paper; as he drank his tea. Most things were now back to normal in North Bend. Spencer stood and watched things transpire while holding little Annabelle.

Annabelle looked into Spencer's eyes and holding her arms out wide, smiled and said, "Ta-dah!"

Spencer returned a, "Yes, indeed."

From up the sidewalk came a shrieking scream; it was Annabelle's mother, accompanied by her father.

Annabelle's mother approached them, tears in her eyes, "Oh, my God, Annabelle, where have you been? We have been frantic not knowing where you were."

Annabelle's father lifted her out of Spencer's arms, saying, "Darling, are you all right?"

Annabelle said shyly, "Yes daddy; did you see the magic?"

Annabelle's father said, "Finding you is all the magic I need, Dear. Thank you, Sheriff Harrington, for finding Annabelle."

Spencer replied, "I'm glad you folks are back together; I think she is a bit hungry."

Annabelle's mother said, "Yes, thank you; we will get her right home, cleaned up and fed. And we will be forever grateful to you, Sheriff."

With that, Annabelle and her mother and father made their way back up the street and headed home, with Annabelle's wagon and doll in tow.

Jarl stood away from the group, looking out over the valley; he held out his hand, palm up, toward the sky. As he stood, a puff of smoke appeared above his hand. The smoke started swirling, and the Black Orb automatically appeared and settled into his hand. It had done its work, keeping all the Bigfoot hunters at bay, and the town's people occupied while he had had the opportunity to train Dan Simmons. But not all of the things that the Black Orb had changed, returned to how they once were.

———————

Dave Notworst was back on the job, following up on a report of an abandoned vehicle up ZT145, a silver Subaru station wagon. When Dave arrived at the location, he saw inside the car, a stack of papers, copies of Dan Simmons' notebook. They were the same copies stolen from his home at the time his .45 disappeared. Farther up the road, Dave spotted another vehicle. It was Pete Davis' 1948 Willys-Overland truck. Dave thought to himself, "Why would Pete leave this pristine truck way out here in the woods?" He called Spencer to see if he could come up and have a look-see. Under the circumstances, this was out of Dave's jurisdiction. Within an hour, Sheriff Harrington pulled up on the Cedar Creek Watershed Road. Spencer got out of his patrol car and walked over to Dave, who was still looking over the Subaru.

Spencer asked, "What is going on, Dave?"

Dave answered, "Well, I came up here this morning on a report of an abandoned vehicle, and along with the Subaru, I found Pete's truck just up around that corner."

Spencer surmised, "Pete would never leave his truck out here in the woods; that is the only thing he loves."

Dave agreed, "That's exactly what I thought; now take a look here in the front seat of the Subaru."

Spencer peered into the front seat, standing a bit away, and without touching the car said, "Looks like the missing copies of Dan Simmons' notebook."

Dave queried, "Do you know whose car this is?"

Spencer nodded, "Well, yes I do, it is Miss Rebecca Love's car."

Dave quipped, "So you know that female troublemaker?"

Spencer said, "Yes, indeed; I took her into custody, shortly after the break-in at the General store."

Dave asked, puzzled, "Why did you let her go?"

Spencer responded, "I had no evidence to hold her."

Dave spoke sharply, "Well, looks like you do now."

Spencer said, "I will call in for a tow and impound both of these vehicles; it looks to me that Pete and Rebecca are tied together somehow."

Dave queried, "Like maybe they are both looking for that reward money?"

Spencer had both cars towed to the impound lot and hoped that soon one of the owners would show up to claim his or hers. Spencer had suspicions about Rebecca, and he had been suspicious of Pete for years. As he had predicted, things in a small town sooner or later come full circle. Spencer was ready to let them play into his hands. And Spencer had a hunch that that would be happening soon.

Jarl returned to the group to find Rebecca and Saga conspiring. Jarl picked up their thoughts. Saga had become attracted to Pete and had been longing for another mate. Saga and Rebecca saw Jarl approaching and confronted him with their proposal. They wanted Pete to stay in the Bigfoot commune and become attached to Saga. Jarl could see the problems this would create and wanted nothing to do with the wishes of the females. They persisted, considering how lonely Saga was, and claiming that she found Pete special and she wanted to care for him. Jarl broke off the conversation without answering to them and went to find Dan. Dan was sitting cross-legged with eyes closed, meditating.

Jarl spoke by thought making Dan open his eyes, "You must leave soon, and the ones that followed you must leave too."

Dan responded, "I feel that I have much more to learn from you and your kind."

169

Jarl indicated mentally, "You know too much already; it is a great risk that we have taken. Your female is interfering with us, and she must be sent back now."

Dan returned by thought, "Rebecca? What has she done?"

Jarl avoided answering the question, "That does not concern you; she must leave now."

Dan agreeing, replied, "Okay, but what about me? Can I stay if you send the others away?"

Jarl grimaced, "Only for a short time. But your female must leave now."

Dan realized he could not argue with Jarl; he was the leader and, Dan had previously agreed with his requests. With that, Jarl summoned the group into a council circle. This meeting was called to resolve the circumstances of the humans invading their protected domain. Jarl relayed to them that the time had come for all humans that had come into the valley to leave. The only one that didn't understand what was going on was Pete. He did not have the ability to read thoughts or to project his thoughts to others. Dan did notice that when Pete first arrived, he had a horrid stench about him and that he had this unhealthy green tint to his skin. But the longer he had been here his color improved, and the odor was dissipating.

Pete watched as the creatures looked at each other and nodded and shook their heads from time to time, but he did not comprehend what was taking place. He had no idea he was about to be sent back to civilization.

Jarl continued to state how he needed to deal with the unusual circumstances. With all Sasquatch in agreement, Jarl waved his arms, then straightened them, pointing at Rebecca. She then became two-dimensional, a flattened image, a thin line and then disappeared. She was gone. Dan felt alone again; something, or some emotion, had just left him; it felt painful; there seemed to be a missing piece inside him.

Pete started yelling, calling Jarl a big ugly monkey. Jarl waved his hand and Pete could not talk. Jarl did this because

Pete had become verbally exuberant. It was painful for Jarl to listen to; besides Jarl assumed it was some type of insult.

———————————

Spencer Harrington was back at his office, standing in front of the double doors that led into the building. He stood on the front porch drinking a cup of coffee, looking out into the street deep in thought about the town's circumstances. As he stood there blowing on the hot coffee, out of thin air appeared Rebecca Love directly in front of him. Spencer made a step backward and dropped the coffee mug onto the steps, shattering it. Rebecca stood there, disoriented and confused, unable to move. She looked up and down the street. Rebecca was trying to figure where the heck she was. When she finally recognized where she was, Sheriff Harrington grabbed her by the arm.

Spencer said, "Hello, young lady, you are just the person I wanted to talk to."

Rebecca still confused, looked at Spencer and said, "I'm back!"

Spencer answered, "Yes, you are; please step into my office."

Spencer helped Rebecca into the office and escorted her to a chair. He asked her, "Miss Love, we found your car up Cedar Creek Watershed Road. Do you know how it got there?"

Rebecca boldly responded, "Well, I drove it there and parked it there."

Spencer reached into his desk and retrieved the missing copies of Dan Simmons' notebook. Looking back at Rebecca, "Do you recognize these?"

Rebecca replied, "Yes, those are copies of some papers Dan Simmons had written."

Spencer continued, "And how did you come by them?"

Rebecca, becoming a little angry responded, "I found them; they were on the ground outside the ranger station."

Spencer pushed the questions at her rapidly, "Did you steal them from Ranger Notworst's cabin?"

Rebecca responded, "No. I think I need a lawyer!"

Spencer, beginning to get frustrated with her, "Okay, Miss Love, I am placing you under arrest."

Spencer read Rebecca her rights and locked her in the cell. All the evidence was pointing at Rebecca for the three break-ins; only there was nothing in her possession except for the copies of the notebook. Spencer had an uneasy feeling about her guilt and had a gut feeling it wasn't her. But still, she had the copies. He knew more evidence would be required to get a solid conviction. He knew he needed to make his future questioning count once she had a lawyer. He gave her a phone book so that she could try and locate a lawyer that was willing to drive to North Bend from Seattle. This would provide Spencer time to dig a little deeper to see what he could find. He locked up the sheriff's office and headed to the impound lot to go through Rebecca's car; he wanted to get more evidence.

As the day closed and evening approached, all sat in a circle awaiting the fire-gazing. Dan sat, and Saga approached and sat in front of him; her thighs against her stomach and her feet flat on the ground. She placed a handful of berries in front of him along with a small bundle of roots and a water bag. She looked into Dan's eyes; he could see the sadness in her eyes, hurt and longing deep within her.

Saga projected her thoughts, "You know I miss my beloved."

Dan answered, "Yes, I can see you're hurt."

Saga projected again, "I need your help."

Dan responded, "There is nothing I can do; I am just a visitor here and must obey Jarl."

Saga nodded, "I know, I know." She rose and continued to serve the meal.

Soon the sun was setting, and they all joined in the grunt-chanting, all except for Pete, he had nothing to do with this foolishness. Soon a small flame appeared in the center of the circle. It grew and became a massive fire, hanging just above the ground. The Sasquatch and Dan began to fire-gaze, Dan longed to know more. What should he ask the flame? What questions did he still need to ask? He looked far into the flames as if he were looking at a mountaintop. His time was short here, and he had so much to ask. He thought about Rebecca, and he sensed she was in trouble; she needed his help. He stared into the dancing flames. His heart was warm, and content; he let his feeling flow and be absorbed by the fire. The dance began; the blaze drew him in; soon they were one and the same. The questions were unending, flowing from Dan into the flame. Soon Dan was engulfed as he levitated and oscillated inside the fire.

He was inside his dream again; he was deep in the forest, among the cedar trees, walking through the thick moss that covered the decaying forest floor. He walked to a pool of water surrounded by large trees; the massive roots were tangled, and they were reaching out from the bank into the depths of the pool. Above the pool floated an apparition; its head was a bright light radiating rays of light. Its body was 20 feet tall but, actually, there was no body at all, just a gently flowing white translucent gown, like bed sheets flowing and wrapping and unwrapping around an invisible entity. The slow-moving gown shifted about the phantom, as it hung above the pool of water. Hauntingly, it was staring at Dan as he approached the pool.

This voice vibrated at the base of his skull, within the reptilian portion of his brain. "Know this, a warrior creates his own enemies to conquer and, without this dynamic, the warrior would not exist. Strive for a world without warriors. When confronted, stand as strong as a granite wall, be impenetrable. Do not allow the warrior within your mind to defeat you. This way the warrior cannot turn you into his enemy."

It was celestial; from beyond this world, and it spoke to him. "You have all the knowledge you need." The spectral vision then slowly retreated into the black pool from which it came. The forest grew dark as the light dimmed and became extinguished by the pool.

Chapter 15

Full Circle

Dan Simmons woke early, before the others. He sat and watched the sunrise, knowing, today he must leave. He understood why; the Sasquatch needed to protect their hidden Eden. His thoughts were clear; his future was taking shape. Once away from this paradise, there were things he needed to set in motion. It was time to make changes for humanity's sake. The work would be, but now he had a purpose, a direction he needed to move. He possessed the power and knowledge to change the destructive nature of man effectively. Searching for Sasquatch was no longer a goal. In the future, he may need these genetically advanced creatures to help him. They had saved his life and in a short time gave him special powers and an understanding that would transform him forever. He was now more than just an anthropologist but a transformed humanist. From studying the past, he could reshape the future. As Dan sat cross-legged contemplating his situation, he wondered how his experience had opened up for him new motivations. He had now reached previously unused portions of his mind, an expanded awareness; supernatural abilities that drove him to an ever-deepening purpose, surpassing his previous ambitions. Humbled, he was dedicated to this new commitment to the preservation of mankind and the entire planet. He would be able to save a species bent on consuming resources, transforming them into one that could live in ecological harmony with nature and all other creatures. However, what would he be able to do with dysfunctional people like Pete Davis?

———————

During the night, while fire-gazing, Saga was determined to have her way. She physically bonded herself to Pete. This meant that Pete could not get farther away than 15 feet from Saga. Pete woke up and decided he needed to make his way from camp to the brush to relieve himself. When he got up and started to walk toward the forest, he bumped into an invisible wall. Pete tried again; this time in a different direction, still slamming into the wall. Each time he tried, he would get 15 feet from Saga and then be stopped. Dan was observing this and, out of curiosity, he walked over to Pete.

Pete pleaded, "You have got to help me; these Bigfoot things have done something to me."

Dan asked, "What's wrong?"

Pete responded, "I can't get away from this hairy monkey-faced Bigfoot she-devil, this one here," pointing at Saga.

Dan said, "I see; I'm not sure what to say, and I don't know what to do."

Pete begged, "You have got to do something. I just want to get out of here and go home."

Dan, acting dumb, said, "Well, Pete, I don't know what is going on."

Pete pleaded even more desperately, "Go talk to that big monkey over there; he seems to know what is going on. Maybe he can get me loose."

Dan replied, "That is Jarl, and I will go and speak with him about your strange dilemma."

As Dan walked toward Jarl, Saga was going about her daily tasks. As she took a step, Pete was forced to take a step in the same direction. Pete fought it for a while, trying not to step but being compelled by Saga's movements. He had no alternative, except to step in the direction that Saga was headed. Pete decided to just lie down on the ground in protest, but as Saga took a step, Pete was dragged along, leaving a skid mark in the dirt. Finally, Pete gave up and started walking behind Saga. Pete felt defeated, chained to a female, something he vowed he would never let happen. And not just a female, but "this hairy, monkey-looking Bigfoot thing."

Dan petitioned Jarl to release Pete from this debilitating chaining to Saga. Jarl told Dan that there was nothing he could do. Saga had bonded herself to this man, the one that Jarl wanted to be gone from their home. Their sanctuary kept the Sasquatch safe from the dangerous ravages of man. Jarl, in a way, was also linked to this horrific spectacle of mankind. Jarl no more wanted Pete there than Pete wanted to be there.

Jarl responded to Dan, "Forget about that man; you must leave today; you must go back and change things in your culture. Change mankind, change his destructive nature, make this planet whole and pristine again. Teach him to live in peace with his environment and to stop violating it."

Dan nodded in agreement and commented, "I now know my future; I will try."

Jarl continued, "You must do, not just try. Do you understand?"

Dan nodded his head, "Yes."

Jarl offered, "If you need me, you can contact me through the Zemi."

Dan asked, "How do I do that?"

Jarl reminded him, "You fire-gaze; use your thoughts; project yourself to me; I will do the same."

Dan acknowledged, "If you say so."

Jarl gruffly answered, "I don't say! I tell! Do you understand?"

Dan again conceded, "Yes."

Jarl said, "Come to the group now; you must go out from us."

All of the Sasquatch had formed into a circle, a type of

ritual to send Dan Simmons back, to expunge him from their home. They had lived their lives in isolation from mankind for millennia. But there had been an urgent need to cure the planet's illness. It was necessary to take Dan Simmons hostage, to make him their bond-servant but, with this servitude came a tremendous personal awakening and future responsibility.

Dan Simmons meant to take a step forward in human evolution. His renaissance would spawn a new age for humanity, an enlightened intelligence, compassion, and respect for all living creatures. His new goal included all plant life and microorganisms. The eco-chain of life would now have a deliberate bond of survival, a co-existence.

Jarl and Dan walked to the center of a circle that the other Sasquatch had formed; Pete was still struggling to get away from Saga. Dan stood in the center with Jarl. Jarl nodded his head at Dan and told him to shapeshift and return to his home. Dan stood focusing intensely, but it was difficult; there was a choking sensation, and his tears welled up.

Pete kept shouting out, "Simmons, don't you leave me; you can't leave me here!"

Dan looked at Pete and smiled, "I have no control over this; I must leave."

Pete was standing, pressed up against the invisible wall; he was pounding his fists against a barrier that didn't seem to be there. Pete shouted again. He was almost sobbing as he pleaded, "Damn it, Simmons, you can't leave me here with these stupid mountain monkeys. I don't know what this female is going to do to me. I am begging you. Hell, they may eat me when you're gone. I don't want to end up as a pile of Sasquatch dung."

Dan gently responded, "Pete, I am sorry, you must do the best you can with the situation you are in. I hope the Sasquatch gods have mercy on your pathetic soul."

As Dan focused, he saw himself morphing into a hawk; bending his knees, then leaping into the air, arms outstretched, he rose from the ground. His arms changed to wings; his body became light, and the wind lifted him from the ground. It felt good to fly, being one with the wind and sky. Dan looked down at the group; all were standing with arms raised toward the heaven, with uplifted open palms toward him. Pete was on his knees, pleading to be rescued. Dan soared higher into the atmosphere. He could see the circle of mountains that protected this valley --- the valley of the Sasquatch, the valley of his new-found friends. He soared higher, reaching the peak of the tallest mountain, and then he could see it --- the congested existence of mankind, the buildings and the roads --- and I-90. Dan circled the mountain peak for one last look into the valley, then turned and flew toward his destiny.

Farnsworth P. Huntington III was a pro bono attorney that drove up from Portland to represent Rebecca Love. Dressed in a cheap corduroy sports coat with suede leather elbow patches and jeans. This was set off by a hand-painted tie of a hula girl protruding from an unbuttoned jacket, accentuated by a basketball-sized pot belly. His friends called him "Worthy," but not for his competence. His hair was shoulder length, and he only shaved twice a week, today being toward the end of the cycle. He stood outside the jail cell and addressed a sleeping Rebecca Love.

Clearing his throat, "Ahem, Miss Love? Miss Love, I'm here to represent you."

Rebecca rolled over and opened one eye, "I'm Rebecca Love."

Farnsworth, started out in his high-pitched voice then attempting to bring it lower, said, "Hello, Rebecca, I am the attorney you called to represent you. You can call me Worthy."

Rebecca called out, "Thank God; I haven't done anything wrong; this sheriff has me locked up for no reason."

Worthy, speaking as he cleared his throat commented,

"Ok, let's get your side of the story, and then we will go over the charges."

Rebecca explained that she found the copied pages of Dan Simmons' journal lying on the ground outside of Ranger Station 5. She told him that she didn't steal anything from anybody. Worthy explained that she was being charged with three break-ins. He said that the current evidence was very damaging, mostly because she couldn't explain where she had been during the crimes and couldn't account for where she had been for the last 5 days. She was unable to say why her car was abandoned on the Cedar Creek Road and why the pages were found in her car. Worthy told her that the sheriff's evidence had some holes and that would help her case. Sheriff Harrington hadn't connected all the dots to the puzzle yet, and his allegations would more than likely have trouble standing up in court. Nevertheless, this was a serious crime and the itinerate circuit judge could decide either way. This meant, if they couldn't present a clear-cut case, Rebecca could be spending some time in the women's correction center at Gig Harbor. Rebecca broke down and started crying and tried to explain through the spasmodic verbosity that was audible between sobs. Worthy talked confidently but didn't really have a plan of attack. What made it worse, Rebecca was a physical mess and was in need of a shower and some clean clothes. Worthy could barely stand to talk with her over the stench. She smelled like she had been living in a goat barn for the past week.

Worthy asked, "How long have you been in jail?"

Rebecca answered, "About 24 hours; why?"

Worthy suggested, "I will get the sheriff to get you a shower and some clean clothes, and then we will get the details on paper and plan our strategy after that. Sound good?"

Rebecca said, "Yes, I'm getting pretty ripe; I can't stand myself."

With that, Worthy left to talk with Spencer to explain that Rebecca had civil rights and it was just human decency to get her cleaned up. Spencer apologized and said he would see to it that Rebecca got what she needed. Worthy then asked Spencer where he could get a meal. Spencer gave Worthy directions to the Double D Diner. Worthy headed up the street to the diner, the wind blowing up the back of his hair and the sides of his sports coat as he walked up East North Bend Way.

There was no one in sight. The streets were clear of pedestrians; there were no cars; the red flashing light above the intersection swayed back and forth in the wind. It was flashing on and off and on and off. A red-tailed hawk descended into the middle of the street, spreading its wings to slow its descent. Just before it touched the ground, it transformed into a man; the momentum carried him forward as he slowed until he regained his average walking speed and proceeded up East North Bend Way. Dan Simmons was back; he could feel his muscles ache from fatigue; his beard was several inches long; his clothes were torn and filthy. He looked like a refugee from a disaster. But his determination was strong, his will was focused, and his direction set. As Dan walked up the windy street, he spotted an elderly man dressed in a dark suit on the opposite side of the street. The man was walking the other direction, and he tried to keep his suit jacket from blowing open. The gentleman had swirls of smoke trailing him, and the bottom edges of his suit coat glowed like embers. Then Dan noticed a slight smell of Barbecue in the air. Dan thought, "is that Bottomdolr? I thought he quit smoking?"

Spencer was standing inside the double doors to the sheriff's office. Spencer stood there with a cup of coffee in his hand, pressing the cup up to his lips, blowing over the top to cool the brew. As he stood idly enjoying his well-deserved break, walking up the street came Dan Simmons. Spencer's mouth dropped open; he then dropped his second favorite coffee mug; it smashed on the floor, spewing hot coffee onto the double doors and Higgins' desk. Spencer pressed his hands against the glass doors staring out into the street in amazement and disbelief. Walking up the street just outside his office was the SOB that started all this confusion, the one man that turned this town into a circus. The ringmaster himself, the culprit, the agitator, the Bozo driving this loony bus, the one person everyone was looking for. Spencer's face was red, and veins were popping out of his neck; the whistle on his internal tea kettle was blowing at 1000 decibels; his inner boiler was about to explode. Spencer shoved one of the double doors open with such force that it wedged itself open against the handrail. Storming out into the street, he was going to subdue Dan Simmons, even if he had to hogtie him. With clenched teeth, Spencer approached Dan Simmons.

As he reached Dan Simmons, Dan turned and said, "Hello, Sheriff Harrington, just the man I wanted to speak with."

Spencer was never brought back to his senses so abruptly. Quickly regaining his composure, he said, "Well, yes, you're just the man I wanted to talk with too."

Dan responded, "Great! Can we go into your office and talk?"

Spencer replied, "Yes, please come in. I would offer you a cup of coffee, but all my coffee mugs are broken."

Spencer motioned for Dan to go ahead as they walked into the Sheriff's office. Spencer tried to dislodge the door from its wedged position against the handrail but it wouldn't budge. Dan walked through the door; he was then spotted by Rebecca. She jumped up and grabbed the bars of the cell yelling to catch his attention.

Rebecca shouted out, "Dan, hey, I'm here; the sheriff is accusing me of stealing."

Dan walked over to the cell and put his hands over her hands that were clenching the bars, "It's okay, I'm here to help you."

Rebecca began crying, "I'm so afraid; I didn't do anything wrong; they are talking about me having to go to prison, I don't know what to do. I didn't steal anything; really,

I'm innocent."

Dan calmly reassured her, "Don't worry; I am here to make sure that doesn't happen."

Rebecca, sighing, said, "Thank you, thank you." She pressed her cheek against Dan's hand. She calmly said, "I knew you would come."

Dan commented, "My first task is to clear your name. Don't worry."

Spencer cleared his throat from across the room, "Ahem, Mr. Simmons, a word with you, if you please?"

Dan spoke without looking around, "I'll be right there."

Dan smiled at Rebecca and then walked toward Spencer's office. Once Dan was inside, Spencer shut the door quietly.

Spencer asked, "Okay, why don't you start from the beginning, from when you left your vehicle up on Cedar Creek Road?"

Dan smiled, knowing, that whatever he told Spencer, he wouldn't believe. So, Dan decided to tell Spencer the whole truth and leave out no details. Spencer smiled back as he pushed the button on the small handheld tape recorder. Dan started out by telling Spencer he had been looking for Bigfoot, Sasquatch, or Yeti, whatever one wanted to call him. Spending nights and days in the woods, under camouflage, waiting for a chance to take a picture or record the sounds was his driving force. He wanted to find any evidence of Sasquatch's existence, from looking for hair stuck to trees or possibly some Bigfoot dung. He told Spencer of the night he left the Jeep, how he had been taking pictures of Sasquatch, that the creature chased him, and lifted him off his feet. Waking up in the cave, he saw these spooky eyes staring back at him through the dark. The Sasquatch nursed him back to health, spending countless hours teaching him how they lived. He had learned from them how to disappear, to shapeshift, how to fire-gaze and to time travel in dreams. He was shown how to change into a bird and how to soar into the heavens. He was now given a mission to save mankind from its own destruction and rebuild the eco-system. He was chosen to end human conflict and convince men to live in harmony with each other and with nature.

The hair was sticking up on the back of Spencer's neck. He thought to himself, "I need to get this guy in for a psychological evaluation." He wondered if he could get that done before Rebecca's trial date, which was fast approaching. Spencer started to speculate that maybe Dan Simmons and Rebecca Love were in this together, that the two of them were on some kind of drugs; that's what George Wallis, the General Store owner, had suggested. And after Dan Simmons' story, Spencer was leaning in that direction. It really seemed to make sense to Spencer. Whatever the truth was, he most assuredly wasn't going to get it from Dan Simmons. Spencer strongly recommended to Dan to stay in the North Bend area until the trial and to definitely stay out of the woods. He gave Dan the keys to his Jeep and told him that he will find it over at Bill Sales' used car lot. Spencer told him to go home and clean himself up before coming back to the sheriff's office because he smelled, well, awful. Dan took the keys and said he would heed the warning. He had no plans of leaving town without getting Rebecca freed. Dan said goodbye to Rebecca and headed up the street to Bill Sales' Used Cars. As he walked up the street, he pulled the Zemi out of his pocket and looked at it in the palm of his hand with its brilliance glistening in the sunlight. As he waved his hand over it, the small tape recorder on Spencer's desk began smoking and shooting out sparks. This small incineration didn't last long, but the tape was destroyed. Dan smiled as he continued walking up the street.

Spencer spent the rest of the day putting together evidence and pictures of the break-ins. The worst charge against Rebecca was the missing government issued .45 caliber revolver, taken from Dave Notworst's cabin. This was not only the biggest charge, but he knew that because it was stolen from a government employee and was government property, the circuit judge was going to throw the book at the accused. However, Spencer felt very uncomfortable with the evidence; he just didn't want someone that was innocent going to jail. Being falsely accused was something that made Spencer feel not only uneasy but something he swore he would never let happen. Spencer felt that he just didn't have enough facts to go to trial. He must have missed something important, some small bit of evidence. Spencer decided to go back out to the impound lot and look over Rebecca's car again. He was to meet with the prosecuting attorney tomorrow, and he needed to find something more than just Dan Simmons' copied journal.

Spencer made arrangements for Rebecca to shower at a local boarding house run by Nell Gwynn, a former owner of a well-known house of ill repute in Seattle. She was now an honest businesswoman. Spencer trusted her to keep his prisoner confined. And she would make sure she got what she needed as far as clothing and personal items. Spencer escorted Rebecca out of the office, locking the double doors behind him. He then made sure she was comfortably situated in the patrol car. He pulled up outside the boarding house and was cheerfully greeted by Nell.

Nell spoke, "Hello, Officer Harrington. How are you today?"

Spencer responded, "I'm well; please make sure my guest is well taken care of, whatever she needs. Oh, and make sure she has a couple changes of clothes and get her something dressy so she can appear in court."

Nell answered, "You got it, Spencer; give me a few hours to get her cleaned up."

Spencer asked, "Can you put her up for the night and get her a home-cooked meal?"

Nell replied, "Okay, anything else?"

Spencer concluded, "No, that should cover it. See you in the morning. Rebecca, this is Nell. She will get you whatever you need. If you need some personal effects from your house, she can send someone over there to fetch those too."

Rebecca said politely, "Okay, thanks."

Spencer answered, "No problem." Looking at Nell, he said, "Thank you, Nell."

Nell winked, "Anytime, Spencer."

Spencer slid back into his patrol car and headed back to the impound lot. Nell was sweet on Spencer, but Spencer preferred to keep their relationship distant and professional. And by professional, Spencer meant professional; past professions were best kept in the past. Spencer pulled into the driveway of the impound lot. Putting the patrol car in park, he swung the door open and stepped out. Spencer proceeded to the County garage and had obtained the keys from the mechanic, Gilbert Whistler, and unlocked the gate and slid it open. The sun was starting to set, so he didn't have much time left. Unlocking the Subaru, he opened the driver's door. As he looked in, there wasn't much to see. Rebecca Love was clean; the car was spotless. Then he saw the shiny corner of the tin can sticking out from under the passenger seat. There it was --- the evidence he needed. Spencer reached across the seat and retrieved it. He began to smile because it was not just any tin, but a tin of Prince Oscar Sardines. Spencer pulled out his pocket notepad, flipped through the pages, and there it was in bold blue ink. Things missing from Chief Ranger Notworst's cabin, one .45 revolver, Dan Simmons' journal copies and five tins of Prince Oscar sardines. Spencer now was more convinced than ever that he was on the right track. He shut the door of the Subaru. While contemplating the new evidence that he had so far, he spotted the pristine 1948 Willys-Overland pick-up truck that belonged to Pete Davis. "What the hell happened to that crusty old bugger?" Spencer thought to himself, "The guy must have gotten drunk and ended up shacked up with some new woman friend, most likely some big hairy type of gal. That would fit Pete Davis just right." Spencer laughed loudly, "Big hairy ugly woman, one that wouldn't let him go."

Leaning on the tailgate of Pete's truck, he looked into the bed, and noticed a pry bar lying on the floor, but did not give it a second thought. He decided to head back to the office; the sun was going down, and he was pleased that he found another nugget of evidence. Things were stacking up against Rebecca, and frankly, Spencer was beginning to feel more confident.

Chapter 16

Trial by Fire

Judge Andrew Phineas Arbuckle was the circuit court judge assigned to the case of the State versus Rebecca Love. He was best known for his strict verdicts and was proud that none had ever been overturned. At the ripe age of 89, feeling his years left were probably few, Judge Arbuckle was impatient and in a big hurry to find fault. Judgment was on its way to North Bend, and he was about to test Rebecca Love's morality. The court date now set to start in 7 days, and Spencer was meeting with the prosecuting attorney assigned to the case. He was unpacking a new box of coffee mugs he had just purchased from the General Store. Rebecca was back in the cell after spending the night at Nell Gwynn's boarding house, provided with fresh clothes, a meal, and a good night's sleep.

The front door opened and in walked a smug Rupert Longarm, the prosecuting attorney from Seattle. He was tall and wore a black fedora and trench coat, even though it was a warm summer morning. The look made him take on the appearance of a henchman or a 1940's G-man. Rupert was a man that had had his sense of humor removed early on, and he desired to only deal in facts. Rupert prided himself on a track record of winning. He had a reputation for putting more criminals behind bars than his predecessors, regardless of whether the accused were guilty or not.

Rupert inquired pretentiously, "Sheriff Harrington?"

Spencer straightened and turned seeing the tall man and answered, "Yes, I am Sheriff Harrington."

Rupert, puffing out his chest, said, "I am the prosecuting attorney sent from Seattle, here to try Miss Rebecca Love. May I have a word with you in private?"

Spencer graciously answered, "Right this way," pointing toward his office.

Once inside, Spencer shut the door and said, "Have a seat."

Rupert started speaking immediately, "I'll get right to the point; I need to go over all your evidence and then question the accused. Does she have an attorney yet?"

Spencer responded politely, "Yes, a Mr. Farnsworth Huntington, from Portland."

Rupert replied, "I know him; he was almost disbarred over some tree-huggers attacking a group of clam diggers harvesting Geoducks out of season. It involved some ruckus between some hippy protesters with signs and foreigners invading some protected clam beds on Orcus Island. It seems that a group of Japanese tourists with rented clam shovels unwittingly headed into the protected area. The protesters attacked them with their signs, and it turned into quite an international incident. Huntington was in the group of protesters and took most of the blame; the newspapers called it the Huntington Clam Bake. I don't think he's going to be much of an opponent."

Spencer said indifferently, "Well, okay, here's the file." With that Spencer tossed a rather thick Manilla envelope on the desk for Rupert to examine. "Let me know if you have any questions; I have some business to attend to."

Spencer said goodbye and left the room. His instincts were usually pretty accurate, and sensing Mr. Longarm's arrogance, he immediately didn't like this guy. As Spencer was exiting the room, he shut the door behind him. Rupert opened the envelope and started laying the documents out on the desk in some semblance of order and groups. He found nuggets of damning evidence to use against Miss Rebecca Love. The one card he could play if the case started falling apart would be her fringe lifestyle. She was an outspoken survivalist, well documented by the Student Affairs at the University of Washington. The evidence included some very damaging reports of her claiming to be a survivalist. Indicated in the statements were self-incriminating language that she had said, "... that if need be, she would take anything she needed from anyone, at any time and by any means necessary." Comments Rebecca had made in the school newspaper, "The Daily," and also at organized gatherings where she demonstrated survival techniques and explained how to acquire supplies at no cost. Rupert thought to himself, "Some of these kids of the millennial generation do believe in the Zombie Apocalypse." Rupert was pleased with his skills in research and that his methods had never failed him.

Farnsworth P. Huntington III entered the sheriff's office and nodded to Spencer and stated, "I would like to talk with my client."

Spencer promptly replied, "Go right ahead; just to let you know the prosecuting attorney is in my office going over the evidence file. I don't want you to be surprised."

Worthy acknowledged his thoughtfulness, thanked him and said, "No problem; can you let me in the cell?"

Spencer walked over, unlocked the cell door and swung it wide open.

Worthy asked, "Do you want to lock us in?"

Spencer replied, "No, I don't think she is going to make a run for it."

Worthy answered, "Thank you, Sheriff."

Spencer smiled unemotionally and then went back to his paperwork.

Worthy went over the events step by step with Rebecca,

making notes and then asking more questions. As the morning proceeded, Worthy was hoping for something to stand out to turn this case in their direction. But no such luck, the more Rebecca talked, the worse her situation appeared. Worthy realized that there was a lot of coaching necessary in order to avoid incriminating statements. Rebecca liked to expound excessively on all questions asked. Worthy explained that she just needed to answer the question asked and, if at all possible, to answer only yes or no. Rebecca tried but felt that she needed to say more to protect her innocence. Worthy explained that these long-winded answers were in no way helping her case. Rebecca was an honest person, just too honest, but sometimes less is more. Toward the end of the meeting, Rebecca was starting to get the point, but she was not comfortable with it. Then Worthy got to the place in the story when Rebecca made her way into the mountains to find Dan Simmons. He soon realized that an insanity plea might not be out of the question. Rebecca told in great detail of living with the Sasquatch for several days, and how Dan Simmons had been living in the Bigfoot commune. She explained how some of the things had happened, and that she and Dan and the Sasquatch had been in a hidden valley to the east of North Bend.

Worthy cautioned, "Rebecca, we cannot tell this story to the court, you won't end up in prison, but in a psych ward for the rest of your life, with a state-issued butterfly net."

Rebecca conceded, "I see what you mean; what shall I tell them if they ask where I had been for lost time?"

Worthy asked, "Why were you up there in the first place?"

Rebecca replied, "I was looking for Dan Simmons."

Worthy coached, "Okay, that is all you have to say."

At that moment, Rupert Longarm stepped out of Spencer's office; he noticed that Worthy was with Rebecca; he then walked over to the cell. "Good morning, Miss Love, and Mr. Huntington," said Rupert. "I would like to set up a time to depose your client, counselor."

Worthy asked, seemingly annoyed, "What do you have in mind?"

Rupert responded, "Tomorrow morning; say around 10 a.m.?"

Worthy agreed, "Okay, we will be here."

Rupert responded, "Great, see you then." With that, Rupert left the sheriff's office.

It was now Worthy's turn to look at the evidence. When he walked into Spencer's office, he could see all the neat piles in which Rupert had stacked the evidence. This compilation could give Worthy an edge, an insight into Rupert's plan of attack. Worthy studied the collections without touching them. Then he looked at the evidence in each pile. There wasn't much evidence collected, and it didn't take Worthy long to go through each division. Nothing stood out to him, nothing really linking Rebecca to the crimes. The only thing so far that connected her to one break-in were the copies of the journal and one can of sardines. "Pretty flimsy bit of detective work," thought Worthy. It was evident to him that Rebecca wasn't the mastermind behind the three break-ins. Fingerprints lifted from the crime scenes, and the beer can did not match Rebecca's. As for that can of sardines, you could buy them in any store from Maine to California, so not clear-cut evidence. There were a bunch of pictures of crowbar marks used to pry open the doors at the General Store and the second-hand store. But no crowbar was found, no .45-caliber revolver, no banjo, no cases of beer, no beef jerky. There was not much to build a case on; Worthy was feeling very confident that any attack Rupert was planning was mostly hot air, and a lot of far-reaching connected dots.

The next morning all persons summoned were gathered at the sheriff's office. Rupert and Worthy were ready to depose Rebecca Love along with Dan Simmons, Chief Ranger Dave Notworst, Sheriff Spencer Harrington, Oscar Madison, Tommy Wells, Mitch Cochran, Ranger Tom Willkie and Gilbert Eriksson. Rupert wanted to question Wendy Storms and Higgins, but their whereabouts were unknown. The first one to be interviewed was Rebecca Love. She went into Spencer's office while the rest waited in the lobby. Spencer's office was crowded with Rupert, Worthy, the stenographer and Rebecca Love. As the questioning proceeded, outbursts could be heard from Spencer's office. The interrogations were profoundly probing and invasive. Shadows moved back and forth across the frosted office door window. Rebecca cried at one point and then came silence. After 45 minutes to an hour, a shaken Rebecca Love emerged from the office, her face buried in a man's handkerchief, crying softly. Without stopping Rebecca headed back to her cell and slammed the iron-barred door shut and flopped down on the cell bunk. Sobbing and crying into the pillow, Rebecca lay face down, muffling her anxious sobbing.

Next, Dan Simmons was summoned; he stood and walked confidently into the office. Rupert gave the door an excessively hard swing closed, rattling the glass when it shut. As the interview wore on, no expression at all appeared on Dan Simmons face; he maintained a real poker face throughout the entire process.

One by one, they each went in and came out, each leaving the office wearing a frown or a cross look on their faces as they emerged. Finally, the interrogations ended.

With only a few days left before the trial, Rupert and Worthy began to interview the town's selected jury prospects. Not an easy task. The first prospective juror was a Philbert Bottomdolr. Quickly eliminated because the breast pocket of his suit, or the handkerchief in it, burst into flames, and then smoldered after he extinguished with his hand. One by one they were either eliminated because most had heard the stories about Rebecca Love and had formed biased opinions with possible damaging conclusions. After two days of questioning potential jurors, the attorneys completed the chore, and everything was set to go to trial.

The day before the trial was to commence; Judge Andrew Phineas Arbuckle arrived in North Bend. He pulled into Nell Gwynn's boarding house parking lot in his 1972 model 164 Volvo sedan with weathered leather interior. Finding a suitable parking spot, Judge Arbuckle placed the car in park and turned off the key. The Volvo engine sputtered and surged and choked and coughed and sputtered again and again as if it were trying to restart itself numerous times, and with a final knocking sound shuttered to a stop. For an encore, it backfired a puff of black smoke out the tailpipe. Judge Arbuckle chuckled, patted the dash with his hand and said, "Atta girl, Jessabelle, we made another trip; hope you can make it back to Seattle, old girl." Judge Arbuckle pulled the door handle and shoved the door open with his foot. Slamming the door shut with his right hand, he left his shiny fingerprints in the faded blue paint.

Judge Andrew Phineas Arbuckle chose Nell's boarding house at which to stay, on purpose. He had known Nell in Seattle. Nell had come before Judge Arbuckle on numerous occasions for running a questionable house of suspicious goings-on. It was Judge Arbuckle who convinced Nell to change her lifestyle. Once a tall man, the Judge now walked hunched over, making him about average height. Showing snow on the roof, Judge Arbuckle still had a fire in the furnace and twinkling blue eyes. As he opened the door to the boarding house, he was quickly greeted by Nell with a big hug and a kiss on his cheek.

A giddy Nell giggled out, "Judge Arbuckle, how wonderful to see you!"

Judge Arbuckle grinned broadly and responded, "Nell, you're just as pretty as the day I first sentenced you."

Nell giggled again, "Oh, Judge, thanks; you know how to make a girl blush."

Judge Arbuckle said, "I'm glad you still can."

Nell continued her bubbly talk, "Judge, I see you still have that great sense of humor. I have you set up in room 15, the best room in the whole place; it has its own bathroom."

Judge Arbuckle commented, "Thank you, Nell; I think I will take a nap before I have to head to the courthouse."

Nell responded, "Okay, Judge, I will have your bag brought up for you. See you at dinner; we're having your favorite tonight, fried chicken."

With that, Judge Arbuckle winked at Nell and said, "Good to see you again, kid," and made his way up the staircase to room 15.

That afternoon was the arraignment hearing; it was set to proceed in the courthouse, it was short and ended quickly. All interested parties were present. The bailiff walked near the podium and announced loudly, "All rise." Everyone stood up. Then he clearly stated, "The Honorable Judge Andrew Phineas Arbuckle, presiding, the case number 941, State versus Rebecca Love."

As he sat down, Judge Andrew Phineas Arbuckle softly exclaimed, "Be Seated."

Judge Arbuckle started to shuffle papers on his desk; he then stated, "Miss Rebecca Love you are charged with three counts of burglary, three counts of larceny, three counts of breaking and entering and one count of grand larceny. Counselor Farnsworth Huntington, how does the defendant plead?"

Worthy stood up and nervously cleared his throat, "Ahem, Your Honor, my client, Rebecca Love pleads not guilty to all counts."

Judge Arbuckle nodded and spoke, "Duly noted, Counselor; have the record show that Miss Rebecca Love enters a plea of not guilty. The court is adjourned until tomorrow morning at 9:00 am."

The next morning Dan Simmons was in the sheriff's office early; he had brought a skirt and blouse for Rebecca to wear for court. Rebecca was in the ladies' room getting dressed, and when she emerged, she had transformed --- from the normal tom-boy in cargo pants and a tank top to a slender young woman in high heels with the look of a professional young lady. Dan could not believe his eyes, not even a resemblance to the former person. Spencer was bent over looking at paperwork on Higgins' old desk. Glancing up, he did a double take. The first glance was like he was seeing someone other than Miss Rebecca Love; the second look confirmed that in fact, it was Rebecca.

Spencer smiled, "This may sound unprofessional but, Miss Love, you look absolutely stunning."

Dan followed suit, "I would have to agree with you, Sheriff; she sure did clean up nice."

Rebecca walked farther into the room, struggling in the high heels, "Thank you, I'm glad you approve. I can't say that I'm comfortable in this outfit. And whoever invented pantyhose should be strangled with a pair."

Dan chuckled but quickly gathered composure, "Well, you need to look your best in court, and I think you nailed it."

Rebecca with a blushing smile said, "You think so?"

Spencer addressed Rebecca, "Okay, Miss Love, I need to put the handcuffs on you to escort you over to the courthouse."

On their way to the courthouse, Rebecca, Dan, and the sheriff were joined by Worthy. He was still attempting to coach Rebecca on courtroom etiquette, what to say and when to say it and when not to say anything and let your attorney do the talking. He continued telling her she should not speak unless directly asked a question, and that would most likely happen when under oath and on the stand. Rebecca kept nodding her head in agreement. The group reached the courthouse steps and entered. They walked up the first flight of stairs, and stood outside the courtroom doors, preparing their minds for the morning in court. Rebecca could feel herself starting to hyperventilate, becoming dizzy, so she asked for a drink of water. Dan Simmons went to the nearby water cooler and pulled a cone-shaped cup from the dispenser. Filling it almost to the top, he returned to Rebecca and held the cup to her lips for her to drink, as her hands were still cuffed. She gulped down the full cup. She leaned back and nodded back to Dan who crumpled it and tossed it into a trash can. Then she smiled and told them she was ready. Spencer opened one of the double doors to a packed courtroom. The entertainment value of this trial alone was the talk of the town, and no one was going to miss the spectacle. Some of the attendees took time off from work, and many even packed lunches. The circus had come to town, and everyone wanted to witness it. Rebecca was shaky, almost stumbling in the high heels, as she entered the courtroom, trying not to make eye-contact with anyone. Once they reached the defendant's table, the sheriff unshackled her, and she sat down. Whispers from the crowd filled the courtroom. Worthy then sat next to her, placed his briefcase on the table and proceeded to remove folders and copious legal notepads, handing a pencil and notepad to Rebecca in case she wished to jot down notes or messages for Worthy to read.

The courtroom door flew open, and a most pretentious Rupert Longarm, dressed in his trench coat and fedora entered; everyone else in the courtroom dressed in light clothing. The courtroom was already getting warm, and the slow-moving ceiling fans tried to circulate the muggy air. But Rupert had ice water in his veins, and like a reptile, he acclimated to the surrounding temperatures. He swaggered into the courtroom and made his way to the prosecutor's table without making eye-contact with anyone. Plopping his briefcase onto the table and removing his fedora and coat, he sat down and pushed himself back into his chair; he tilted his head back giving an air of being under perfect control. When Rupert had first entered the room, Rebecca perceived that the room had just darkened and she took on a feeling of heaviness and doom. She could feel panic creeping back into her body. Dan Simmons was sitting right behind Rebecca and could sense her anxiousness. He reached into his pocket and rubbed the Zemi; the darkness left Rebecca immediately, and she shrugged off Rupert's domineering character and put her focus back on the proceedings, looking straight ahead calmly.

The bailiff walked near the podium and announced loudly, "All rise." Everyone stood up. Then he loudly stated, "The Honorable Judge Andrew Phineas Arbuckle, presiding, the case number 941, State versus Rebecca Love."

Judge Andrew Phineas Arbuckle entered the packed courtroom then loudly exclaimed, "Be Seated."

Judge Arbuckle adjusted his glasses and moved a few things around on his desk; he then stated, "Miss Rebecca Love, you are being tried for three counts of burglary, three counts of larceny, three counts of breaking and entering and one count of grand larceny. Counselor for the defense has entered a plea of not guilty? Okay, let's move this thing along; Prosecution, your opening remarks."

Rupert stood and walked over to the jury box. He started making eye-contact with members of the jury. "Ladies and Gentlemen of the jury, I intend to prove beyond a shadow of a doubt that Miss Rebecca Love, with premeditation, broke into Chief Ranger Notworst's home stealing a revolver. Not just any revolver but a government-issued revolver, so not just personal property but government property, your property, taxpayer property ---a felony in the state of Washington. Then she proceeded to burglarize two other places of business. Total accumulated value of the stolen property estimated at $4,375. 00 and damage totaling $2,678.00. Miss Love, a self-proclaimed survivalist, who lives by the self-absorbed rule that anything is open to being acquired by any means and used anyway she pleases. This woman teaches survival training on how to obtain needed supplies through looting and pilfering. She promotes the idea that if you are in need, take what you want; helping yourself is the first rule of survival. This woman has been living in your town, in the shadows, watching your every move and looking for opportunities to take what she needs. Honest people like yourselves, people who are willing to help a neighbor or a stranger in need, become her victims. Rebecca Love is just waiting to take advantage of this honest Christian community. Don't let her innocent looks fool you; she is a calculating predator waiting to pounce. Don't let her demeanor mislead you; listen to the facts and the evidence and do your civic duty to put this criminal behind bars where this sociopath belongs. Thank you." Rupert returned to the prosecutor's table and sat down.

Judge Arbuckle addressed the defense attorney next, "Mr. Huntington, you may make your opening remarks to the jury."

Worthy stood up and walked over to the jury box, standing with his belly pressed up against the handrail, which made his stomach look like it was taking a bite out of the handrail. "Ladies, Gentlemen, I would like to commend you for your willingness and openness to hear the facts and the real evidence in this case. You see, it is the evidence that will overwhelmingly prove that my client, Miss Rebecca Love is innocent. Yes, Miss Love is a self-proclaimed survivalist, as many, many people are these days, with such uncertainty in the world today. Remember the cold war days between Russia and the United States. Remember how people were building fallout shelters and stocking up on food and supplies in the 1960's? The feeling of those days was almost total hysteria. It consumed the behavior and attitudes of citizens in those days. And what happened? --- nothing! Neither nation used nuclear weapons and everyone survived; we are still here, alive and doing well. Whether today it be from paranoia or merely a simple interest by a cautious generation, these preppers are an ingrained part of our society. If someone is a survivalist, it only means that if there is an apocalyptic disaster, someone like Miss Love knows how to survive. Look into your hearts; keep your eyes and ears open and make an honest decision in these proceedings by considering the evidence. Remember, Miss Rebecca Love's future is in your hands. I know you will make the right decision, thank you." Worthy pushed away from the handrail, and his potbelly sprung back into its protuberant shape.

Judge Arbuckle called, "Prosecutor, you may call your

first witness."

Rupert spoke, "I would like to call at this time, Gilbert Eriksson."

The old Swede approached the bench, the bailiff swore him in, and he sat down, smiling ear-to-ear from all the attention he was getting.

Rupert started, "Please state your full name for the courtroom."

The old Swede, answered, "I'm the old Swede."

Rupert stated forcefully, "Give your real name, your complete given name please."

The old Swede replied, "My mother calls me Gilbert."

Rupert, getting irritated, roared "Your whole name please!"

The old Swede, "Gilbert L. Eriksson; I'm of Viking descent."

Rupert sarcastically responded, "We don't need a DNA sample, just a name. Mr. Eriksson, do you know the defendant?"

The old Swede answered, "You mean the cute little filly over there?"

Rupert turned to the court recorder and said, "May the court, please note that Mr. Eriksson is pointing to Rebecca Love."

The old Swede grinned and responded, "Yes indeed; that's her."

Rupert asked another question, "Mr. Eriksson, did Miss Love ever ask to buy a weapon from you, any type of firearm?"

The old Swede said, "Yes sir, it was over at Murphy's Pub. She wanted some kind of self-protection."

Rupert continued the questioning, "Did you sell her one?"

The old Swede stated, "I did intend to, but she didn't have enough money. So, she didn't buy it."

Rupert, turning toward the judge, concluding, "Your Honor, no further questions."

Judge Arbuckle nodded to the defense attorney, "Mr. Huntington, your witness."

Worthy approached the witness stand, "Mr. Eriksson, do you mind if I call you that?"

The old Swede grinned, "Everyone calls me the old Swede; call me that."

Worthy continued, "Okay Mr. Swede, do many people ask to buy guns from you?"

The old Swede responded, "Well, hell yes; I deal in guns; everybody buys guns from me."

Worthy pressed on, "So Mr. Swede, it would be common for someone to walk up to you, say at, Murphy's Pub and want to buy a gun?"

The old Swede just beamed; he was in his element and enjoying the popularity, "That's what I said, Sonny; you gonna keep asking me the same questions?"

Worthy, acting a bit frustrated, said, "Thank you, Mr. Swede, Your Honor, no more questions."

Judge Arbuckle nodded to the witness and said, "Mr. Eriksson, you may step down."

The judge turned to Rupert. "Prosecutor you may call your next witness."

Rupert called out loudly, "Prosecution calls Ranger Tom Willkie to the stand." Tom Willkie strolled up, was sworn in and sat down.

Rupert asked, "Do you know the defendant?"

Tom looked at Rebecca, "I've seen her pokin' aboot; she's been up at the ranger station asking for maps, eh?"

Rupert continued, "Did you see her the night Chief Ranger Notworst's cabin was broken into?"

Tom replied, "You bet; it was pretty dark, eh."

Rupert asked, "What was she doing?"

Tom answered, "Not sure; she looked as if she was pickin' trash up. It was kind of hard to tell it was her; she had on a bunnyhug, eh?"

Rupert, unamused, "What is a bunnyhug, A? Is there also a bunnyhug B and C?"

Tom replied, "Ya know, a sweatshirt with a hood, bunn-yhug, eh?"

Rupert turned to the judge, "Your Honor, that's all the questions I have at this time."

Judge Arbuckle turned to the defense lawyer, "Mr. Huntington, your witness."

Worthy approached the witness stand, "Hello, Ranger Willkie, tell me, could you tell what Rebecca Love was picking up?"

Tom answered, "Papers."

Worthy walked over to the tagged evidence, picked up the copies of Dan Simmons' notebook and held them up, "Could have they looked like these?"

Tom responded, "Yea, sure could have; I mean they were all the same size and scattered everywhere, looked just like them, eh?"

Worthy looked to the court recorder, "Would the court take note that Ranger Willkie has identified evidence item 11 as the possible trash that Rebecca Love was picking up in the parking lot on the night of the break-in at Chief Ranger Notworst's cabin."

Rupert jumped to his feet demanding, "Objection, Your Honor, counselor is leading the witness and trying to make the witness draw a conclusion."

Judge Arbuckle, jarred awake from a dozing off moment, spoke, "Objection sustained; the jury will disregard that last statement; court recorder, strike that from the record. Mr. Huntington, that's your first warning; don't let it happen again."

Worthy acquiescing to the judge's comment, "Yes, Your Honor; no more questions."

Judge Arbuckle called to Rupert, "Prosecutor, your next witness."

Rupert looked at the judge, "Your Honor, the prosecution calls Tommy Wells to the stand." Tommy stepped up to the stand, was sworn in and sat down.

Rupert stepped in front of the witness, "Mr. Wells, have

you ever seen the defendant?"

Tommy replied, "Yes."

Rupert stated, "Please tell the court, and our distinguished members of the jury; where did you see Miss Love?"

Tommy said, "It was during the Search and Rescue mission looking for Dan Simmons."

Rupert prodded, "Please recount the details of that encounter."

Tommy started, "Well, we had just found some footprints, and Oscar and Joe and I were headed down this ridge in the direction the footprints were headed. I looked back and saw Rebecca looking at the big friggin' footprints, the ones that were huge. We found Dan Simmons' last footprints, and it looked like some big thing picked him right off the ground. The thing was huge, Bigfoot prints, couldn't have been anything else. She was knelt down looking at the prints. These prints were not a bear; they were friggin' Bigfoot prints; I'm talking Sasquatch; couldn't be nothin' else."

Judge Arbuckle interrupted him, "Okay, son, I'm going to stop you right there; I am going to give it to you straight; I am not going to tolerate nonsense in my courtroom. I don't know what your personal life is like, if you are a dope-head, or you're delusional. But in my courtroom, keep your bull dropping drivel and harebrained opinions to yourself. This is a courtroom dealing with evidence and facts. I don't know if you think you're being funny but, myself, I have no sense of humor, especially when it comes to stupid knot-heads that think Bigfoot, Sasquatch or the Boogieman are real. You got me, young man?"

Tommy naively and shyly responded, "Yes, yes sir, sorry Sir."

Judge Arbuckle spoke turning to Rupert, "You may continue, Prosecutor."

Rupert returned to questioning, "So you did see Miss Rebecca Love that day."

Tommy replied, "Yes, she was following us."

Rupert abruptly concluded, "No more questions, Your Honor."

Judge Arbuckle turned the questioning over to the defense, "Mr. Huntington, your witness."

Worthy smiled and commented, "Hello, Tommy, did you see Rebecca after that?"

Tommy stated, "Yes, at Murphy's Pub; she was talking to the old Swede."

Worthy probed further, "Any other time?"

Tommy spoke, "Yes, outside the General Store, the day after it was robbed. The sheriff took her away in the police car and towed her car."

Worthy ended the questioning, "Okay, Tommy that's all. Your Honor, no further questions for this witness at this time."

Judge Arbuckle glared at Tommy, "Step down."

Judge Arbuckle, "Let's keep moving here; times a-wasting. Prosecutor, next witness."

Rupert stepped forward, "Prosecution calls Mitch Cochran to the stand." Mitch walked up to the stand and was sworn in, and took a seat.

Rupert proceeded, "Mr. Cochran, do you know the defendant?"

Mitch answered, "Well, I don't know her, but I have seen her."

Rupert continued, "And where would that have been?"

Mitch responded, "Well when I was conducting flights over the mountains during the search for Dan Simmons." Mitch was very nervous and afraid of what he mistakenly might say, or that he would possibly reveal something he shouldn't.

Rupert pressed on, "In your own words, what did you see?"

Mitch was beginning to shift in the seat, "Well, I was flying my chopper over this clearing, and I spotted her running down the hill. She seemed in a big hurry. It was up near the cliffs where they found some of Dan Simmons' stuff in a cave."

Rupert pursued the line of questioning, "Was she running from something?"

Mitch answered, "Well, I don't know; she was just in a big hurry."

Rupert pressed the inquiry, "Did you see anything she might be running from?"

Mitch was sweating and starting to become unglued, "I saw a bear, a big bear."

Rupert seemed interested in pursuing this story, "Okay, spill it, Cochran, what did you see?"

Mitch blurted out, "It was the biggest damn bear I ever saw; it was running on its hind legs."

Rupert, inching forward, proceeded, "Running on its hind legs? I didn't know they could do that."

Mitch was extremely agitated and exclaimed, "It was crazy; I didn't either; the stupid thing was wearing a hat."

Rupert surprised now, continued, "What?! A hat?!"

Mitch's story was picking up momentum, "It was wearing this camo jungle hat, but the damn thing wasn't smiling. I'm telling you it wasn't smiling; it wasn't smiling at me. The damn crazy thing wasn't smiling and it sure as hell wasn't a Bigfoot; hell, no, it wasn't a Bigfoot. I'm sure of that." Mitch was definitely attempting to protect his reputation.

Judge Arbuckle interrupted the session quickly, "Okay, I'm going to stop you right there; what the hell is in the water up here in North Bend, Mr. Cochran? Are you trying to get some free publicity for your business? Do you think you can make up some stupid story about some Bigfoot and drum up business for your sightseeing helicopter business? Not in my courtroom! What is this town promoting; some kind of Bigfoot festival? Do you know you are about to be found in contempt of court? Would you like to spend time in jail?" Judge Arbuckle was getting heated up and looked at the courtroom. "If I hear the word 'Bigfoot' one more time in my courtroom, someone is going to jail. Is that clear?"

Judge Arbuckle turned to the counselor, "Prosecutor, proceed; Mr. Cochran, watch yourself."

Rupert responded quickly, "Your Honor, no more questions."

Judge Arbuckle turned to the defense, "Mr. Huntington, your witness." Judge Arbuckle pursed his lips together tightly and stared at Mitch.

Worthy stepped up, "Hello, Mr. Cochran, do you need a drink of water?" Mitch nodded his head, and Worthy poured him a glass from the decanter. After a long drink, Mitch set the glass down, staring up at the ceiling.

Worthy started his questioning, "Mr. Cochran, you're a veteran, a decorated veteran, Purple Heart, right?"

Mitch answered, "That's right, 'Nam."

Worthy continued, "I'll bet you saw some crazy action in those days that you were there."

Mitch responded, "Damn crazy."

Worthy proceeded, "But I bet you kept a level head when things got crazy, right?"

Mitch answered, "I never lost my cool; I saw a lot of guys go bonkers, berserk, bugshit. But not me."

Judge Arbuckle cautioned, "Mr. Cochran, watch your language; no foul vulgarity in my court."

Mitch agreed, "Yes sir."

Worthy continued, "When you're flying, you need to make sure you have a clear head; there are a lot of things you need to keep track of, right?"

Mitch nodded and replied, "Yes, Sir."

Worthy proceeded, "Even in your regular life; you stay clean, no drinking, always have a clear memory of events?"

Mitch conceded, "Yes, Sir, clear as a bell."

Worthy continued, "The night of the break-ins, didn't you see Miss Rebecca Love?"

Mitch responded, "Yes, I did."

Worthy pressed on, "And where was that?"

Mitch said, "The Double D Diner. I was having dinner, and she was sitting in a booth by herself."

Worthy queried, "And what time was that?"

Mitch answered, "Oh, it was late, around 12.30, maybe 1 a.m."

Worthy continued, "And did you watch her leave?"

Mitch replied, "Yes, we left about the same time; she was short about 75 cents to pay her bill, and I gave her my change."

Worthy pressed on, "Did she go straight home?"

Mitch responded, "Yes, I drove the same direction she did; I watched her pull in her driveway."

Worthy continued to question, "Do you recall the time?"

Mitch answered, "Yes, it was 1:35 a.m. when I drove past her driveway."

Worthy concluded, "Your Honor, no more questions."

Judge Arbuckle nodded and spoke to the witness, "You may step down, Mr. Cochran. I am going to call a recess until tomorrow morning at 10 a.m., and we will continue the questioning. Court adjourned."

Rupert Longarm turned and looked at Rebecca, eyes cold, emotionless, staring into her soul. Rebecca looked back; she could see flames in his eyes. Burning, evil, the devil lived in this man. His soul was black; she could see the torment he wanted to inflict on her. Rupert Longarm was not a man but a minion, a servant of something dark. Truth had nothing to do with what drove him; his existence was for something other than justice. If they still burned witches, he would be the one to convict them.

Chapter 17

Light Diminishes Dark

After the sun had set, Rupert Longarm made his way up the dark road to the impound lot to have a look through Rebecca Love's car. He had a feeling that there was some overlooked evidence still to be found. The chain link fence gate was slapdashly locked with a long rusty chain and he quickly slipped through the gate gap. Once inside, he pulled out a large flashlight and started to look around for the silver Subaru. It didn't take long, and he spotted it alongside the shabby, weather-beaten county-owned garage. Parked next to it was Pete Davis' 1948 Willys Overland Truck. Checking the door handles on the Subaru, he found it was locked up tight. "No problem," thought Rupert. Reaching under his overcoat, he retrieved a stolen coat hanger from the Hyway Motel. A little twisting and straightening and fine tuning, Rupert had constructed a key of his own. He slipped the looped end of the coat hanger between the rubber window seal and the driver's window. Just a few turns and adjustments later, Rupert had the looped end of the device around the door lock, swiftly lifting it up, click, the Subaru driver's door unlocked. He looked through the car, including everything in the glovebox. Finding nothing, nada, a big zero, but this wasn't going to stop Rupert, no way, not in the least. He walked around the car and leaned on the bed of Pete's truck. Then he spotted it --- the crowbar. Reaching over the bedrail he grasped it. Looking closely, he noticed green paint on the fulcrum end of the cane shaped crowbar. It seemed a familiar shade. Then he remembered, the photographs he had seen of the break-in at the General Store. If not a perfect match, it was close enough. He returned to the Subaru and opened the hatch on the back of the station wagon. Lifting the floor panel that covered the spare tire, he tossed the crowbar on top of the spare tire. Shutting the hatch and returning to the driver's door, he pushed the electric lock button; all the locks on the car clicked down and locked. Rupert then slammed the driver's door and headed back to the gate to make his exit from the impound lot.

The next morning, Rupert Longarm was up early and sitting on the steps of the sheriff's office, waiting for Sheriff Harrington to arrive. When Spencer pulled into the parking lot, he couldn't help notice Rupert sitting on the steps. Spencer got out of his car and walked over to the front double doors of the building.

Spencer greeted him, "Good morning, Mr. Longarm, what can I do for you?"

Rupert said, "I would like to go over to the impound lot and look through Miss Love's car, and I would like to do it before court starts this morning. Is that possible?"

Spencer graciously agreed, "Well, let's go right now; I have some time before I need to open the office. Come on, let's make it quick; we can take my patrol car."

The two got into Spencer's patrol car and headed to the impound lot. When they got there, the gate was open and Gilbert Whistler, the mechanic who worked for the county, was standing outside the garage smoking a cigarette. As they pulled up and parked, Gilbert waved and at the same time blew out a big puff of smoke.

Spencer spoke, "Good morning, Gilbert, may we have the keys to the silver Subaru?"

Gilbert smiled and said, "Sure thing, Spencer, I'll be right back."

Gilbert returned with the keys, attached to an eight-ball fob. Spencer held out his hand, and Gilbert dropped the keychain into his palm. Spencer tossed the keys into the air, then snatched them with the same hand as he walked toward the Subaru. Sorting out the correct door key, he unlocked the driver's door and then pushed the unlock button on the driver's armrest controls. Spencer turned and looked at Rupert Longarm.

Spencer motioned with his right arm, "There you go, Mr. Longarm, take your time."

Rupert nodded and said, "Thanks, this won't take long."

Rupert Longarm knew what he was looking for but tried to make it appear convincing that he was doing a thorough search, but he was just pretending as he skimmed through the car. Spencer watched him with concern. This action just didn't seem like the kind of behavior one would expect from the supposed in-depth prosecutor he purported to be. Spencer felt a bit suspicious as he looked on; something didn't seem quite up to snuff; his stink detector was pegging on the high side. Rupert was moving quickly as if he were looking for a lost tube of lip balm, or a missing cell phone that could be easily detected. When Rupert started in on the glove box, he didn't even take the time to scan through the paperwork. Moving about from the front seat to the back seat, rapidly opening and slamming doors, then Rupert reached the hatch on the back of the station wagon. His movements now slowed as he raised the door with one hand, slowing its ascent with his hand while resisting the upward force from the door pistons. Spencer watched this slow-motion activity with particular interest, looking for the expressions on Rupert's face for clues. Unaware, Rupert was revealing by his body language that he was attempting to deceive. Spencer studied his every move. Rupert didn't even take the usual time to look in the back of the cargo area but immediately lifted the cover over the spare tire. Then he smiled exposing his teeth, like a shark preparing to bite deep into its prey.

Rupert, producing a glowing visage, clamored, "Well, Sheriff, what do we have here? It looks to me like you missed some evidence, and quite incriminating, might I add."

Spencer in an exasperated tone answered, "What do you think you have discovered?"

Rupert reached into the cavity and retrieved the black crowbar, rusted on the ends, except for the smudged green paint.

Rupert continued arrogantly, "I would have to say; this just might be the crowbar that broke into the General Store and the second-hand store. In fact, I would say that this green paint on the end is an exact match to the paint on the General Store. What do you say we head over there and see if it is a match, Sheriff?"

Spencer could feel his temper rising; he knew he had looked over every inch of this car, and that crowbar was not there before, puzzled as to how he could have missed it. Feeling some guilt of having overlooked such a crucial piece of evidence didn't sit well with Spencer, and the way Rupert acted made him very suspicious. Spencer tossed the keys to Gilbert and told him to lock it up. Spencer and Rupert returned to the patrol car and headed in the direction of the General Store. On the way, Spencer grew inwardly furious; how dare this pompous, haughty, self-important nitwit find fault with his investigation. Spencer was sure that there had been no crowbar previously in the spare tire compartment. Rupert just seemed too pleased with his find, which caused an irritating rash around Spencer's neck where his tight collar met his skin. This was an embarrassing turn of events. All Spencer could hope for at this point was that the paint of the General Store wouldn't match the smudged paint on the crowbar. As they arrived at the General Store, Spencer drove around to the back-parking lot.

Both men jumped out of the patrol car and slammed the doors at the same time. Each was trying to get to the jimmied back door before the other. Rupert had the crowbar in his hand. As he approached the door, he held the crowbar up to where the wood trim had been scarred. Rupert began to smile, again showing those shark teeth. Holding the blade of the crowbar up to the gouge in the wood, it not only had the same shade of green paint but the wedge shape matched the width of the gouge. Rupert was beaming, as he stood back up; he pushed his chest out parting the opening of his over-coat.

Rupert, now appearing to gloat, said in a cocky tone, "Well, Sheriff, what do you say we run over to the second-hand store and see if we have a match there, too?"

Spencer huffily remarked, "Get in the car!"

Both men jumped back into the patrol car and headed in the direction of the second-hand store, 'It Lives Again.' As the two in the patrol car arrived, Hillary Upshaw was just opening the front door. Like adolescent lads, they both opened the doors of the vehicle and again slammed them in unison; the two men walked briskly, as in a race, toward Mrs. Upshaw. As they reached the steps, the two struggled to get up the narrow passage between the handrails. They squeezed up the steps and stopped just behind Hillary Upshaw. She turned and peered over the top of her glasses at the two.

Mrs. Upshaw, admonishing but smiling, said, "My, my, what in the blue blazes do you two silly boys want?"

Spencer spoke first, "Mrs. Upshaw, this is prosecutor Longarm, and we would like to have a look at your back door where your establishment was broken in. Would you mind if we have a look?"

Mrs. Upshaw eyed the two up and down, "You two are quite an irksome duo; yes, right this way; follow me."

Spencer and Rupert followed Hillary through the store and to the back door of the second-hand store. She opened the door with the skeleton key she had on her keychain. With the door open the two men rushed by Mrs. Upshaw and out the back door. There it was plain as you please, the damaged doorjamb. Rupert still had the crowbar in his hand, and he held it up to the damage. Sure enough, it was the same size wedge-shaped scar as the General Store's. Again, Rupert smiled with his razor-sharp teeth; this time his eyes twinkled.

Rupert asked, "Sheriff, can you please take me back to the courthouse; I have a new piece of evidence to enter into the court documents." Spencer nodded and thanked Hillary Upshaw for letting them examine the back door. After pleasantries, both men again walked quickly toward the patrol car as the grudge match continued. Neither man spoke as they drove back to the sheriff's office. Spencer kept going over the evidence in his mind, quietly working through the events. He was confident that Rupert had a dirty hand in the new evidence, but he just couldn't work it out. Rupert, on the other hand, was elated with the prospect of putting this trial to bed. To him most of the pieces fit; now all he had to do was convince the jury. Rupert began mentally putting together his delivery and chaining events together to tighten the noose. Spencer was concluding that he had seen the crowbar before, but how could that be, but in the back of his mind, he was convinced he had. This new evidence was out of place, a fit, but not a fit; it was like playing poker with someone dealing from the bottom of the deck. You have a feeling you're being duped, but you don't know how.

Spencer pulled into the parking lot of the courthouse, and before he had stopped, Rupert was out of the car and running toward the courthouse, crowbar gripped in his right hand.

Spencer drove across the parking lot and pulled into a parking spot near the sheriff's office and got out of the patrol car. Still thinking over the whole morning, he unlocked the front door of the sheriff's office. The phone in his office was ringing, and he caught it on the fourth ring. The call was Nell Gwynn; she had Rebecca Love ready for court, and he needed to come and get her. He made the arrangements and a time for him to transport her back to court. He ended the phone call and went back to his desk to go over the evidence to see if he could find anything that would lead to the crowbar. He sat in his chair looking at each photograph and wondered where the hell he had seen that crowbar. Time was running out, and in his heart, he knew for sure Rebecca was innocent, but the missing puzzle piece was not materializing.

The media was once again back in town. North Bend was quickly becoming a circus. Several people were dressed in Bigfoot outfits and wandering the streets. One was seated at the coffee shop drinking a double espresso latte and eating a blueberry scone. Two other people were standing outside the courthouse with picket signs that said, Free Love. They were dressed in hippy clothes, with matching psychedelic head-bands and vests, protesting the incarceration of Rebecca Love. Walking up the street was another newcomer walking his dog that was dressed in a four-legged Sasquatch outfit. Over in the park, another pair dressed in Bigfoot costumes were playing Frisbee and putting on a show for several by-standers, who cheered with each incredible catch. In the crowded courtroom, three Bigfoot made it into the gallery to watch the day's proceedings. As Judge Andrew Phineas Arbuckle pulled into the courthouse parking lot, he was una-mused at the sight of two Sasquatch holding 'Free Love' signs.

Spencer escorted Rebecca Love into the courthouse, ac-companied by Dan Simmons and Farnsworth P. Huntington III. They walked in the front door and up the steps to the second floor and down the hall to courtroom B. The court-room was again packed with spectators looking forward to the anticipated outcome. As they walked to the defendant's table, Rebecca felt like a dessert cart in a fancy restaurant. Everybody glared at the delicacy. Spencer removed the cuffs from Rebecca, and she sat at the table. Dan Simmons sat be-hind Rebecca, and Worthy sat next to her. Sitting up straight and shoulders pulled back, she looked forward, saying a pray-er that the truth would be found.

Once again, the bailiff walked near the podium and

spoke loudly, "All rise." Everyone stood up. Then in an audible voice announced, "The Honorable Judge Andrew Phineas Arbuckle, presiding, case number 941, State versus Rebecca Love."

Judge Andrew Phineas Arbuckle entered the courtroom and walked to the bench, sat and said, "Be seated." He continued, "I am not amused at the actions of the people of this town; I don't think that idiots dressed up in monkey-like costumes is the least bit amusing, and I won't tolerate it in my courtroom. You three buffoons there, dressed up in Bigfoot attire, you make a mockery of my court, and you could be found in contempt of court and find yourselves in the county jail for 30 days. Do I make myself clear?"

Silence fell over the courtroom; the three people in Bigfoot costumes hung their heads and nodded in agreement.

Judge Arbuckle opened the session, "Okay, Mr. Prosecutor, call your first witness of the day."

Rupert Longarm addressed the court, "I would like to call Sheriff Harrington to the stand."

Spencer walked to the witness stand and was sworn in by the bailiff. Rupert stood and stepped out into the courtroom, smiling at the jury.

Rupert spoke arrogantly, "Good day, Sheriff, please state your occupation to the courtroom."

Spencer complied, "I am the elected sheriff of North Bend."

Rupert continued, "And have you been conducting an investigation of some thefts in North Bend, the same thefts that Miss Rebecca Love is being tried for?"

Spencer answered, "Yes."

Rupert walked to the prosecutor's table and picked up the crowbar. "Sheriff, do you recognize this crowbar?"

Spencer nodded answering, "Yes."

Rupert looked at the judge, "Judge Arbuckle, I would like to enter this crowbar as evidence."

Worthy spoke out quickly, "Objection, Your Honor, this evidence was not on the original discovery list."

Judge Arbuckle asked the prosecutor, "Explain, Mr. Prosecutor."

Rupert spoke deliberately and loudly, "With the accompaniment of Sheriff Harrington, this item was discovered, just this morning in an automobile belonging to Miss Rebecca Love. The sheriff is a witness to the fact."

Judge Arbuckle promptly replied, "Objection overruled; the evidence will be allowed; proceed, Mr. Prosecutor."

Rupert continued, "Sheriff Harrington, did you witness the discovery of this evidence?"

Spencer responded, "Yes."

Rupert, resumed his questioning, "Please, in your own words, describe what happened after the crowbar was discovered?"

Spencer through gritted teeth, "We took the crowbar over to the General Store and found that the paint smudge on the crowbar matched the paint on the jimmied door. The damaged wood on the door frame was the same width as the crowbar tip."

There was a gasp throughout the courtroom.

Rupert continued, seeming delighted at the progress of this question and answer period, "And what else was discovered?"

Spencer responded, "We proceeded to 'It Lives Again,' the second-hand store owned by Mrs. Upshaw."

Rupert urged, "And what was found there?"

Spencer proceeded to answer, "We examined the back door of the store to find that the wedge-shaped damage was of the same size as the tip of the crowbar."

Rupert proceeded with almost rapid-fire questions, "What else?"

Spencer begrudgingly said, "There was a smudge of green paint on the door jamb that matched the paint on the crowbar and the paint on the General Store."

Rupert asked, "Sheriff, have you ever had Miss Love in custody, before arresting her for these break-ins?"

Spencer responded, "Yes."

Rupert pursued the issue, "Sheriff, please explain those circumstances."

Spencer continued to answer, "The morning I got the call that there was a break-in at the General Store. As I was taking a statement from the owner, I saw the silver Subaru station wagon belonging to Miss Love parked out front."

Rupert pressed on, "And you impounded the car at that time, is that right?"

Spencer answered, "Yes. I took her in for questioning but had no evidence, so I let her go."

Rupert's questions were relentless, "Did you search the car at that time?"

Spencer almost feeling hounded, "No, but my deputy did; he found nothing unusual."

Rupert proceeded to query, "So, you didn't find the crowbar at that time?"

Spencer, seeming agitated, "No."

Rupert continued bluntly, "Wouldn't you say that there is an element of incompetency in your methods?"

Worthy jumped to his feet, "Objection, Your Honor, leading the witness and forcing the witness to draw conclusions."

Judge Arbuckle, seeming agitated with the proceedings, "Overruled; I'm going to allow it. I too am curious as to the procedure in gathering evidence. Prosecutor Longarm has a valid point. Proceed."

Rupert pressed on, "So, Deputy Higgins was the first one to search the car?"

Spencer responded, "Yes."

Rupert asked, "And where is Deputy Higgins now?"

Spencer stated, "I have been unable to locate Deputy Higgins."

Rupert pushed on with his questions, "And what happened to the deputy?"

Spencer gritted his teeth and growled out, "He walked out of my office, got in a car that drove off, and hasn't returned."

Rupert queried, "Who hired the deputy?"

Spencer answered, "I did."

Rupert abruptly ended the questioning, "Your Honor, no further questions at this time."

Judge Arbuckle turned to the defense attorney, "Mr. Huntington, your witness."

Worthy approached the witness stand, putting his bent elbow up on the hand railing and smiling at Sheriff Harrington. "Sheriff, good morning, can you tell me who initiated this last search of my client's vehicle?"

Spencer answered, "Prosecutor Rupert Longarm."

Worthy asked, "How many times has this vehicle been searched for evidence?"

Spencer replied, "Once by deputy Higgins, twice by myself and then by Mr. Longarm."

Worthy continued, "And this evidence didn't appear until the fourth search?"

Spencer frowned, "Yes."

Worthy abruptly ended, "Your Honor, I have no further questions at this time."

Judge Arbuckle turned to the Rupert Longarm, "Mr. Prosecutor, you may call your next witness."

Rupert said, "I call Miss Rebecca Love to the stand."

Rebecca's breakfast became uneasy in her stomach; a slight panic sensation rushed through her body as she stood up and made her way to the witness stand. Standing by the witness stand, the bailiff swore her in. She sat in the witness chair, scared to death, but showing no evidence of the fear in her mannerisms. Sitting up tall, she watched Rupert Longarm approach.

Rupert asked, "Miss Love, is this your car?" Rupert held up a picture of Rebecca's Subaru, showing it not only to Rebecca but moving it about for the jury to see as well.

Rebecca agreed, "Yes."

Rupert pressed on, "Do you know the General Store and the second-hand store?"

Rebecca shifted uneasily, "Yes."

Rupert continued to probe, "Have you ever been in either of them?"

Rebecca responded, "Yes, I have been in both of them."

Rupert kept up his inquiry, "So you would have a general knowledge of what they have for sale?"

Rebecca agreed, "Yes."

Rupert pushed on relentlessly, "So, if you needed something, you would know where to go to get it, right?"

Rebecca obviously irritated, "Yes."

Rupert asked, "Okay, Miss Love, calm yourself; would you like a glass of water?"

Rebecca responded, "No."

Rupert asked, "Miss Love, are you in love with Dan Simmons?"

There was a sea of whispering filtering throughout the courtroom, bound to perpetuate future rumors in the community.

Judge Arbuckle slammed his gavel down in a loud, sharp report, "Quiet! Hush that irritating whispering. I won't have it in my courtroom. Or I will clear it, understand?" Silence once again settled on the courtroom. "Proceed, Mr. Prosecutor," the judge droned.

Rupert returned to his questions, "Please tell the court; what is your relationship with Dan Simmons?"

Rebecca squirmed a bit, "I am interested in his research about evolution, and the possibility of the existence of Bigfoot."

The courtroom broke into hysterics; some people were laughing, some shaking their heads. The three dressed in Bigfoot outfits started howling, stood up and performed victory dances and high-fived each other. Judge Arbuckle's face turned bright red as he smashed the gavel down again and again. Judge Arbuckle instructed the bailiff to arrest the three buffoons in the monkey outfits and charge them with contempt. The three Bigfoot were quickly escorted out of the courtroom and taken over to the sheriff's office and locked in the cell. The decorum returned to the courtroom; only then did Judge Arbuckle continue the proceedings.

Judge Arbuckle looked over and addressed the witness, "Miss Love, I am not going to tolerate nonsense in my courtroom; that includes talk about mythical creatures or any reference to irreverent things like fairy dust. Do I make myself clear?"

Rebecca choked out, "Yes, Your Honor."

Judge Arbuckle turned back to Mr. Longarm, "Mr. Prosecutor, you may proceed."

Rupert continued the questioning, "Miss Love, are you a self-proclaimed survivalist?"

Rebecca answered, "Yes."

Rupert asked, "Have you ever instructed classes or given lectures on the subject?"

Rebecca again concurred, "Yes."

Rupert relentlessly pursued, "Did these classes or lectures teach people how to obtain needed supplies, by any means possible, such as breaking into businesses to steal whatever they needed?"

Rebecca was becoming restless and agitated, "That is taken out of context; that was meant to teach survival skills in case of a national disaster."

Rupert increased his intensity, "Miss Love, just answer the question, yes or no."

Rebecca answered back hotly, "It's not a yes or no question."

Judge Arbuckle intervened, "Miss Love, answer the question, or I will add contempt of court to your list of problems."

Rupert repeated, "Miss Love, did these classes or lectures teach people how to obtain needed supplies, by any means possible, such as breaking into businesses to steal whatever one needed?"

Rebecca lowering her head answered sedately, "Yes."

Rupert turned to the judge, "Your Honor, I would like to refer to the photographs taken by Sheriff Harrington at the investigation of the two break-ins. The bailiff handed a manila envelope to Judge Arbuckle. "And also, the photographs taken this morning with the crowbar discovered in Miss Love's car." The bailiff handed another envelope to the Judge. Rupert asked Judge Arbuckle for the extra copies of the photographs to show to the jury. Rupert then handed out the copies to the members of the jury to inspect as he continued. Judge Arbuckle shuffled through the photos as the jury passed the copies around among the group.

Rupert addressed the judge and jury, "As you can see the photos that were taken by Sheriff Harrington the day of his investigation match the photos taken this morning. By looking at today's photos, the size of the crowbar tip matches the damage to both break-ins; also, you can see that the paint on the crowbar matches the paint on the damaged door jamb of the General Store." Rupert strutted over to the evidence table and picked up the crowbar and then over to the jury box. Holding up the crowbar tip with the paint on it, Rupert showed it to the jurors as he strolled the length of the jury box. Then he walked over to the witness stand where Rebecca Love was seated.

Rupert passed the crowbar before Miss Love's face, "Miss Love, do you recognize this crowbar?"

Rebecca pulled away, "I have never seen that thing before."

Rupert rudely continued, "But Miss Love, it was found in your car. Can you explain that?"

Rebecca answered sharply, "I haven't seen my car in two weeks since I left it up on Cedar Creek Watershed trail with the keys still in it. Anybody could have put that in my car, including you!"

Judge Arbuckle, seeming irritated with this whole scene, "Miss Love, this is your last warning; just answer the question."

Rebecca retorted showing her irritation, "No."

Rupert smugly responded, "Just what I suspected that you would say. Your Honor, no further questions at this time."

Dan Simmons began rubbing the Zemi in his pocket; at the same time, he could see the expression on Judge Arbuckle's face change.

Judge Arbuckle was still looking through the photographs; stopping at one, and then turning it upside down with a puzzled look on his face. He asked the bailiff, "Are all these photos from the break-ins?"

The bailiff answered, "Your Honor, there is a description on the back of each photo."

Judge Arbuckle flipped the photo over and read the description on the back. Then he asked, "Miss Love, please raise your left hand."

With a confused look on her face, Rebecca raised her left hand.

Judge Arbuckle continued to speak, "The description on the back of this photograph states that it displayed a handprint left by the perpetrator at the break-in at the second-hand store. It shows a handprint with one missing finger; I would say it is the ring finger on the left hand. Miss Love clearly has all of her digits on her left hand."

There was a low rumbling sound of voices throughout the courtroom; all the jurors rose to view a copy of the photograph mentioned by Judge Arbuckle, that was now being held by one juror. It was an obvious oversight that had come to light. Spencer sat in the courtroom, his thoughts were racing, putting together pieces, the tumblers in his mind were all lining up and the evidence now pointed in a different direction.

Judge Arbuckle addressed the courtroom, "I am going to adjourn court for lunch; we will continue at 2:00 this afternoon." The Judge slammed the gavel down, stood up and left the bench and walked out of the courtroom. The rest of the courtroom then began to empty.

Spencer turned and whispered to Dave Notworst who was standing next to him, "Dave, you have got to come with me." Dave nodded with compliance at Spencer. Dave followed Spencer out of the courtroom and across the parking lot to the sheriff's office. When they walked through the double doors of the sheriff's office, the three Bigfoot imposters were standing at the bars of the cell. One had his hand over his mouth, the second had his hands over his ears, and the third had his hands over his eyes.

Spencer didn't appreciate the attempt at humor and said, "I was going to let you knuckleheads out of jail, but I think you need to stay in there for a while longer."

Spencer and Dave entered the office, and Spencer shut the door.

Spencer spoke, "Dave, I need you to come along with me as a witness."

Dave answered, "Sure, whatever you need."

Spencer queried, "Dave, think back, who do you know anyone that is missing a finger on their left hand?"

Dave thought for a minute, shaking his head back and forth, "Spencer, I am drawing a blank."

Spencer asked again, "Think about it, someone you know, he lost his finger one drunken night at Murphy's Pub."

Dave still drawing a blank said, "I don't recall."

Spencer coaxed, "Sure you do; he was playing five finger roulette with a knife on the bar at Murphy's Pub when he missed and cut off his own finger."

Dave looked Spencer in the eyes; Spencer was staring back at Dave; they both said at the same time, "Pete Davis."

Spencer asked, "Dave, I need a witness to go over and search Pete Davis' truck.

Dave responded with enthusiasm, "Okay, let's head over to the impound lot and have a look."

Both Dave and Spencer headed out of his office and out the double doors of the Sheriff's office as the three Bigfoot were pleading for their release. As the two men drove over to the impound lot, Spencer realized where he had seen that crowbar before; it had been lying in the back of Pete Davis' truck. Spencer had seen it when he found the sardine tin in Rebecca's Subaru. He had leaned on the back of Pete's truck and saw it lying in the bed. Spencer suspected that someone must have moved it from the truck into the back of Rebecca's car. But how was he going to prove that? When they arrived at the impound lot, the gate was open, and Gilbert Whistler was standing in the doorway of the garage smoking a cigarette.

As they pulled to a stop and stepped out, Gilbert asked, "Gentlemen, what can I do you for?"

Spencer said, "We need to search Pete Davis' truck."

Gilbert responded agreeably, "Help yourself; it's open."

Spencer and Dave walked over to Pete's truck, and one opened the driver's door while the other opened the passenger side door. Dave flipped the bench seatback to look behind the seat, nothing. Spencer looked under the passenger side seat and found a tin of Prince Oscar Sardines. Spencer smiled at Dave as he pulled out the tin from under the seat. Next, Spencer looked at the glove box. He reached up, wrapping his finger around the latch and pushed inward on the button with his thumb. The glove box popped open emitting a slight click. Spencer slowly lowered the door. And there it was --- the missing .45 caliber revolver stolen from Dave's cabin. Spencer smiled at Dave; Dave was nodding his head up and down. But how did that crowbar from the back of Pete's truck get into Rebecca's car? Gilbert Whistler was standing behind Spencer as he pulled the .45 from the glove box.

Spencer turned and looked at Gilbert, "Does anyone else have a key to the impound lot beside you."

Gilbert replied, "No, just me."

Spencer said, "Well, I suspect that someone has been tampering with the evidence in this impound lot, and I would like to get to the bottom of it."

Gilbert spoke, "If anyone has been messing around the lot, it would be on the surveillance tape."

Spencer, surprised, smiled and said, "What? You have surveillance cameras?"

Gilbert said, "Yes sir, ever since that drunk broke in the lot and stole the road grader; he wiped out every mailbox from here to about 3 miles that away," Pointing up the highway with his greasy finger.

Spencer, grinning, chuckled, "Well, let's have a look."

The three men went into the garage and sat in the broken and stained armchairs squeezed into the tiny office. On the desk was a monitor, keyboard and a mouse. Gilbert typed in a password and moved the mouse around clicking here and there that ran the surveillance tape back 24 hours. The videotape sped in reverse, but it didn't look like it was running because of the seeming lack of movement. Then the tape started forward; at the gate there appeared a dark shadow; it squeezed through the locked gate, and walked over to the silver Subaru. The figure popped the lock on the car door and started going through the car. The tape showed the culprit reaching into the back of Pete Davis' truck and retrieving the crowbar. The figure moved to the back of the Subaru, opening the hatch and placing the crowbar on top of the spare tire. Locking up the Subaru, the character turned as he walked away; the spotlight on the corner of the building lit up his face for the camera. It was Rupert Longarm, visibly captured on tape.

Spencer started laughing, "Gilbert, can you make a copy of that segment for me?"

Gilbert assured him, "No problem; I will burn you a CD. Hell, I can print you out that frame of his face, if you want."

Spencer answered, "Great! Dave, we need to get back to the courthouse and show this to Farnsworth before court starts."

Dave concurred, "Okay, let's get going."

Spencer grabbed the CD and the printed photo of Rupert Longarm, thanked Gilbert for the help and out the door the two men ran. Speeding out of the impound lot, they headed up the street toward North Bend. As they arrived at the courthouse, Worthy was just walking up the steps to the front door. Spencer pulled into a parking spot and shouted at Worthy.

"Hey, Farnsworth, hey!" shouted Spencer.

Worthy stopped halfway up the steps and turned to see Spencer running toward him. When Spencer reached him, he was out of breath but still tried to explain the new turn of events. Worthy patiently listened, trying to get Spencer to slow down and take a few deep breaths. Finally, Spencer got out the whole story and explained the new evidence and how they had found the missing .45 and the surveillance tape that showed the clear photo of Rupert's face. Worthy began smiling with the news about the great revelations which would help him win his case and free Rebecca Love from incarceration. The three men then made their way into the courtroom. Worthy sat at the defendant's table, and Spencer, Dave, and Dan Simmons sat just behind Worthy and Rebecca Love.

The bailiff shouted, "All rise! The Honorable Judge Andrew Phineas Arbuckle presiding." Then the grumpy Judge Arbuckle walked into the room, sat down, and stated that everyone may be seated. Judge Arbuckle scanned the courtroom gallery. There in the second row was Philbert Bottomdalr, smoke rising from his head like steam lifting from a lake in early morning. Judge Arbuckle slammed the gavel down three times, stood up and pointed the instrument at Bottomdalr. "There is no smoking in this courtroom; bailiff take that fool out of here!" Judge Arbuckle added, "May we now proceed?"

Worthy stood up and spoke, "Your Honor, if I could, may I approach the bench?"

Judge Arbuckle nodded as he said, "What is the issue, Mr. Huntington?"

Worthy stated, "During the lunch break, Sheriff Harrington and Chief Ranger Dave Notworst have uncovered paramount evidence affecting this case."

Judge Arbuckle said, "This is highly inappropriate; what have you got?"

Rupert jumped up and opposed, "I object, Your Honor, this last-minute introduction of evidence is not acceptable."

Judge Arbuckle addressed Mr. Longarm, "Mr. Prosecutor, may I remind you that you yourself introduced new evidence this morning? I would suggest that you hold your water! Mr. Huntington, you may approach the bench."

Worthy explained the new evidence, showing Judge Arbuckle the missing .45, and a hand-written statement from Sheriff Harrington as to where the gun had been found, the CD of the surveillance tape and the photograph of Rupert Longarm's activities in the impound lot. Judge Arbuckle looked over the top of his glasses at Rupert Longarm as Worthy continued to explain the aspects of the evidence. Worthy nodded his head at Judge Arbuckle in agreement, turned and walked back to the defendant's table.

Judge Arbuckle spoke, "I am going to allow this new evidence, and declaring a mistrial based on the evidence and evidence-tampering by the prosecution."

Rupert Longarm stood and started to protest but was interrupted by the courtroom doors being forced open. Into the courtroom burst, a half a dozen men dressed in blue windbreakers with yellow letters FBI printed on their backs. They rushed up to the prosecutor's table.

The lead FBI agent addressed Rupert, "Rupert Longarm, you are under arrest for conspiracy with criminal intent for the purpose of promoting organized crime."

The agents quickly read Rupert his rights and cuffed him and escorted him out of the courtroom. Everyone in the courtroom looked on in astonished amazement as all this activity transpired. Even Judge Arbuckle watched in stunned silence. The FBI agents were gone as quickly as they had arrived, but with Rupert Longarm in tow.

Chapter 18

All's Well

The next day, things seemed back to normal --- no camera crews, no visitors masquerading in Bigfoot costumes; the town of North Bend was back to the quiet buzz of the town's people going about their business. Dan Simmons was briefly happy for the quiet, no need to attend to any business. He decided to take a walk on a country road near his house. The morning was a bit cool, and the crispness caused him to walk at a faster pace to keep his body temperature up. He walked briskly and covered a tremendous amount of ground. Dan decided to walk up a dusty road that turned into a wooded trail; the air grew cooler as the path became shaded. As he walked along, he noticed that the birds were no longer singing, and the other sounds of the forest were absent too. There was no breeze, so the trees were not moving; the leaves were not rustling. The physical exercise had made him feel warm, and he was a little out of breath, so he stopped to rest just a bit. While resting, he scanned his surroundings to take in the natural beauty of the scenery. From behind a stand of Aspen trees, appeared a large cougar, mouth open, swaying back and forth as he walked, the tail slowly whipping back and forth. The cat seemed unafraid and was staring in Dan Simmons' direction. Dan stood perfectly still and tried to blend in with his surroundings, hoping not to be noticed. As he stood in silence, from the other side of the Aspen grove lumbered a giant grizzly bear. These two creatures would never have ventured this close without threatening to create a confrontation.

Dan remained still and didn't move; the two-large animals slowly moved toward him. Dan prepared to shapeshift and fly away. When they were 30 feet away, the pair instantly changed as they walked. One was Jarl, and the other was Gunnarr. At that moment, Dan realized that there must be something urgent for them to appear in broad daylight.

Jarl projected his thoughts first, "We need you to come with us."

Dan inquired earnestly, "What's wrong?"

Jarl stated as if the need were urgent, "It is the human that Saga has bonded to."

Dan asked, "Pete? What's wrong with Pete?"

Jarl replied, "They both are unhappy."

Dan asked somewhat alarmed, "What has Pete done now?"

Jarl commented, "He has done nothing wrong actually; they do not want to live bonded to each other. It is too difficult for them."

Dan sought further clarity, "So, can't Saga just un-bond herself from him?"

Jarl responded, "No, they both would die from extreme sorrow if they broke the bond."

Dan continued with another query, "Well, what can be done, and what do you need from me?"

Jarl spoke candidly, "They must be paired."

Dan was puzzled, "Paired? What does that mean?"

Jarl explained, "It is like being bonded, but the two can move about without having to be just a few feet apart as in bonding."

Dan asked, "So if I understand you correctly, this pairing is like, marriage?"

Jarl grimaced slightly, "If that is what you call it, yes, marriage."

Dan being concerned inquired, "And Pete is okay with this?"

Jarl confirmed, "Yes, he doesn't want to die, and he doesn't want to live closely tied to Saga."

Dan pursued the inquiry, "So, how can I help?"

Jarl said, "To do this, the human requested the aid of something called a man of God."

Dan's demeanor changed to amazement, "A man of God?" Then Dan understood, "He wants a priest, or minister or something of that sort."

Jarl nodded and answered, "Yes, you must bring a priest!"

Dan, not feeling comfortable but willing to comply, said, "I will find someone that is a man of God and bring him to your camp, and then you can proceed with the pairing."

Jarl snorted lightly and grinned but demanded, "Good; today."

Dan, realizing that these things have a way to manifest themselves and work out somehow answered, "Yes, I will bring a man of God."

Jarl, still grinning, showing his fangs, replied, "Good."

The two Sasquatch stepped back, then the two shapeshifted and were gone. Dan found himself standing alone. He wondered, "Where am I going to find a man of God, one that would be willing to marry a man, a human, and a female Sasquatch?" He was sure there was something in the Bible that forbids this kind of an act, but he didn't want to think about it. The thought made Dan feel a bit ill. He walked back toward his house at a quick pace, pondering the whole way how he was going to pull off this feat. How was he going to explain, or convince someone to marry a man to a beast? Dan thought to himself, "Don't feel the worries, let them go, feel the positive and in time all will be revealed." This is just a small problem compared to the problems Jarl is expecting him to conquer in the future. Dan continued to wonder, and told himself, "Just let it flow, and things will happen; the pieces will fall into place." Dan reached his house and propped his walking stick up against the door jamb just inside his home. He grabbed the keys to his Jeep and went back out the door. As Dan drove along, he pondered where he could go to find a man of God? He decided to go to the sheriff's office and ask the advice of Sheriff Harrington; he knew everyone, and what they did for a living. That was his plan.

Dan pulled into the parking lot of the sheriff's office and parked in one of the many vacant parking spots. As he walked into the office, Sheriff Harrington was talking to a gentleman dressed in a black suit and black shirt, and he just happened to have a white collar around his neck. Dan interrupted the conversation by his presence. Spencer stopped talking and looked at Dan.

Spencer greeted him warmly, "Hello, Mr. Simmons, how can I help you today?"

Dan cleared his throat and spoke, "Well, I was hoping you could tell me where I might be able to find a minister or a priest."

Spencer smiled and looked over at Billy Bob Compton, then back at Dan, "Dan, this is your lucky day; I would like to introduce you to Reverend Billy Bob Compton."

Dan, a bit surprised by coincidence, "Well, I am delighted to meet you."

Spencer turned to Billy Bob, "This is Dan Simmons; the man that was missing for several weeks."

Billy Bob smiled and extended his hand, "Nice to meet you, Sir. Why may I ask, are you looking for a minister or priest?"

Dan cleared his throat again feeling a bit uneasy about what he wanted, "Well, I have a difficult situation; two of my friends want to get married today, and they are in a bit of a hurry."

Billy Bob chirped, "Have they applied for a marriage license? I can do the ceremony, but they need a license."

Dan replied, "That is not going to be a problem; they

have everything they need."

Billy Bob answered, "Great! My fee for a marriage cere-mony is one hundred dollars; is that in your budget?"

Dan grinned and said, "No problem; are you available now?"

Billy Bob, hesitating a little, responded, "Let me check my busy schedule." Holding up an empty hand and flipping through imaginary pages, responded with a quick, "Yes, it so happens that, at this very moment, my schedule is clear and I think I can squeeze you in."

Dan, smirked at the humor, "Great, let's go. I'm parked just outside."

Billy Bob commented, "I'm right behind you, Sir." He smiled at Spencer, "Thank you for your help, Sheriff. Good day."

Spencer waved good-bye as the two men rushed out of the sheriff's office and back to the parking lot. They jumped into the Jeep, and Dan pulled onto the street and headed for the most secluded spot he could think of that would work. Fifteen minutes later, Dan pulled the Jeep into an open field just off a small dirt road. There were no houses.

Billy Bob asked somewhat perplexed, "Where are all the people; the bride, the groom?"

Dan motioned, "Follow me; they are this way."

They walked some distance into a field of grass. The seed tassels of the tall grass slapped against their waists as they walked. Reaching the middle of the field, Dan abruptly stopped.

Billy Bob, skeptically asked, "Okay, where is this wed-ding?"

Dan replied, "One moment." Dan grabbed Billy Bob's arm and immediately shapeshifted, and they became invisible instantly.

When they reappeared, they were standing near a lake within the hidden Sasquatch valley --- the home, the sanctu-ary of Dan's friends, the ones that had saved his life. The very place that Dan had learned to acquire all of the new powers that had transformed his life. Billy Bob was very uneasy and unsure of what had just happened. He had been deceived and thought that this Dan Simmons must be some kind of magician. He wondered, "What unholy place had he been brought too? But, it was beautiful, and how could an unholy place be so beautiful?" Billy Bob turned around and around, taking in the pristine beauty that surrounded him. He thought, "This must be a true Garden of Eden. Even the air is pure and clean. I feel younger just by breathing it in." Billy Bob had never seen such a place or ever imagined that one even existed in this world. He looked at Dan Simmons, and Dan was smiling back at him, knowing just what Billy Bob was feeling.

Dan said, "This is where the wedding is going to take place."

Billy Bob, still puzzled, asked, "Where is everyone?"

Dan reassured him, "They will be here shortly."

Billy Bob blurted out, "What a perfect place to hold a wedding." He was feeling pleased to be officiating this ceremony and in such a beautiful, pristine spot on God's earth. For the moment, he had completely forgotten about how they had just recently arrived here.

But, not all perfect things, are just that, perfect. The wedding party arrived in a flash. Billy Bob saw the creatures suddenly appear in a circle around him. He let out a loud gasp, his knees buckled, and down he went. Billy Bob, the needed man of God, had passed out at the sight of six hairy giants. Six, yes, there were six. Dan was surprised to see six and not the original five Sasquatches. Then Dan gradually realized that one of them was Pete. Dan walked over to Pete to take a closer look. Pete's appearance was in the process of changing; he no longer had a bald head but was growing reddish-brown hair, and his hockey-player smile had changed too. No longer did he have that big gap in his teeth, but he was now growing fangs. Two fangs protruded upward from his bottom jaw, and two top fangs grew downward, just inside the bottom ones. He had grown in height too, about a foot taller than he had been. The only clothing, he was wearing were his pants; his shirt was absent. In the shirt's place was a hairy chest except for a few tiny patches of skin on his chest and abdomen. The back of his arms and feet were covered with reddish-brown hair also. Dan realized that Pete Davis was becoming a Sasquatch. He also sensed that Pete had learned to read thoughts and could communicate telepathically.

Dan transferred his thoughts, "Pete, you have changed."

Pete responded, "Something is wrong; I don't feel the same; this she-devil has cast a spell on me."

Dan grinned, "Well, why would you want to marry her?"

Pete glanced about uneasily, "I don't have a choice; if I don't, I will die."

Dan replied, "Well, that's a good reason. Hum, death or Bigfoot, tough choice; I guess it could be worse."

Pete asked in surprise, "Worse? How could something possibly be worse?"

Dan grinned again, "Believe me, Pete, it could be worse."

Pete changed the subject, "I see you brought me a priest; what? Is he drunk? Or, has he passed out?"

Dan explained, "He's a minister and no he's not drunk; he's in shock; he took one look at you and passed out. I wish I had a mirror so you could see yourself."

Pete responded, "No, I don't want to know, I don't want to see myself; I know it's bad." With that being said, Pete raised his chin and let out a mournful howl.

Dan, trying to put Pete at ease, said, "Well, Pete, you know, you gotta roll with the punches."

Pete, in a demanding tone, uttered, "Well, wake him up; let's get this silly thing over with."

Billy Bob was starting to come around and sat up; then he opened his eyes, and looked around, muttered a few indistinguishable sounds and then passed out again. Dan walked over to one of the female Sasquatch and took a water bag from her hand. He walked back over to Billy Bob lying on the ground. Dan located the opening in the water bag and proceeded to pour the entire bag on Billy Bob's head. Billy Bob woke up, gasping for air and sputtering through his water-soaked beard. Dan knelt down next to Billy Bob and explained that everyone was in costume for the wedding; they were all dressed in Bigfoot costumes just for this unique wedding in this remote location. He reiterated that these people are all in costume. Billy Bob, wanting to believe anything that resembled reality, went along with the story just to maintain his sanity. Besides he needed the hundred dollars because --- well, he was --- broke. Billy Bob got to his feet with Dan Simmons' help. Dan placed his arm around Billy Bob's waist and walked him over to where the bride and groom were standing. Saga was wearing a ring of flowers around her head and had a bouquet of wildflowers in her hand. Pete stood next to her and showed his teeth; he could not close his lips because the protruding fangs pushed them apart. He looked as if he were growling. Billy Bob thanked Dan for helping and Dan stepped back away from him. Billy Bob took out his Bible and opened it to a particular section.

Billy Bob began, "Dearly beloved, we are gathered here today to witness the union of this man?" Billy Bob wasn't quite sure if Pete were a man or beast, maybe both.

Dan leaned in and whispered the name, "Pete Davis."

Billy Bob continued, "This man, Pete Davis, and this Beast? Billy Bob looked over at Dan for some reassurance.

Dan whispered, "Saga."

Billy Bob resumed the ceremony, "And this beast, Saga, in holy matrimony."

The ceremony proceeded well until Billy Bob got to the part at the end of the service that states, "I now pronounce you man and beast; the groom may now kiss the bride." Pete made some comment that he would rather eat a road apple.

The wedding was now over, and Pete Davis and Saga were paired for all eternity. Dan shook Pete's hand and congratulated him and told him he had a heck of a gal.

Dan then turned and kissed Saga on her cheek and winked at her. Dan thought he saw her blush, but he wasn't sure. Dan said his goodbyes, grabbed Billy Bob's arm and shapeshifted, and the two men disappeared.

Billy Bob and Dan Simmons reappeared in the middle of the same grassy field from which they had left. Dan pulled out his wallet and handed Billy Bob a single hundred-dollar bill.

Dan cautioned, "You cannot tell anyone what happened here today. Do you understand?"

Billy Bob nodded and agreed, "What sane person on God's green earth would believe me? I don't want to end up sounding like the old Swede!"

Dan answered, "Good point; thank you, Reverend; where can I drop you?"

Billy Bob remarked somewhat sheepishly, "How about Murphy's Pub; I could use a post-wedding libation."

Dan replied heartily, "You got it, and I'll buy."

Every life has a twist or turn that is unexpected; it wasn't any different for Wendy Storms. Somehow, she and Higgins ended up in the biggest little city in the world, Reno, Nevada. Wendy had lost interest in becoming a famous news anchor and set her sights a little higher; she took a more glamorous job in the entertainment field. She definitely had the looks, and she could dress the part, mostly because she could walk in those extremely tall high heels. And that is what showgirls do, dress outrageously, but when you start out, you have got to pay your dues and work your way up. Wendy got hired by Willie Flynn, nightclub owner, talent agent and owner of Wet Willies, a casino so far off the strip --- it might even have had a different zip code. Wet Willies Gentlemen's Club was starting at the bottom of the entertainment industry, but Wendy was now the most requested pole dancer in the joint.

Wendy knew she was on her way up and there was no stopping her; she was going to drive her way to the top, no matter how many claw marks she needed to leave behind her in that climb to success. Higgins also got a job in the entertainment business, but he seemed to be a bit more successful than Wendy. Just out of dumb luck, Higgins happened to be applying for a job at the Reno police department after a boasting session when he was bragging about his prowess as a deputy in North Bend. Higgins was telling the desk detective about how he had single-handedly subdued an unruly bunch of bikers at Rattlesnake Lake, just a few months before. This bit of luck happened when a television producer gathering information for a re-make of a cop show overheard him. Si-mon Schuster, the producer, overheard Higgins' self-inflated version of the incident and he immediately signed Higgins for his new show, a re-make of Reno 911. Higgins thought he was going to be the next Brando, just when everyone thought his head couldn't get any bigger.

───────────

Philbert Bottomdolr's life had pretty much returned to nor-mal. He had breakfast and his tea every Sunday at the Double D Diner. He would sit for hours and read the sports section of the Sunday paper as he let his tea cool. But after the black orb had incinerated him, he began having after death experi-ences; he was now able to prognosticate --- not catastrophic events but sports outcomes. Not just any predictions, he be-gan predicting outcomes of the local high school basketball and football games. He was spot-on every time. Every game for which he predicted the outcome, he was correct. He even began predicting the final scores, which made the local town's people upset because he was ruining the sport and the local high school's spirit, especially when they lost. Can you imag-ine how hard it would be to play a game knowing that your team is going to lose? So Philbert quit predicting the local high school sports outcomes and moved on to professional sports. This decision made the local people happy but brought in a bad element to North Bend. Bookies from Seat-tle heard about Bottomdolr's talents and started showing up at the Double D Diner on Sunday mornings. Philbert was being pressured to tell them who was going to win so that the bookies could hedge their bets. Philbert Bottomdolr was no idiot and could see the writing on the wall. He started giving false outcomes and bad scores, and soon most of the bookies left North Bend and ultimately labeled Philbert a hoax.

Philbert Bottomdolr scared off the last of the bookies pretty bad. Not by a threat but by just lighting the bookie's cigar. A couple of bookies cornered Philbert outside the Double D Diner trying to pressure him into forecasting an upcoming Seahawk's game. One of the bookies pulled out a cigar during the shakedown. Bit off the end and spit it on the ground, looking at Philbert the bookie demanded, "Hey, Mac, you got a light?" Philbert obliged by sticking his index finger of his right hand to the end of the cigar. Philbert winked as a flame popped from the end of his finger. The bookie's mouth dropped, and the cigar hit the ground. The two ran to their car and sped off, never to return to North Bend.

Chief Ranger Dave Notworst did marry Betsy, but she chose not to take his last name. Happily married, she still went by Babette F. Spunkmeyer, which she felt was better than Babette F. Notworst. Dave didn't care about her decision to retain her name, and he also didn't want to change his name to Dave Spunkmeyer-Notworst. But what's in a name anyway? But the subject would arise again when Betsy got pregnant. Dave and Betsy made a beautiful couple, and they loved each other dearly, and this marriage had a fairy-tale ending. It helped to have a nudge from a little black orb which put this bliss in motion.

With the lasting image of the wedding of Pete Davis and Saga, Billy Bob Compton could no longer stomach the thought of continuing to be a minister, especially, if he continued to live in North Bend. The chances of possibly encountering a similar wedding gave him chills. He took a job at the Double D Diner washing dishes and busing tables. But he didn't waste his time; he took an online course for law enforcement. When he finally earned his diploma, he applied for an opening at the North Bend Sheriff's Office. Sheriff Spencer Harrington was pleased to offer him the open position that Higgins had left. Billy Bob was not only the number one candidate for the job, but he was also the only one who applied. Spencer was no longer a one-man operation, and Billy Bob was a step up from the former employee. As time went on, Billy Bob became a real asset to Spencer, and he relied on the deputy in many situations. After a year of service, Spencer actually felt comfortable taking a long-needed vacation. He always wanted to go to Reno Nevada.

As always when the fourth of July rolled around, there was the North Bend celebration and parade. Pete Davis' 1948 Willys-Overland pickup truck always led the parade, but the Willys was now driven by Gilbert Eriksson the 'old Swede. But to keep the celebration safe, Sheriff Harrington had to make sure that Gilbert spent the previous night in the jail cell instead of keeping his barstool warm at Murphy's Pub. The first-year Gilbert drove Pete's truck in the parade, he was quite hung-over and took out a fire hydrant on North Bend Way, which flooded the street and soaked many bystanders. Also, that same year was the first year for the "All Sasquatch Un-Synchronized Marching Drill Team." People came from all over the United States to be part of this event; it became one of the main highlights of the parade. Hillary Upshaw and her "It Lives Again" second-hand store started renting Bigfoot costumes for the parade; she also started selling them too. She became a big hit on eBay and her little shop became the go-to place to buy Sasquatch or Bigfoot costumes.

Not everyone fared well, however; Rupert Longarm found himself in hot water, so hot it would be considered a rolling-boil of hot water. It seems that he had been taking bribes from the Chinese Dark Society of the Triads. The Triads wanted to control the ports and waterfronts of Seattle and Tacoma. To push out the other organized crime syndicates, the Triads bribed Rupert only to prosecute their rival gangs. Rupert not only indicted the other gangs but helped to fabricate evidence. Rupert was in reality a soft little worm, and the FBI soon convinced him to turn states evidence and rat out all the members of the Triad gang. After testifying against the Triads and exposing the members, he was placed in witness protection. Because of the blatant threats, Rupert's life was in danger. Rupert Longarm ended up in Barrow, Alaska, a town where its inhabitants are afraid of vampire attacks because of the extended periods of darkness. But Rupert felt that assaults by vampires were easier to survive than the Triads.

Rebecca Love had returned to Seattle and re-enrolled in school. Dan Simmons was unsure where he would end up now. Not too concerned about the future, Dan sensed that something big was about to happen. One evening he sat on a chain sawed stump in front of an open campfire in his backyard. He relaxed and opened his mind as he stared into the flames. They danced, reflecting in his eyes; the sky was clear, and the stars were bright; the smoke rose straight up into the sky. Dan wondered how his Sasquatch friends were doing and assumed they were doing the same as he was, fire-gazing. He let his thoughts flow and became entranced by the dancing flames. Soon, he was one with the fire. Warm, colorful thoughts drifted through his head. He could feel his heart open and his mind became free. Soon, he was no longer sitting in front of the fire but standing on a flat stretch of white sand; in the distance, deep blue mountains surrounded the sand floor. The stars were so intensely bright that his mind seemed perfectly clear. In the distance, he could see a figure approaching. The closer the figure got, Dan could tell it was a man. He was a simple man dressed in peasant clothes. The approaching man was wearing sandals and carried a bedroll slung over his shoulder secured only by a sisal rope. When he reached Dan Simmons, he stopped and looked him in the eyes. The humble man looked eerily like David Carradine. Then he spoke to Dan.

The humble man spoke, "What is it you seek?"

Dan asked, "Can I call you Grasshopper?"

The humble man responded, "No, you may not! Again, what is it you seek?"

Dan said, "I seek direction."

The humble man answered, "Look inside; feel inside; what is it that drives you?"

Dan, getting frustrated, replied, "Can you just tell me instead of asking me questions?"

The humble man spoke again, "I cannot! Look inside; what do you see?"

Dan stopped, closed his eyes and tried to feel and see inside his spirit, "I feel loneliness."

The humble man said, "Then you know how to change that. Look past that and tell me what you see?"

Dan exclaimed, "I see a newspaper on my front porch."

The humble man spoke, "Open it; what do you see?"

Dan answered, "I see the want ads."

The humble man asked, "Do you see more?"

Dan said, "It is the employment section."

The humble man asked, "Do you have your answer?"

Dan asked, "I'm supposed to get a job?"

The humble man said, "I ask the questions here! As the sun rises, the bird sings."

The morning sun was shining on Dan's face when he woke; he could hear a distant neighbor's rooster crowing. He got up and went to the bathroom to wash his face. Then he went to the kitchen and made a pot of coffee. As he waited for the coffee to perk, there was a thud at the front door. Dan walked over and opened it. There on the front porch was the morning paper from Seattle. Dan picked it up and returned to the kitchen and poured himself a cup of morning joe. Sitting at the kitchen table, he unfolded and then parted the newspaper, opening right to the employment section. A rectangular box surrounded the most significant ad on the page. In bold letters at the top, it said, "Wanted Diplomatic Liaison," and below in smaller letters, "No experience required." Dan left the kitchen and took a shower and got dressed, then fixed breakfast. At precisely 9 am, he pulled out his cell phone and dialed the number in the ad. A soft female voice answered the phone and Dan explained he was calling about the advertisement for the Diplomatic Liaison. The voice told him to email his resume to an email address, and they would get back to him. That afternoon Dan's cell phone rang and a masculine voice was on the other end and an arrangement was made for Dan to drive to Seattle for an interview.

The next day, Dan arrived in downtown Seattle, forty-five minutes ahead of his interview. He drove around the Henry M. Jackson Federal Building until he turned a corner. As he made the corner, there was a car pulling out of a street parking place. Dan maneuvered his Jeep into the spot. The parking meter was broken, and a locked blue canvas bag hung over it. Dan thought, "Free parking, it must be a sign." He headed into the lobby and pushed the button on the elevator, and the door opened immediately. Dan thought, "Another sign?" Then he pushed the button for the 13th floor. When he reached the floor, the doors slid open, and he walked into a very sterile and orderly-looking office. There was no receptionist, only phone on the wall and a sign above it that said, "Pick Up Receiver." So, Dan followed the direction and picked up the phone. A soft voice answered the phone. Dan told the person who he was and the door next to the telephone, emitted a buzzing noise and then popped open, swinging with a creak and opening about 5 inches exposing plush carpeting. As Dan opened the door the rest of the way, he could see the receptionist. She smiled and instructed him to go to the right and down a hallway to the office of Durkin

Mills. Dan softly knocked on the designated door, and from inside the office, a masculine voice said enter. Dan opened the door and shut it behind him.

The meeting with Mr. Durkin Mills went very well and was short. Mr. Mills was impressed with Dan's background and education and told him he was a perfect fit for the job. The job was in New York City, and he would be supplied with a driver and an apartment and an office at the United Nations Building. He also would be allowed to hire an assistant of his choosing. With that, Dan accepted the position immediately, and Mr. Durkin Mills instructed him to go to the 9th floor and get photographed and fingerprinted. When he was done with the process, Dan was given a new Black Passport stamped with his vital information under his picture; it also stated, "Diplomatic Immunity." He was given a large sum of cash for travel expenses and two plane tickets that could be used at any time on any carrier. He was told that he needed to report in two weeks to his supervisor, a Graham Buckfuller. Dan thanked the man who gave him his documents, and he left the federal building and headed back to his car. Dan whispered, "Just one more stop." He started his car and headed for the University of Washington campus. He pulled into the visitor's parking lot and headed for the campus housing. Dan had been here many times, and he had a pretty good idea where he was going. He crossed the campus and headed for Mercer Court, walked up one flight of concrete steps, then he stopped. Dan was standing outside room 222. Taking a deep breath, he knocked on the door. The door slowly opened, and there stood Rebecca Love. She let out a screech and jumped up wrapping her legs around him and threw her arms around his neck and immediately started crying. "I didn't think I would ever see you again," she sobbed.

After Dan was able to get her calmed down, and the crying subsided, he told her he needed to talk to her about something very important. Rebecca offered him a glass of wine, and they sat and talked on the couch. Dan explained that he had taken a job in New York City and would be leaving within the next two weeks. Rebecca's eyes teared up, and she was on the verge of crying again. Dan calmed her down and told her that he had a proposal for her, but it wasn't marriage. Rebecca calmed, took a few deep breaths, then nodded that she was ready to listen. Dan explained what his job was and that he was given an opportunity to hire an assistant to accompany him. He told her that all expenses would be covered, but there was a lot of traveling involved. Rebecca dabbed at her eyes with a tissue and was sitting straight up, staring into Dan's eyes as he explained. Dan then asked Rebecca if she would be interested in the position. Rebecca let out a huge scream and kissed Dan hard on the lips. When she was done kissing him, he said, "I guess that is a yes."

The day that Dan Simmons left North Bend for his new career in New York City, he drove up North Bend Way past the sheriff's office. Standing out front were Sheriff Spencer Harrington, and he was talking with Chief Ranger Dave Notworst. As he drove by, Dan waved goodbye to the pair. And both Spencer and Dave waved back.

Dave looked at Spencer, "I'm sorry but, I am not going to miss that guy."

Spencer added, "That makes two of us."

Dave released a big sigh and said, "Thank God; this town is back to normal, and the camera crews and kooks are gone."

As Dave and Spencer stood on the front steps of the sheriff's office, a white van pulled into the parking lot and stopped. A man dressed in a plaid shirt and a khaki vest and cargo pants climbed out of the van and walked over to the two men.

Khaki vest greeted, "Hello, gentlemen, do either of you know where I could find a Dan Simmons?"

Spencer furrowed his brow and lowered his eyebrows and grunted in a disconsolate tone, "You just missed him; I heard he's on his way to New York City."

Khaki vest, in a cheerful voice, said, "My name is Bill Woods; I'm from the National Geographic Channel; I am here to investigate a possible sighting of the North American Sasquatch."

About the Author

Daniel L Simmons currently lives and grew up in the Pacific Northwest of the United States. Avid traveler and adventurer he spent most of his life as a blue-collar class. These acquaintances have given him an understanding of the different depths of personalities. As a traveler, new experiences gave him an understanding of other cultures.